Maker

of

Angels

Dean Sault

[signature]

#1016

DISCLAIMER

Copyright © 2013 Dean Sault
All rights reserved.
ISBN-13: 978-1493631483
ISBN-10: 1493631489

DEDICATION

This book is dedicated to Carlan Steward, 1945-2013.
As my business partner and close friend for over thirty years,
Carlan encouraged me to pursue my writing when I lacked
confidence. He covered for me at work, so I could write,
and he was always among my greatest supporters.

I love and miss you, buddy.

ACKNOWLEGDGEMENTS

I would like to thank my beta readers whose valuable feedback polished this story to its final state. My creative ideas often come with reckless abandon, and, in my zeal, I overlook issues that should be addressed. Dedicated beta readers often save me from myself as they identify those places where I need to improve. Thank you my friends. My success is your success.

Chapter 1

"Beer." I slapped two bits on the bar. "Where's the best grub in town?"

"Ain't no real eatin' place here in Tumbleweed, boy. Got some jerked meat under the bar, but you best drop by the Empty Nest for a visit with Miss Nelly if you want good food."

With breath betraying a mighty need for tooth doctoring, he leaned closer and whispered, "You can get your manly needs settled at the same time. Costs the same for grub as for the friendship, if ya know what I'm saying."

He winked.

"Thanks, but I just need food. Where's the town blacksmith? Horse went lame a few miles out of town. I think there's a rock under his shoe"

"Willy runs the livery right next to the Empty Nest at the west end of town. He ain't a real blacksmith, but the boy's good with a hammer and anvil. Fixing that shoe shouldn't be no trouble, even for him."

A man stumbled up to the bar next to me and demanded another shot of whiskey.

"Charlie, you had enough," the bartender said. "It's still daylight, and you're already drunk. Go back to the bunkhouse and sleep it off."

This fellow stunk of filthy clothes and soiled britches.

"Gimme a whiskey," he demanded, "or I'll shoot the place up."

He drew his Colt six-shooter and waved it recklessly in the air.

"Put the gun down Charlie!" the bartender shouted. "Zcke, come get your brother 'fore I have to kill em."

The bartender lifted a shortened, double-barreled shotgun into view from below the bar. He clicked both hammers, emphasizing the seriousness of his threat.

1

Despite leaning away from the drunk's weapon, its barrel glanced off the side of my face, sending pain through my temple and cheek. I grabbed the man's wrist to hold his weapon back, and the gun went off.

Chaos filled the bar. Patrons ran for the door while some dove to the floor and crouched behind tables toppled over as shields. Poker cards, money and drinks flew in every direction.

Another round fired from the drunk's forty-four into the ceiling as he struggled against my grip. Ringing filled my ears from the loud retort.

"Let'em go," someone shouted from farther down the bar.

I was not about to release my grip.

"Let go, damn it!" the same voice demanded again.

The drunk shoved me backward, and my stool slipped out from under me. We fell to the floor where I landed hard on my back with the drunk on top. The impact broke my grip on his wrist, and his forty-four's barrel swung toward my face, aiming between my eyes. I jerked my head to one side while frantically grabbing for my own sidearm.

A deafening blast exploded into the floor and splinters stuck into the side of my neck.

An instant later, I pulled my trigger sending a slug into the drunk's abdomen. Violent recoil from the weapon I had never before fired surprised me and the gun wrenched out of my hand, spinning across the floor.

My assailant sat up straight and looked at me with a strange mix of rage and pain in his eyes. He brought the sinister, black tunnel of his high caliber pistol to bear on my face again.

Two loud blasts rang out in quick succession.

The drunk lurched forward. His gun clunked on the floor, and his limp body draped across my head. There was a sickening, dull thud as his face bounced on the hardwood.

Someone immediately dragged the dead man off me, rolling him to where his back faced me. Small dots of blood oozed through his shirt where buckshot penetrated his back and neck. A single, large hole marked where my slug exited just above his belt.

"Damn you, Harvey," a man said from his knees next to the corpse.

The man, with a heavily scarred face, cradled the drunk's upper body in his arms.

"Why'd you kill Charlie?" he yelled at the bartender with an odd blend of anger and confusion. "He ain't never hurt you. Why'd you shoot my brother?"

"He didn't give me no choice, Zeke. He drew on the stranger. You saw it."

The dead man's brother stood up, unceremoniously dumping his brother's body on the floor. He shook a fist at the barkeep.

"Since when does a stranger mean more than town folk? Me and Charlie, I thought we was like family to you. You killed him over some damn outsider. That ain't right."

The sheriff burst through the swinging bar doors with his gun drawn.

"Put down your weapons! That includes you, Harvey. Lay the shotgun on the bar."

With the sheriff in control, patrons began restoring tables and bickering about where they were in their poker games before the commotion. Nobody showed concern for the dead man or for the lawman's interrogation. They just wanted to get back to their poker games.

I was surprised. A man just died, and none of them cared.

The town's lawman quickly determined the bartender acted properly to save my life. The sheriff warned Zeke that he was real close to cooling off in jail, if he did not stop making threats toward me and the bartender.

"Zeke, go fetch Doc Brown to come get Charlie's body, and let the preacher know so he can plan a proper funeral," the sheriff ordered.

The dead man's brother headed out of the bar, but stopped in the doorway to vent his fury at me.

"It's your fault, you son of a bitch!" He pointed at me. "My brother, he . . . he'd still be alive if you didn't grab him. You're a dead man, stranger. You're dead!"

The swinging doors clapped to a close behind him.

"Sheriff, I'm sorry about your town resident, here. I didn't look for trouble."

3

"I know, kid. Unfortunately, it found you. Son, you best not stay in town. Zeke and his brothers, well, they're a crazy clan. Found a sheep man strung up last year north of town. Zeke's family runs cattle, and they hate sheep coming into the county. I never could pin it on em, but I wouldn't be surprised if they done it."

"Thanks, sir. I'll put my horse in the livery for a shoe repair and get some grub. Expect I can be out of town by midnight. I'm not looking for a fight."

The sheriff leaned close to me and whispered, "Don't eat here at the bar. Food's a lot better at the Empty Nest. Tell Miss Nelly I sent you." He winked.

What's with all the winking about Miss Nelly? I thought.

I turned to pick up my gun, and the sheriff stopped me with a firm grip on my shoulder.

"Where are you headed, boy?"

"Sacramento in California, sir. I'm a journalist from Boston, just going out west to cover the gold rush for my newspaper."

"That explains your funny way of talking," the sheriff said about my accent. "Head south when you leave town. Zeke's people will be watching the main roads to the north and east. Nobody goes south."

"Why can't I head west?"

"Hardy Grumman's ranch covers the land west of town. Don't nobody trespass on his spread. Even Zeke's clan fears that crazy German. Ain't no safe water south of town, so nobody will expect you to go that way. Pack enough water for you and your horse for three days, and you can avoid Zeke's family by skirting around the south end of Grumman's spread. I've got extra canteens if you need em."

"Thanks, sheriff. I've got water bags. I'll fill them at the stable. It should be enough for four days, especially if I take it easy on my horse."

He picked up my hat, slapped it against his leg to remove dust and handed it to me.

"If you leave at midnight," the sheriff said, "you should hit a big dry gully about midday tomorrow. Follow it west for two days, then, turn north until you find the main stagecoach trail. That'll skirt you around Grumman's land. Once you get back on the main trail, stagecoach lines maintain regular water stops all the way to Santa Fe. Don't bed down in the washes, boy. Ain't much weather this time of year, but if it does rain, flash floods can kill a man right quick."

I brushed dust off my shirt and picked a couple splinters out of my neck. My gun rested under a nearby table. Returning it to my holster, I slipped the leather retaining loop over the gun's hammer to keep the weapon secure while riding.

The sheriff stared at my weapon and frowned. Deep disapproval creased his forehead as he watched me tighten loose leg straps that kept the holster tight against my thigh. As I reached the exit, he called out to me, but his friendly demeanor vanished.

"Stranger," he said in a cold, harsh tone. "You don't fool me with that bullshit about being a journalist. Make sure you get out of my town, tonight. We don't need your kind here."

Tension lines deepened into a frown, and he glared at my gun as I pushed past the doors.

"What the hell got into that sheriff," I spoke to my horse as he limped beside me on the way to the livery.

Chapter 2

Willy, the stableman, seemed a nice sort. He was easy going and good with my horse.

"Plutus? What kinda stupid horse-name is that?" he asked.

"Plutus was the Roman God of Wealth," I said. "I've come out west to write about the gold rush in California that everyone back home's been talking about. I figured it made sense to ride the God of Wealth on assignment to gold country."

He did not appreciate my humor. The smithy leaned sideways and lifted my horse's leg to study the bad shoe.

"Tell you what," Willy laughed, "this here Plutock, or Pluter, or whatever the hell you called that Roman god, he ain't gonna bring you much wealth with that rock in there. Why didn't you remove the shoe when he pulled up lame? Could'a saved him a might of suffering if you just let him walk bare-hoofed."

"I didn't know I could do that. I let him set his own pace and figured he'd adjust."

"New at this, ain't you, kid?"

"Yes, sir."

"Tell you what, boy, you got yourself one fine quarter horse here. Good sixteen hands and big flanks. Bet he can outrun them Injun pintos. Where ya from?"

His reference to outrunning Indians was unsettling. I had chosen this southern route along the Santa Fe Trail to avoid just such encounters.

"Massachusetts. I finished college in Boston, studying journalism. That's my reason for coming out here. I'm writing about the gold mining experience in California for my newspaper."

Willy stood up after removing the bad horseshoe. He looked up and down my body as if judging me, but he stopped when he saw my sidearm and holster.

"Do yourself a favor, kid. Get rid of that iron. Then, ride this here horse as fast as you can back where you come from. You're heading for a heap of trouble, and you ain't got the slightest notion about it."

Has he heard about the problem at the saloon? I wondered.

His unsolicited advice fell on deaf ears, because I already wanted out of this town as soon as possible, only I had no intention of heading east.

"How long until the shoe's repaired? I'd like to leave town tonight."

"It'll be good as new in about an hour. Leave four bits on the grain barrel over yonder, and take your horse whenever you're ready. Your tack will be hanging on his stall."

"You always this trusting with strangers?" I asked, trying to be friendly.

"Yep." He spat a mouthful of dark-brown saliva mixed with bits of tobacco on the ground close to my boot. "Ain't met a man yet who wanted me to hunt em down and kill em over four lousy bits. Wouldn't wanna be the first, would ya?"

He chuckled at his own joke and walked over to the blacksmith hearth where he began pumping bellows. I believed he meant it. He would kill a man over four bits.

Here I was, only in town half a day, and that livery owner gave me my second lesson about the West. Life was cheap out here. Everything broke down to simple terms. Live or die over a whiskey or four bits for a horseshoe repair. I made a mental note to start my first article with that observation. It would provide a dramatic image to shock the gentile crowd in the big city—might even make a catchy title.

As I walked out of the livery, I chuckled at ideas for dramatic titles.

One Whiskey from Death, I thought. *Will Kill for Four Bits!*

So far, my article material consisted of a dead drunk, a moody sheriff and a horse tender who might kill a man over four bits. I began formulating my first story as I headed up the neatly arranged paver stones to the entrance on the Empty Nest.

"Sure hope Miss Nelly's food is as good as her press," I said under my breath while spanning both porch steps in a single stride.

The sun had dropped low on the horizon and warmth of the day surrendered to a chilly evening breeze. Nights were not near as warm as my trip preparation indicated they should be at this time of year. My new jacket and tight-fitting pants did not cut the chill like the sales clerk in Wichita promised they would. I was beginning to think he took me for a fool and sold me city slicker duds instead of heavier clothes needed for back country travel.

Can't do much about that now, I thought and entered the front door of the Empty Nest.

Nice furniture, bright wallpaper and noticeably clean floors provided a contrast against the rest of this rundown town. It felt good to be in civilized surroundings like back home.

As the entry door closed behind me, it tapped a small bell mounted on a spring at the top of the doorframe. A door opened, and in walked a living goddess with piles of red hair braids, carefully layered above the most perfect lady face I had ever seen. She greeted me with a warm smile. Huge green eyes danced in friendship, and this woman's easy smile made me feel like I was being greeted by an old family member.

"Hi there, cowboy." Her hands bent backwards, propped against her thin waist. "Haven't seen you before. Ranch hands call me Miss Nelly. What's your name?"

I felt a bit awkward while she looked me up and down.

"Name's Colton. Friends call me Cole."

"Cole it is, then. You're obviously not from around here, Mister Cole." She made a point to emphasize my name. "Locals haven't shined boots or shaved clean in months. Let me guess, you've come out west to hunt buffalo?"

Even I knew how rough buffalo hunters looked. I enjoyed her playful sarcasm.

"No ma'am."

I felt a little conspicuous under this attention and unconsciously rested the palm of my hand on my pistol grip.

She noticed and pointed at my gun.

"May I?"

I nodded. Miss Nelly slipped the hammer loop off and withdrew my forty-four from the holster. Palming it with one hand in a confident motion that surprised me, she studied the weapon carefully and sniffed the barrel.

"Been fired recently. Where'd you get this? I've never seen this model. It's a lot lighter than a Walker 44 or a Dragoon."

"Guy in Wichita sold it to me. He said it was the best on the market."

She turned the gun upside down and looked at the trigger guard. I thought that odd. Her fingers ran along the barrel as if she was feeling the smoothness of a fine piece of linen.

"He sell you that holster, too?"

"Yes, ma'am. Taught me how to use the gun and holster proper."

I meant that he instructed me on the use of the hammer loop to keep the gun from falling out of the holster while riding a horse. I'm not sure she took my comment the same way.

"I hope he taught you real good," she said and slipped the weapon back into the holster. "You're going to need it."

Chapter 3

A loose braid of hair slipped down across her face. With her hands lifted high fixing her hairdo, I could not help but notice that her blouse strained mightily to contain her ample lady endowment. I got the impression she wanted me to notice.

"What brings you to the Empty Nest?" she asked.

The young woman looked so damned pretty that I was tempted to follow the implied suggestions of others and inquire about more than grub, but I had been raised to be respectful of ladies.

"I'm just here for grub, ma'am. Seems everybody in town raves about your cooking."

"Is that all they raved about?"

Bartender and sheriff opinions of her cooking were right. Miss Nelly made some fine grub. Plentiful beef chunks mixed with carrots, potatoes and some kind of greens all boiled in a big, iron pot. She made enough for a platoon of hungry cavalrymen, and I soon found out why.

There must have been more than a dozen men at a rustic, plank-wood table in the dining room. Most dropped by after dark for a bowl of her kettle stew. Some ate more than one helping while she flirted with all of them, finding something to compliment about even the ugliest old cowpuncher.

I took my time eating, making mental notes for future stories. Every one of the guests left four bits on the table, a mighty fare, suited more to a fine-China meal in an Eastern restaurant than a steer-wrangler's chow hall, but nobody complained. They all left with a smile, and most took a couple fresh-cooked pan-biscuits with them. I noticed three men went upstairs with Miss Nelly's lady-friends and never saw them again.

It was getting late, and I knew I needed to be ready to hit the trail out of town. Packing saddlebags and adding extra water bags would take some time. Nevertheless, I made sure I was the final man at that table. Growing journalist instincts told me Miss Nelly had a story.

"Had enough?" she asked and took a seat directly across the rustic table from me. A couple of her red braids had worked loose and hung across her shoulders resting softly against the exposed rise of her bosom.

"Would you mind if I have a little more?" I asked, not because I was hungry, but she was just so darn pretty.

"If there's more in the kitchen, it's yours, but don't get your hopes up. Boys ate good tonight. I'll be right back."

Miss Nelly leaned forward, excessively, as she stood up. Firm round breasts bulged against the restraint of her bodice as she did so, and she caught me looking. I was embarrassed. I'd been taught better than that. She just smiled.

Nelly returned with another bowl of food, but instead of placing it in front of me, she straddled the bench next to me in a very unladylike manner. Scooping up a heaping spoonful of stew, she ate it herself and filled the spoon again.

"Your turn," she said and held the offering to my mouth.

I will not lie, being hand-fed by this green-eyed beauty stirred manly feelings.

"My turn."

She savored another bite and ran her tongue slowly across her lips to capture a thin smudge of gravy that lingered.

Mind you, I was no stranger to feminine wiles, but this was a first for me. No lady-friend ever fed me dinner, much less in such an enticing manner. By the time that bowl was empty, I could barely keep my thoughts pure.

"Where are you staying tonight?" Nelly asked sweetly.

"I'm heading south at midnight. I'll probably bed down before dawn for a few hours, and hit the trail again at sunrise."

"Sounds like you're traveling fast. Law hunting you?"

I suppose that was a fair question, especially in a desolate place like Tumbleweed. After all, this town would be the perfect place to avoid territorial law, and why would I be leaving at midnight, if I had nothing to hide? I explained what happened earlier in the day.

"That was you?" she asked. "I heard about it, but nobody told me you were so young and good looking."

My face suddenly felt warm.

"Well, if you really have to leave in the middle of the night, we'd better take advantage of the time we have."

She took my hand and gently tugged me.

I resisted.

"Miss Nelly, I appreciate your good will, but I didn't come here to take advantage of you." I stuttered, "If . . . if that's what you are thinking."

Chapter 4

Miss Nelly lifted my face with both her soft hands. Her face moved so close to mine that when she spoke I felt the warmth of her breath on my lips and smelled the rich stew.

"It's nice to meet someone who respects women. We don't get your type out here in the desert much. Come with me."

She leaned back, pulling a bit more forcefully with both hands.

"Miss Nelly, I only came here for food."

"Do you think I have other intentions?" she asked.

"Well, this is a—"

"Whorehouse?"

"That's what I was told, and I don't want to take advantage of you."

"Do you think I'm one of the working ladies?"

"I . . . I don't know what to think." I lied.

"Let me put your mind at ease, pretty boy. I own this establishment. No man, including you, could afford me if I was a prostitute. Do you understand?"

"Yes, ma'am. I just didn't know what—"

"Let's start over, now that you know I am not one of the ladies. I like you because you're a handsome young man with respect for women and somebody bothered to teach you manners."
She pulled my hands again. I feigned resistance but slowly obliged and followed her back into the main parlor. As we rounded the top of the stairs, she glanced down at my pants.

"Where'd you get those pants?"

"Wichita. Guy told me they are the best a cowboy can buy."

"Really? I hope he also told you they're too small and not suited for riding distances."

I looked down at the ornate leather fringe on my chaps and my new pants. "Too small? How can you tell they're too small?" I asked as she closed the bedroom door behind us.

"Here, let me show you." She dropped to one knee and began to untie my chaps. With amazing speed, she stripped them off and tossed them over the back of a tall wood chair.

"Slip out of those pants."

I hesitated.

"If it will make you feel better, I promise I won't look. Wrap that blanket around you when you're done."

She pointed to a folded blanket at the end of an ornate four-post bed and turned her back to me.

I removed my boots because the pants would not slip over them. Then, I wiggled out of my tight slacks, folded them over the back of the chair and wrapped the blanket around my lower half like a wrap around skirt.

Miss Nelly took my pants and turned them butt up and inside out.

"What do you see?" she asked, holding the inside crotch in front of me.

"Cloth and some stitches. Why? Am I missing something?"

"Real cowboy pants have extra fabric called a saddle cut. These don't. No working cowboy would buy these. They're also too small for you."

"No they're not. They fit fine."

"Did you wear these all day on the trail?"

"Yeah, why?"

"I'll bet you took a lot of breaks during your trip to, uh, stretch your legs."

I thought back.

"Now that you mention it, yes I did. How did you know?"

14

"Cowboys go over size for sitting on horseback all day. These must have been tough on the boys."

She pointed at the crotch area that had annoyed me during long hours in the saddle.

Opening the bottom drawer on a tall dresser, she pulled out a pair of older, well worn jeans.

"These are bigger than those. Try them on."

She tossed me the pants and turned her back to me."

They fit loose, a bit too loose for my taste.

Miss Nelly turned around and said, "Much better. Squat down. Let's see how much room you have."

She was right. I couldn't squat all the way down in my new pants without my man parts getting squashed uncomfortably. These pants also had an extra panel of heavy fabric in the rear end.

I broke into a silly grin.

"What?" she asked.

"How come you have man jeans in your drawer?"

She shoved me playfully.

"Don't tell anyone, but I prefer the loose pants for riding."

Miss Nelly held my Wichita pants up to me.

"These things had to pinch you something terrible," she said. "If you want, you can keep those old ones, and I'll keep these."

That damn Wichita sales clerk did snooker me. I wonder what else he didn't tell me.

Nelly tossed my pants across an overstuffed easy chair and began unbuttoning her blouse.

"Miss Nelly, I did not come here to take advantage of you."

She pulled two long hairpins out of her hairdo and shook her head to free half a dozen braids she'd worn in a tight bun all day. I was amazed how long her hair was. The woven hair tumbled over her shoulders and unrolled almost to her waist. Tiny ribbons at the end of each braid kept them secure. She slipped the bows off and shook her head again. Deep red waves of hair, as thick as harvest hay, bounced playfully over her chest emphasizing the contours.

Nelly ignored my comment and pulled her blouse open revealing a tightly drawn beige corset that disappeared under the waist band of her floor-length, flowered skirt.

"You don't have to stay here, if you don't want to, but at least, be a dear, and untie this corset for me before you leave. The girls usually help me, but they're busy tonight, and it's killing me."

Turning her back to me, Nelly pulled her hair over a shoulder, revealing rows of tightly drawn strings threaded from side to side on some kind of ribbed cloth. She tossed her blouse on the same chair across my pants.

"I never untied a corset before. Where do I start?"

"See the bow in the middle?"

"Yeah."

"Pull the draw strings. Then, loosen the loops until they come out of their hooks. Work from the top to the bottom."

I followed her directions, and she inhaled deeply when the top most section of the binding garment suddenly loosened. Soon, the corset hung loose across her torso with multiple strings hanging to one side. I looked away to be a gentleman.

Miss Nelly turned to face me, holding up her shaping-garment with an arm pressed across her chest.

"I apologize," she said and extended her free hand. "I forgot your name."

Still looking politely at the floor, I answered, "Colton, but my friends call me Cole."

"Very well, Cole. It's nice to meet you."

We shook hands. It seemed an odd formality under somewhat intimate circumstances.

"You too, Miss Nelly."

She inched a little closer. I could smell a subtle sweetness, like week-old flowers.

"May I tell you a secret, Cole?"

16

I nodded and cautiously looked into her eyes.

"Nelly is not my real name. It's just a name I use for my professional image in this town. My real name is Tess. I'd like you to call me Tess, but not in front of others. Is that okay?"

"You bet, Miss . . . uh, Tess."

Without hesitation, Tess reached for my face with both hands and planted her soft, warm lips firmly on mine while holding my cheeks. The corset slipped to the floor. At that moment, I should have pushed away, partly out of being proper and partly because I'd heard about the diseases a man can get from fallen ladies. I returned her kiss, but pulled back slightly.

"What's the matter, Cole? Don't you like me?"

She slipped her arms around me, pressing her bare chest against my shirt.

"Yes. You're beautiful, but I shouldn't . . . what about the risks?"

"What risks are you worried about?"

I was not sure how to say I had heard about sex diseases, so I took a different tact.

"What about having a baby? I don't—"

"So sweet to think of me," she interrupted. "Do you think I would risk getting pregnant? Don't you worry. I assure you, it won't happen. In fact, I am worried about catching something from you. How do I know you are safe?"

I was shocked by her concern.

"I . . . I've never done this before. How could I have any—"

"You're a virgin?" she asked with a mix of surprise and disbelief.

"Yeah," I admitted, a bit embarrassed by being twenty-three and a virgin. My college buddies used to tease me about it.

Tess noticed my nervous fidgeting.

"That explains a lot. I thought you might not find me attractive."

"Lord no. You're beautiful and very attractive in, you know, that way."

"Cole, it's okay to be a virgin. Everyone is a virgin at first, and just to put your mind at ease, I have never been a working girl. I am as clean as you are. In fact, that's why I am so attracted to you. The first moment I set eyes on you, I saw a wonderful young man, a gentleman with manners and respectful of women. You are a wonderful change from all the local men who have been courting me, unsuccessfully, for the last two years."

My thoughts drifted off. She felt so good, and I had never gone all the way with a woman before. I reminded her one more time that I had not come to her place to take advantage of her.

"Thank you, Cole," she replied. "I do appreciate that, but, as you can see, I am taking advantage of you. So, keep quiet cowboy, and enjoy the ride."

Everything started happening fast, real fast. She dropped to her knees and tugged my loose pants down. I wasn't wearing underwear and she expressed delight at what she saw.

Girls back east did not know things like Tess did. That evening went by in a whirlwind. I woke up with her soft, naked body snug against mine with her leg draped across mine at the knee. Swaddled in warm layers of thick blankets, my first experience left me awestruck. It exceeded any fantasy I ever had, and I thought I might spend the rest of my life right there.

Chapter 5

An annoying beam of sunrise streamed through a gap in the curtains striking my face. I shielded my eyes with my forearm for a moment.

"Oh no!" I called out and bolted straight up.

Tess groaned and threw her arm around my waist, tugging me backward.

"Come here, pretty boy," she said. "It's still early."

I pulled free and looked around the dimly lit room for my clothes.

"What are you doing, Cole?" Tess asked, obviously annoyed at being rebuffed.

"I've got to get out of here. Zeke and his clan could show up any time."

"You'll be alright."

"You don't understand, Tess, the sheriff told me about Zeke's people. I got the impression nobody in this town would stand up to them. They plan to kill me."

"Honey, there are things our simple-minded sheriff doesn't understand, like who really runs this town. I have people who will stand up for you. Now, come back to bed."

"What are you talking about?" I asked a bit confused.

"Here's the deal, Cole. As long as you are my guest in this town, Zeke and his boys will not do a damn thing. I'll have a talk with a friend of mine and everything will be fine. Now, come back to bed. I'm not through with you."

She flipped back the covers revealing her fantastic feminine allure. I desperately wanted to trust her. Knowing what that bed had to offer, I threw caution to the wind and decided the risk was worth it, even if I didn't fully believe her.

That's how my adventure in the west began. Tumbleweed offered a few interesting notes for my writing journal, and some memories I'll treasure forever, but this little desert town would never give me the professional status I yearned for when I left the East.

My highly anticipated adventure soon decayed into daily monotony. I wandered around town scribbling notes in my diary. Descriptions of broken down storefronts became repetitive. I documented perpetual drunks and the stereotype, wild-eyed cattlemen who, long ago, forgot how civilized societies work. Boredom got so bad, I found myself getting excited when the occasional stagecoach rushed through town so fast locals barely noticed. And, there was Zeke, always watching me and making that gun-shooting hand gesture when he saw me look back. The man's simmering hatred stayed in check by some invisible power Tess held over him, but I could tell it grew stronger every day. It was just a matter time.

I soon ran out of things to write. Sex never got old, but even with all Tess's charms, I grew restless. My writing demanded fresh material.

How can I escape this trap?

"Morning, Cole. I made flapjacks, bacon and bought some sweet jam for breakfast today. I also put on some fresh coffee. Why aren't you out of bed already?"

"Thanks, Tess. You're so good to me. Hell, you're the only good thing about this town. Have you ever considered leaving here?"

She got a strange look on her face.

"No. I've settled here, and I have no intention of leaving."

"Come with me to Sacramento. I can support us with my journalism, and you can get away from this place."

"Do you have a problem with me owning a brothel?"

"No, of course not. I like the girls. They're all sweet. I was just thinking you might like to see new places, and—"

"I've seen all the places I ever need to see," she said with an angry tone.

"Well, I haven't, and I didn't come this far to end up stuck in a dust town with nothing but drunks and scorpions."

"What about me? Do I count for anything?"

"You're all I care about here. That's why I want you to come with me. Will you consider it? Please."

Tess did not answer. She slammed the door behind her as she left the room. I dressed quickly, making sure to strap on my gun like I did every day in case Zeke had a change of heart.

Breakfast smelled great when I walked into the dining room. Tess was not there, so I went into the kitchen where I found her dumping my pancakes and bacon into the dog's bowl.

"I'm sorry I got you mad," I said. "I was hoping we could travel out west together and—"

"Shut up, asshole. I gave you my body and my protection, and this is the thanks I get. You know I was beginning to think we could have children and raise a family here."

We never talked about having children, I thought. *And I sure as hell didn't talk about turning our relationship into a lifetime deal.*

I began to realize her experience and mine might not be at the same level.

"Tess, I don't understand why you are so set on staying in this God awful town, but I can't stay here. I have responsibilities to my newspaper, and I have a career to build. I'm going to leave later this week. I'd love you to go with me."

Tess's face became deep red, matching her hair. Breathing quickened almost to the point of forcing her wonderful breasts out of their tight enclosures. She stared at me and seemed to be choking back rage. I had heard redheads have bad tempers, but never took stock in stereotypes, at least before then.

"I'm going to the livery to check on Plutus. We'll talk when I get back. There's one more thing I need to tell you, but it can wait until you calm down."

Again, she did not say anything, but I watched her pour an entire pot of coffee out the window onto the dirt. I got the message—no breakfast for me today.

She'll calm down by the time I get back, I thought.

Turns out Hardy Grumman, the German, wanted Tess all to himself. His influence gave Tess her unquestioned power in that washed-out spit of a town. With me out of the way, he would be the only person Tess had left to meet her considerable needs.

A few days ago, Tess and I had attended his birthday celebration. He asked me to take a walk with him and pretty much gave me a choice. Leave town on a horse, or enjoy a free ride on the back of the undertaker's buggy. Real nice about it, though. He never threatened me directly, just kept lamenting about my eventual death, and how bad Tess would feel after the "accident." He warned me not to tell Tess about his ultimatum.

I figured if I could get her to go out west with me, I could solve three problems at one time. Tess and I could continue to develop our relationship, I would build my career, and Grumman's threat would be left behind. Seemed like a great solution to me. I had decided to tell her about Grumman when I got back.

Tess took my decision hard, real hard, about me moving on. When I walked back into the house, she destroyed half her tea setting trying to kill me with China cups and plates. In her outburst, Tess bragged that she sent one of her local fetch-it boys to tell Zeke I lost my protection. Her angry warning saved my life.

That night, I bedded down in the livery stable's loft above Plutus to hider from Zeke. I never did get the chance to tell her how Grumman's threat made it imperative for me to move on. I readied my horse before dawn and waited for first light to escape Tumbleweed.

During my month-long stay, I paid close attention to Zeke's behavior just in case a day like this might ever happen. A lazy man, he usually came to town a couple hours after sunrise, often half drunk before he even got to the bar. Poker with his drinking buddies took most of his morning hours. He would eat lunch at the bar and walk past The Empty Nest trying to intimidate me. Tess sent him away more than once. When she did, he would go back to the bar and drink until he went home after dark to sleep off his boozing.

I planned to be gone before he showed up. Figured I'd miss him by a couple hours if I left at first light. Plutus, being a fast horse, could easily carry me to safety on the German's ranch before Zeke got to town.

He must have wanted me real bad. When Plutus and I shoved out the barn doors, Zeke was waiting. He fired a shot at me from a distance and dove behind a horse-watering trough when I fired back. The whole family of the drunk I killed gave chase.

I left town at a full gallop, headed due west with Zeke and his four dumb brothers not far behind. Plutus needed his head, so I relaxed his reigns and let him set his gallop speed. I never would have believed any horse could run that fast. Leaning forward along his extended neck, I marveled at layers of powerful muscles against my body. He was magnificent.

Plutus reached the end of his wind just as we entered Grumman's territory. Half a dozen armed Hessians fired repeating rifles into the air, cheering as if I had won some kind of derby when I crossed into their ranch. My life and death escape was just entertainment to them.

Zeke and his boys stopped at the sight of the Hessians and shouted every curse word they knew, but they knew better than to enter Grumman's land.

I slowed among Grumman's men to let Plutus catch his wind, but our rest did not last long. They escorted me across the vast ranch at a quick trot. Mr. Grumman even waved to me from a distance as we passed his high country hay barn. His message was clear. This was a one way trip.

Chapter 6

Ten hours after leaving the German's land, I came on the first stagecoach watering station. I pumped fresh water into a small trough and let Plutus drink for a minute before tethering him under the lone shade tree. An old station tender exited the small adobe main building and walked casually over to Plutus and me.

This guy matched the dry, desolate territory. Wearing loose fitting denim pants and an old, fringed frontier coat over a faded red-plaid shirt, the man limped badly and had not shaved in a week or more. One leg bent inward toward the centerline of his walk like it had been badly broken and healed crooked. A wide, dark sweat ring, from years of long hours in the sun, wrapped his hat above an oversized brim that cast a deep shadow across his wrinkled face.

"Howdy, stranger. Fine stallion you got there. Looks a might hot. Got towels?"

I opened one of my saddlebags and produced an old piece of cloth.

"Just this one. It should do." I headed back to the water trough.

"Let me get a couple more. Ain't got nothing else to do. I'll help ya wipe him down."

After drenching three dirty cloths, he began wiping down my horse's head, neck and legs to cool him while I stripped off my saddle and horse blanket. Once Plutus seemed reasonably comfortable, I returned him to the water trough for a deeper drink. I worked through college in a racing stable and knew how dangerous it was to let a hot horse drink without limit. Figured Plutus needed the same precaution.

"Where you headed, feller?" the old man asked.

"Gold country. Where I come from, we hear stories about men getting rich in the Sierra Nevada Mountains near Sacramento. You ever hear those stories down here?"

The old man laughed a high-pitched cackle.

"You believe everything ya hear, boy?" he asked more in contempt than a real question.

"Are they not true?"

"Get some hay into the shade for your horse and come set a spell. I got pan biscuits and antelope gravy cooking. You hungry?"

"Yeah. Been riding all day."

He helped me spread fresh hay for Plutus before we entered the low-roofed adobe station for food. Nagging curiosity about his reaction to my gold prospecting comment bothered me, but it's not in good taste to look after one's own questions first.

"Didn't catch your name, mister," I said.

"Didn't offer no name, stranger. Better that way."

"Fine by me," I replied, a bit annoyed by being rebuffed. "Nothing personal, I—"

"Good policy to keep people at a distance," he interrupted. "Don't get caught up in nobody's business, that way. You might be a nice guy, or you might be a wanted killer. Makes no matter to me. My job is to keep this station open. Stages stop here four times a day, and they need fresh horses. I got to keep the well primed, make sure the coffee is fresh and provide a meal or two, but, most important, I got to take care of the horses."

I dredged a hot roll through gravy in a metal bowl. It was delicious.

"Like that meat?" he asked. "Shot that buck antelope on the high range two days ago. Salted some of it. The rest is in the smoker out back. That's the last of the gravy from a few steaks I cooked for myself."

"I haven't even seen an antelope yet."

"Big herds. Up in high grasslands right now. Summer rain brought out fresh sweet grass up there. Antelope follow the grass. Ain't no grass down here."

"You didn't seem impressed with the gold stories. Mind if I ask why?"

The old station keeper added a second helping to both our bowls and sat across from me.

"Boy, that's a fast draw forty-four on your hip. How many men you killed?"

I was shocked by his question.

"I never killed anyone, at least not intentionally." I thought back to the drunk in the bar. "Bought this gun in Wichita. Why do you think I've killed anyone?"

"Gun fighter. You got the look. Slick type. Good looking, probably hang out in card rooms. Yep, gunmen, I'd say."

He reached across the table and grabbed my hand.

"Soft hands, too. Not much good for hard work. You got the look, boy."

I sat in amazement at conclusions he reached from cursory observation.

"But, I know the truth," he said as he bit into a biscuit. "Want to know how?"

I nodded, completely baffled by his comments.

"That horse, boy. Gunmen are a cold-blooded bunch. Don't care nothin about horses. You took real good care of that stallion. Sure, you're packing a killer's tool, and you look the part. Coulda fooled me if I didn't see you with that animal. You ain't got the stuff of a killer."

"Thank you, I think. What does that have to do with gold?"

He stopped eating and looked at me with his head crooked slightly to one side.

"You really don't get it, do ya?"

All I could do was shrug in confusion.

"Kid, you look the part of a hired killer, or maybe a card-player gunman. There're all the same, but you ain't neither of those things. The way a man looks is his story. Stories can be real, or they can be tall tales. People ain't no different. You boy, you're about as fake as those rich gold miners. I been there, I know. Tried my hand at pan'n the American

26

River's north fork. Got a few ounces of gold, but damned near killed me. Gold stories you read back east are about as real as you would be in a gunfight. Fake, kid, you're a fake."

"If the gold stories are not true, then where are they coming from?"

The station keeper chuckled. "How much do you think this meal is worth?"

I tried to figure out his trick reasoning.

"Depends on how hungry am I."

He tipped his hat back on his head.

"Very good. Now, you're starting to figure things out."

At this point, I really did not have a clue what he was getting at, but apparently my answer hit on some line of reasoning.

"Boy, this here two-bit meal would fetch five dollars in gold country."

I could not believe it. That was a month's wages for a lot of folks.

"Are you joshing me?"

"Nope. That's why nobody gets rich pan'n gold. Yeah, lots of guys bring in a few ounces a month. At twenty-one dollars an ounce, five ounces earns over one hundred dollars. That's enough to make a man rich in a year, right?"

"Seems that way to me."

"What if a sluice pan costs twenty dollars? Or one egg fetches two dollars. Yeah kid, miners make small fortunes, but shop keepers and water barons take it all from em."

Two dollars for an egg! That's not possible, I thought.

After eating, the station keeper had to tend to the corral horses, so I returned his courtesy and helped out. While he added fresh hay to the feeder, I primed his pump and filled the large water trough for his animals. I also brought Plutus to the small trough for another long drink. He would need to be well hydrated for the long ride ahead.

We both heard the approaching horses long before they came into view. Several mounts, moving fast, from the sounds of them.

"Boy, go inside," the station keeper ordered. "Don't show yourself until I say it's safe. Fast-moving horses in the heat of day usually means trouble. There's a rifle leaning against the wall behind the door."

Chapter 7

I watched events through the door hinge crack.

The old man busied himself pumping water into the front trough when three men rounded the bend into sight. Their horses galloped with tongues hanging out, a sure sign of exhaustion and overheating.

"Hey old man, our horses need water."

"Help yourselves, boys. Water's free."

The men dismounted but made no effort to cool the horses before letting them drink.

"You boys ought to cool them down a bit, or they might get cramps,"

"We ain't got time for that, old man. How bout we swap these horses for three fresh horses in that corral?"

"Sorry, boys. Those belong to the stagecoach company. They ain't mine to trade."

The leader of the men looked tough. A long, red scar crossed his face, and his nose showed the flat widening of a fighter. I knew his type in boxing circuits back home.

"Listen, old man, we can work this out real friendly, or we do it the hard way. I see six horses in that corral and a fine looking stallion under that tree. How much will you take for three of them?"

"Like I said, mister, these animals ain't mine. Can't make a deal. Why not sit a spell, and let these critters cool down? I'll even wipe em down for you."

The tough looking leader pulled out his six-shooter and pointed it at the old man.

"I asked you how much, old man. Name a fair price, or we'll help ourselves."

One of the riders, a young guy with long, scraggy brown hair, dismounted and headed toward Plutus.

"I'm taking that one, John," he called out.

"No you ain't, Bobby. That's mine soon as we settle up with this here station keeper."

"Bullshit," he called back. "I seen him first. I'm taking him."

Plutus did not like the approaching bandit. He got real skittish and started pulling against his lead rope. When the man grabbed his tether, Plutus reared up and kicked at him. One hoof glanced off the man's cheek, knocking him to the ground.

"You son of a bitch!" the man shouted as he got up and pulled out his gun.

"Bobby! Get away from that horse. I told you, he's mine," the leader yelled.

"I outta kill that damn horse," he shouted and aimed his gun at Plutus.

I lost my cool and stepped outside.

"Drop your gun, or I'll kill you where you stand!" I shouted and pressed the old man's rifle firmly against my shoulder while aiming directly into the eyes of the leader.

"No call for threats, mister," he said. "We're just having a horse trade negotiation. Why don't you drop that rifle before somebody gets hurt?"

He turned his gun away from the old man as he spoke, so as not to provoke me.

The man near Plutus took cover behind the tree trunk and leaned out to aim his sidearm toward me. Screened by three exhausted horses, I ignored him for the moment. I don't know what possessed me, but I had gained the initiative and knew, instinctively, I had to use it.

The old man apparently understood that, too. "You boys best not fool with Pete, here. Man's a killer. Look at his holster."

The lead bandit stared at my sidearm for a long moment before returning his firearm to its leather sheath.

A shot rang out from the nearby tree. The bullet whizzed above head. When the shooter leaned out from the tree for a second shot, I swung the rifle over the saddle of the nearest horse and fired. I immediately returned my aim to the leader's chest before he could draw.

Bark splattered off the tree, snagging the man's exposed arm. The shooter's gun spun across the dirt. He yelled in pain and fell into view holding his upper arm where my bullet embedded in bone.

The station keeper noticed when the third horse thief quietly drew his revolver and attempted to hide behind his animal.

"Pretty stupid move, pulling that gun," the old station keeper called out. "Texas Pete killed twelve men in the Territories. Fastest gun in these here parts. You boys best put away your weapons and leave while you can. Get stupid if you want. I got extra room in my cemetery up that ridge. It's your call, boys."

I lifted my rifle at the leader's head.

"You get it first, if he comes around with that gun," I said in as menacing tone as I could.

"Put it away, Frank."

"He can't get both of us. Draw on him," the man called back.

"Put the goddamned gun away—now! He already shot Bobby."

I heard the distinct sound of the handgun uncocking and sliding back into its leather.

"Show your hands," I called to the third rider. He raised his hands above the horse.

I handed the rifle to the old man. "Cover them. I'm going to check the guy I shot."

It felt strange to say that. I'd shot two men, now, and did not feel remorse for either of them.

As I approached the tree, I noticed the injured man had retrieved his firearm. I brushed my jacket back off my gun holster, slipped the hammer loop free and withdrew the forty-four in case of the worst.

"Bobby, don't make me kill you." I cocked the hammer, making sure he could hear the metallic click. "Toss your gun out where I can see it, and I'll help you tend to your wound."

"You ain't taking my gun. No man takes my gun!"

The leader of the group called out to the injured man.

"Do what he says, Bobby. He's Texas Pete. Guy's a gunfighter. His kind kills cause they like it."

Bobby listened to reason and tossed his gun a few feet away.

After confiscating weapons from all three men, I made them sit against the side of the building under rifle point while the stationmaster cleaned and bandaged the young fellow's wound. Their horses had recovered somewhat but still needed proper care. I hated to send those animals back on the road, but these guys had to go.

"I unloaded your rifles and tied them into the scabbards. If I see you try to untie them, I'll kill you." I pointed the station keeper's rifle at the leader. "You get it first."

"What about our handguns?" he asked.

I handed the rifle to the old man, opened each gun's cylinder and pushed out all the rounds.

"Reload down the trail. If you show your faces back here, I'll shoot you on sight. Tumbleweed is about ten hours out if you take it easy on your rides."

The men left at a fast trot. I wondered how much longer those horses would last.

Plutus settled down after the stranger left. Gunshots unnerved him. I noted that for future reference in case I had to use a firearm while riding.

Back inside, the station keeper leaned his rifle against the wall.

"Done good, kid. Thanks for standing up for me. Them are some bad sorts. Ain't never seen em before. Hope I never see em again."

"You're welcome, pops." I liked this old guy.

"What's your name, kid?"

"Colton. Colton Minar. Yours?"

"Call me Mack. It ain't my real name, but it's what people who know me use."

"Why not use your real name, Mack?"

"Shit, kid, if your daddy named you Julius, you'd find a nickname, too."

Chapter 8

I was filling water bags for travel when a stagecoach reined to a stop. Butterfield Overland, in wide letters, appeared under a thick layer of trail dust. The stage came from the west. A gentleman wearing high-society duds climbed out followed by three young women who also looked much too sophisticated to be traveling in such rugged country.

Mack began unhitching six tired horses.

"Check number three, the mare," the driver called to Mack. "She picked up a limp about an hour ago."

I helped Mack switch out the rig and wiped down the tired animals for him while he went inside to attend to the travelers.

After I got the hot horses cooled, I went inside and found Mack weaving tales of hunting buffalo, street gunfights and shootouts with gold thieves up in the Sierra Nevada Mountains. His stories sounded real, but I wondered if he actually did all those things, or if maybe he should have been a storybook writer.

Mack warned the driver and shotgun rider about the gunmen we experienced earlier in the day, and then he announced chow would soon be served.

My shirt was sweaty and soiled from handling the horses, so I excused myself and went outside to rinse it before dinner. After cleaning out my sweat in the horse trough, I wrung out the wet shirt and hung it to dry on a corral post alongside the building.

"You live out here?" A woman's voice startled me.

I spun around. The youngest of the three girls leaned against the fence with her arms crossed on the top railing. With her chin resting on her forearms, she looked like any college girl back home, only dressed in a flowered riding skirt instead of school dress.

"No, miss. Just passing through, like you."

"Oh, I thought you live here, because you were tending horses."

"Naw, just helping Mack out. He's the station tender."

"That's nice of you." She stepped through the slightly opened gate. "Do you always 'take care' of strangers?"

I was not certain why she emphasized "take care," but it certainly piqued my interest.

She touched my chest with one finger and ran it down my exposed abdomen, slowly bumping over each muscle until stopping on a jagged scar just above my belt buckle.

"How'd you get this?"

I could not bring myself to tell the silly truth about falling out of a tree onto my family's picket fence, so I took a little license with the facts hoping to impress the fair maiden.

"Got on the wrong side of a steer's face. Pretty near gutted me 'fore I broke his neck and pulled the horn out. Doc stitched me up." As a tough-guy afterthought, I added, "Beef never tasted as good as that one did."

She opened her hand and tenderly passed it over my abdominal muscles and the scar. I wondered how old she was. Despite looking to be a younger girl by her face, the way she filled the notch in her vest left no doubt about her womanly attributes. Add blue eyes and a slight scent of lilac, I was mesmerized.

"Betty Sue," a man's stern voice called out. "Where are you? Are you okay?"

"Yes, papa," she replied. "I'm just talking with--"

"What's your name?" she asked quietly.

"Cole."

"I'm just talking with Cole, daddy. I'll be right there."

She smiled at me, ran her fingers down my chest and headed into the station.

I put on my shirt despite it still being moist and entered the building to the familiar smell of Mack's gravy and biscuits. Betty Sue sat next to the gentleman and two equally handsome ladies sat on his other side. If I had to guess, they were all sisters, Betty Sue being the youngest.

"This food tastes like pig slop," the gentleman complained and threw his spoon down. "I'm paying top dollar for a six-horse coach, and this is the best you can do?"

His comment was directed to the stagecoach driver, but it clearly bothered Mack.

"I'm sorry, Mr. Guillard," the driver replied. "We're at the mercy of local game in these remote relay posts. There's not much around here."

"You'd think a premium operation like Butterfield could stock such stopovers with real food and a competent chef."

Mack squirmed under the criticism. It angered me. People of his class back home often insulted servants and anyone they perceived as lesser in social stature. One time, I opened my mouth in defense of a Negro stable hand and lost my job. I knew wealthy jerks like this.

"Guillard, perhaps you'd like to join me in a little hunt after dinner," I suggested. "I'm sure your exceptional skill with a rifle, and talent with a skinning knife, can provide us with better fare than this."

His attention snapped to me.

"Arrogant little pisser, aren't you?"

"I don't insult people who feed me or carry guns for my protection."

"Boy, mind your tongue! I eat no-talent, cowhands like you for lunch. You don't know who you're talking to."

"True, sir, and you should know that I don't much care who I'm talking to."

The man raised his walking stick and struck across the table at me, landing a stinging blow across my shoulder. As the stick bounced off me, it hit the table, and my unfinished bowl of Mack's food spun into the air, splattering on my freshly rinsed shirt. I jumped to my feet.

Mack seized the opportunity.

"Sir, you best apologize to this young feller." Adding drama to the urgency in his voice, the old station manager jumped up with a hand held out in a stopping motion toward me. "He didn't mean to hit you, Pete. Please, don't kill him."

The gentleman looked back and forth between Mack and me in confusion.

"Look at that killer's gun," Mack said to the man. "He ain't got no horse hands, neither. Not a callous on them. Boy's a gunfighter. Stopped in for rest and helped me out. If I was you, I'd apologize."

He winked to me when he turned his face away from Mr. Guillard to carry on his act.

"Kid, I don't want no bloodshed here. This old man, he's just tired from the long ride. He didn't mean you no harm."

Mr. Guillard stared at my holster. He apparently knew enough about weapons that his face went white. He leaned back on the bench, sliding his walking stick out of sight as he did.

"Sorry," he mumbled in false remorse. "It's been a long trail, and I'm exhausted. I didn't mean to hit you."

"Maybe I was out of line, too." I tried to diffuse the tension. "I'll be back after I wash this gravy out."

I pulled out my shirt to display the wet stain and shook my head in disgust. When I turned the corner, heading to the corral's water trough, Betty Sue called out behind me.

"Cole, daddy sent me to clean this for you. Daddy's not usually so bad. Thank you for not hurting him."

She removed my shirt and scrubbed off the food before hanging it over the same fence post where it dried a short while ago. It was dripping wet, so I lifted it from the post and twisted the cloth as hard as I could to squeeze out excess water. I made sure my muscles stood out.

Betty Sue stepped close.

"Betty! Betty Sue," her father called in anger. "You've been out there long enough to clean his shirt. We're leaving. Get in the coach."

With a panicked look, she planted a hot, probing kiss on my mouth, and pulled away long before my lips were ready.

"I'll be in Saint Louis all summer," she whispered quickly. "Two doors south of the Bissell Mansion. Come see me."

She placed a hand between her legs to pull her travel skirt up so she could run to the stagecoach. Her father glared at me when I walked around the corner without a shirt. I nodded to him, knowing how much his type hates to lose power.

The stage driver called to me, "Would you mind riding with us, mister? I'll pay a good wage for a gunman like you. We're trying to reach the next station under the full moon, so we'll be moving fast, and those men Mack mentioned can't be too far ahead."

"Thanks for the offer, but I'm headed west."

As the stage rumbled away, Betty Sue leaned out her window and maintained eye contact with me until the carriage rounded the bend. I gave momentary thought to abandoning my journey and heading for Saint Louis.

I stayed at the station until late evening helping to hay and water the stock. We checked out the limping mare, and Mack found a loose shoe. He quickly replaced it.

Sun was getting low, and I wanted to hit the trail before dark. I liked traveling in moonlight, especially during a full moon. It was cooler, and I enjoyed safety in darkness.

"Here's some fresh-smoked antelope jerky for your travels," Mack said. "Do you have to go? You're welcome to bed down here for the night."

He handed me a heavy cloth wrap containing a generous gift of his long-term meat supply.

I did not tell Mack about my troubles in Tumbleweed. Zeke and his boys might not give up so easily. They would be at a least a day behind me because they had to travel around the German's ranch. It would be best for the old man if I keep moving, although I couldn't resist staying long enough for one more fill of the delicious gravy and biscuits before saddling Plutus and heading into one of the most colorful sunsets I had ever seen.

Mack's last words to me?

"Get rid of that gun, kid. It'll get you killed."

Chapter 9

Light from the moon lasted deeper into the night than I expected. Trail ruts from years of stagecoach and pioneer wagon wheels made it easy to follow the trail. I kept on until the moon got low on the horizon some time in the early morning. I used the last of the moonlight to find a flat elevation above the trail for my camp. Plutus rested with a long lead rope tied to the base of a thick Manzanita tree while I gathered dead wood a fire.

As long as Plutus was quiet, I knew I had nothing to worry about, so I leaned against my saddle using my blanket roll to soften the back rest Early morning light in the east lifted me out of deep slumber. Warmth of my blanket kept me comfortable against the early morning chill. My fire burned down to a bed of red coals, but I knew it would stoke up in short order.

Suddenly, Plutus began bucking franticly and snorting. The Manzanita bush, anchoring his lead rope, shook violently with each jerk of his head. I leaped up to settle him before the plant's roots might yank free of the hardpan soil.

"Plutus, whoa, boy. Calm down."

I grabbed his lead rope while he reared back, slashing the air with his front hooves. My hand slid down the rope to untie his tether from the base of the stout bush.

"Ow!"

Sharp pain stabbed through my hand. I knew instantly from the distinct warning sound.

Rattlesnake!

I yanked my hand from under the branches and watched a huge diamondback rattlesnake slither away as fast as it could.

Two puncture wounds oozed blood and some other yellowish fluid. Intense burning set in and quickly migrated up my arm.

39

Instinctively, I sucked as hard as I could on the holes, repeatedly spitting out a bitter tasting mixture of blood and venom. My fire was just a bed of coals, and I knew I would need hot compresses to help bring the toxins out. I also knew I did not have much time until I could not function.

After throwing my remaining wood on the smoldering embers, I removed a small pan from my bedroll kit and filled it with water to heat on the edge of the fire. Mack gave me a couple extra horse-wiping clothes that I ripped into strips and dropped into the water. Despite working as fast as I could, nausea and dizzy spells began to accompany violent tremors in sporadic waves.

Every article I had read on the subject of rattlesnake bites before heading into this adventure warned about symptoms and stages of deterioration. They were right.

Within minutes, my hand swelled and turned dark red.

The thin blade of my skinning knife easily cut an incision between the two fang holes. Journals I read before this trip said to do that, but I remembered wondering if I could ever bring myself to make such a self-inflicted wound. It was amazing how little pain mattered when worried about death, besides, my hand was on fire from the venom. Blood ran down my wrist and dripped away.

Less than fifteen minutes had passed, and I was already losing function. The cut seemed to run out of fluid, so I stopped sucking and placed hot strips of wet cloth over the swelling, hoping to draw out more poison. It did not help.

Tingling moved up my arm, and I felt weak all over. My heart raced, partly from venom and partly from anxiety. I considered mounting Plutus and trying to make it back to Mack's station, but I knew that was nearly a day's ride, assuming I could remain alert.

Wood on the hot coals flared while I leaned against my saddle trying to lower my heart rate. I read that, too. Staying calm was supposed to slow the effects of the venom.

Breathing became difficult, and my vision blurred. I replaced the hot compresses and crawled back to my resting place. Pain exceeded anything I ever felt. My hand and lower arm were on fire. I retched violently and began to shake.

I do not know how long I had been unconscious, but when I woke, my fire had grown quite large, and my hand was on the ground next to me covered in dirt and leaves. Pounding in my head was fierce and vision lapsed in and out of focus. My arm looked to be twice its normal size and was an ugly black and red. I lay, bare-chested, against my blanket and saddle in late afternoon sun. My boots were gone, and to my great alarm, Plutus was nowhere in sight. Food, water and weapons lay right where I left them.

Propping on my good elbow, I saw my shirt draped across several branches on a nearby bush, and my boots were stuck upside down on branches stripped of leaves. I tried to get to my feet but the slightest movement sent massive waves of pain and nausea through my body.

Have I been robbed, I wondered. *They only took my horse. Doesn't make sense. Why would they leave my weapons and valuables?*

Through my drowsy fog, I heard horse hooves and a snort like Plutus would make when he was being rambunctious. I tried to move but could not reach my gun or rifle, both out of reach on my bad side.

Plutus came into view as he rounded a sandstone outcropping. A dark-skinned woman rode him using only his lead rope. She looked especially small riding his enormous bulk. He ambled into camp at a leisurely pace, and she jumped off his back with a lithe movement that looked effortless. His lead rope hung limp, and she made no attempt to tether him.

I had seen sketches of Indians before, both men and women, but this was my first live encounter with one. She looked as I expected—high cheekbones, close-set eyes, and long black hair cascading over muscular shoulders and arms. As she approached, she pointed at my bad arm and touched her chest. I had no idea what that meant.

The Native American woman kneeled next to me and removed my bad hand from my thigh where I had it propped after pulling it out of the dirt pile. She pushed it onto the ground and spat onto her palms. Rubbing the moisture on the back of my hand, she scooped a mixture of leaves and reddish dirt, pressing in onto the wetness.

With no obvious threat, and my horse back, I relaxed a little.

Several sticks protruded from the ground on the far side of the fire. They tilted inward above the outer edges of the flames. She pulled one up and offered me some kind of cooked meat wrapped loosely around the wood.

Food made a difference. I devoured her offering and felt better. Across from me, the Indian ate strips of meat as fast as I did.

"Thank you," I said, wondering if she understood. I hoped she would at least sense the friendly tone in my voice.

41

She did not respond, not even a facial tic.

I patted with my good hand on my chest. "Me, Cole."

The Indian woman reached for another skewer of cooked snake and brought it to me. I realized she misunderstood my hand movement as a request for food. I tried again.

"My name is Cole." I spoke slowly and spread fingers of my good hand on my chest trying to make her understand.

"What . . . is . . . your . . . name?"

Again, she studied me without outward sign of understanding. I wondered if Indian language and gestures were different enough from mine as to make communication impossible.

My bad hand began to throb. I pulled it from under the dirt-leaf mixture, and searing spasms pierced up my arm. I fell backward and blacked out.

"Water, drink water."

My sight slowly focused on the Indian woman's face. I gagged on liquid she poured from a rawhide pouch held to my lips. I shook my head attempting to escape the choking fluid.

"Stop," I wheezed.

My good hand grabbed the Indian's wrist, but, as my bad hand attempted to help, some force held it tight to the ground by my side. Leaves and red dirt were piled high on it again.

"Drink," she said. "Need water."

It suddenly dawned on me. She spoke English, and she spoke it clearly.

"Okay, okay, but let me breathe."

She lowered the bottom end of the water bag, and my panic lifted.

"You speak my language?" I asked.

She nodded and scooped some of the spilled poultice mixture of dirt and herbs back onto my injured hand. I noticed a rope wrapped around my bad forearm and running out of sight beneath me. My own body weight pinned my arm and hand tight to the ground.

"Stupid white man. You not be still, so I tie arm down. Must keep hand under medicine one more day."

"If you speak English, why didn't you answer me when I asked your name?"

"You not need name, only medicine."

"Let's try again. My name is Cole. What is your name?"

She ignored me and added several small branches to the fire.

"I go. Find food," she said. "Keep hand on ground."

In a single, fluid motion, she took the lead rope and swung onto Plutus, coming to rest perfectly centered on his back. He reared, unaccustomed to the strange rider, but she leaned into his mane, adjusting smoothly to his halfhearted attempt to buck her off.

"Wait!" I shouted. "How long will you be gone?"

She ignored me. I suddenly felt vulnerable.

Sunlight ended shortly after the Indian left. Night shadows seemed alive with small creatures scurrying about. My hand burned as if it was too close to a woodstove. I was tempted to withdraw it from the Indian's primitive remedy, but the last time I did, the pain got worse.

Maybe she knows what she's doing. On second thought, I wish there was a white-man's doctor around here.

The fire burned down to a glowing bed of coals, but I was unable to do anything about it. I spent hours listening to night sounds while the moon crept across the sky until it began to set in the west. Complete darkness was near when I heard hooves of multiple horses walking along the Santa Fe Trail below my camp. Voices carried up from the riders below.

"Better pitch camp," one rider said. "Gonna be dark soon."

The first voice sounded familiar.

"Old Injun rock-shelter up around the next bend. We'll bed down there."

The second voice exploded in my mind. "Zeke!"

Chapter 10

Rider sounds faded as Zeke and his men continued down the trail toward their camp area. My heart raced until they passed out of hearing range. I found myself gulping air having held my breath too long.

I tried to reach my rifle, but my bad hand remained pinned to the ground by that rope the Indian squaw installed. With a twist of my torso, I rolled away from my weapon hand onto my good elbow. A sharp pain shot up my bad arm and radiated across my chest when the rope hold-down released. My hand jerked up into the night air, and I could barely stifle a shout of pain.

Several strips of rawhide that had held my arm tied down dangled loose from my wrist and forearm. Sharp cramps and persistent throbbing left no doubt about the lack of function in my hand, but I did notice that the pain was more tolerable this time.

My left elbow propped me enough to rotate onto my knees, but the world started spinning and nausea cost me the last of my earlier meal. Nevertheless, I knew Zeke camped within a short ride of here, maybe even within hearing distance. I was determined to get my rifle.

"White man," I heard just above a whisper.

I looked in the direction of the voice, but scattered clouds obscured light from stars and prevented me from distinguishing shapes. Then, I heard Plutus.

Strange, I thought. *I didn't hear him approach.*

"White man," the squaw came close to me in the dark. "Bad men close. We go."

How does she know they're bad?

Without further comment, she moved silently around the camp collecting my gear. She placed my horse blanket on Plutus and cinched his saddle before hanging most of my gear on the saddle horn and leather ties. I picked up his bridle and bit with my good hand.

"No," she said and took it from me. "Horse smart. Not need stupid ways of white men."

The Indian shoved the bridle and bit into a saddlebag. As she inserted my rifle into its scabbard, I grabbed my gun holster to add to the horse's load.

"No," she said. "Not good gun. Only for kill men, not hunt food."

I was not ready to let go of that firearm.

"I'm taking this," I said and hung it over the saddle horn.

She sneered at my decision. With all the gear stowed, she took my aching hand and brushed off residual dirt and leaves. I could not see much in the dark.

Without warning, she lifted my hand to her mouth and sucked on the wound. It turned my stomach. Fortunately, I had already lost my supper, so I just dry heaved while she spat half a dozen times. She rinsed her mouth with water from one of the bags before using the rawhide strips that earlier held my hand tight to the ground to tie strips of red bark over the wound.

I do not understand how that bark worked, but, I swear, the pain went away almost immediately.

"You stay. I come back."

She walked into the dark with my horse following her. Plutus trusted this woman. I could tell, and I had no choice but to trust her, too.

The Indian returned a short time later, without my horse.

"Help make fire big."

She began tossing wood on the coals.

"No," I protested. "Those men are bad. They'll see the fire."

She continued tossing dry wood on the smoldering coals and repeated her instruction.

"Those men are looking for me," I argued. "Don't do this."

The Indian stood erect and looked into my eyes, showing a flash of anger.

"I save your life. Make fire big. It help us get away from bad men."

For the first time, I felt good enough to make my own decision. I thought about my choice.

I can follow her instructions, or, I can demand my horse back and make a run for it.

Who was I kidding? I couldn't ride very far in my condition. I began adding as much firewood to the pile as I could with one good hand.

The fire did not flare right away. Smoke thickened and coals began to glow brighter as the Indian worked faster, piling wood well above chest high.

When this fire ignites, I thought. *They'll see the flames in Boston! I hope she knows what the hell she's doing.*

"Come. Walk soft."

She led me away from the trail up an incline into a boulder-strewn rise. I lost sight of her twice, and each time she stepped back from the darkness to grab my shirt and pull me in the right direction. She finally grabbed my loose-fitting leather jacket and dragged me along faster than I was comfortable walking in pitch dark.

I could feel it as we began a gentle descent, weaving between boulders I could not see, but knew they were there by her detours. She stopped and listened to something I could not hear.

"Look." She motioned in the direction from which we came. "Good fire."

An entire hilltop was silhouetted against the roaring fire we left behind. Residual light from the backlit hill made our vision better and travel easier. This Indian was on a mission, and she meant for me to keep up. Urgency seemed palpable. She let go of my jacket, and I could tell that if I did not keep her pace, she would leave me behind.

We rounded several more large boulders and entered a thick growth of Manzanita scrubs. A small campfire came into view only a hundred feet away. Three men stared in the direction of my former camp.

"What do ya think, Zeke?" one man asked.

"Dunno. Get your guns," Zeke said. "Let's check it out. Might be him."

Their horses were tied to scrub trees at the fringe of the camp and the animals became restless, sensing our approach.

"Want me to saddle em?" a third man asked. He had a thick accent that I could not identify but knew I had heard him before.

"Too noisy. We'll walk. If it's him, we can sneak up better on foot."

Zeke led the group into the darkness along the main trail toward my camp.

"Come. We get horses," she whispered.

"I'm not stealing horses!"

I had read Indians thought nothing of stealing horses, but horse thieves risked hanging under white man's rules, especially in rural areas.

"No steal." She lifted a sash off her shoulder. "Trust me."

I reluctantly followed her to Zeke's horses. She untied the first animal and handed me the rope. Opening her sash, she removed a spiny flower cut from one of the local cacti. After gently lifting the nervous horse's tail, the Indian shoved the thorns against the horse's ass and dropped the tail. Poor thing nearly ran me over as it took off running and bucking. Before the first animal's hoof beats faded in the distance, she sent the other two horses running.

"It take them all day to track horses. We go north."

"I'm not going north. There's a Mexican mission called Los Angeles west of here in California."

"No. Go north, or they kill you."

How does she know that? I wondered.

"They know you go west. I listen to them talk. They find you, how you defend yourself with one good hand? You die."

"Can you go west with me?" I asked, hoping she might be willing to help me.

"No. White men hate Indians. I go north. You come with me, or stay on this trail by yourself. I not care."

She started walking into the pitch-black night in the direction from which we came.

"Wait! What about my horse?"

Chapter 11

"You want horse? Keep up with me."

The Indian set a fast pace. I could not see the ground as I followed her through the dark, but I wanted Plutus back, so I could build distance before Zeke discovered the ruse.

Sounds travel far in darkness. Each gravel-crunching step of my boots threatened to give away our location while the Indian walked without a sound.

Earlier cloud cover passed, and my eyes gradually adjusted to minimal light from stars. I made out her shape just ahead of me. Long legs met a thin waist, and she moved with efficient confidence like a nocturnal predator. For a minute, I forgot she was a savage. It seemed odd to me that her people and mine held so much animosity for each other. I certainly did not feel that way toward her. She could have taken my horse and left me to die.

The squaw stopped so abruptly on the trail that I ran into her.

"Listen," she said and panned her hand toward the trail ahead.

I did not hear anything.

She leaned back into me and whispered, "Man killer. Do not move."

I heard a faint rustle in nearby brush, followed by distant yips of coyotes.

"It move away. Hurry."

My guide set a controlled run. I struggled to keep up with her, gulping air as best I could. Calves burned and my chest heaved by the time we broke into a clearing where Plutus was pulling frantically at his lead rope.

"Get rifle," she demanded.

I grabbed my nearest weapon, the handgun from the holster on Plutus. My right hand collapsed when I tried to hold it, so I switched to my left hand and cocked the hammer with the heel of my bad hand.

"There!" She pointed toward a thicket. "Man killer."

I did not see anything, but heard a low, breathy growl coming from the black void.

"It want horse."

Plutus began rearing frantically. The Indian untied his lead rope and pulled him past me, away from the threat. Then, I saw it. Glowing eyes. Two small green lanterns with large black vertical ovals approached in a silent, steady stalk.

I aimed between the eyes as best I could in the dark and waited for a closer shot. Zeke and his men would hear it, so I would have to make quick work of this threat.

The speed of the beast's lunge caught me unprepared. In an instant, it covered the ground between us and leaped. My bad hand protected my face, but I smelled the hot breath of the mountain lion as it slammed into my chest. Legs wrapped around my torso and claws plunged into my back. Teeth bit down on my gun-holding forearm, and the weapon fired into the animal's side seemingly without effect. I fell backward under the momentum of the heavy cat.

Glints of starlight flashed on metal as my Indian friend leaped onto the predator's back, slashing wildly. She reached around its throat with her blade and cut deep through fur and flesh. The beast released me and fell onto its back, pinning the small woman beneath its body. Her legs locked around the puma's waste while she pressed her relentless attack with fury I had never before seen from a human.

The puma flailed against the Indian's hold, attempting unsuccessfully to roll over. Blood gushed from its throat wound and gurgling sounds muffled attempted growls.

Movements of the great cat slowed. Random pawing of the air quickly led to death convulsions. Pushing out from under the cat, the Indian got to her knees and grabbed my arm. She pulled back my shredded sleeve and ran her fingertips over the fang wounds.

"You live. We go. Bad men know where we are."

She left me kneeling on the ground and bounded into the darkness in the direction she went with Plutus. Moments later, she and my horse returned.

"Put gun away. Must go fast."

I returned the gun to its holster and slipped the hammer loop into place for security. I did not take time to reload that one cylinder, but I made a mental note that I only had five shots left.

We must have walked twenty miles in starlight until morning began to show on the horizon. She would not let me ride, saying it was better use of a horse to carry our goods. My back hurt badly from cougar claw damage, but I continued to match this small woman's drive. I could not let her be tougher than me.

"You still haven't given me your name," I said. "I know you speak English."

For the first time, she smiled. I saw her cheek stick out.

"Why white men always want name?"

"It's a sign of friendship in our culture."

"You not my friend. No white man is friend to Indian."

"But, you saved my life. I'd say that makes us friends."

She stopped walking and released the horse's lead rope.

"Let me see Man Killer wounds."

Rolling back my bloodstained sleeve, she studied the fang marks on top of my forearm in the dim light. Dark red scabs sealed the punctures and dry blood stained my clothes and skin. She flexed my fingers while pressing on my forearm to check for proper muscle tension. Twisting my arm over, she examined smaller holes from the mountain lion's lower teeth.

While the Indian examined my puncture wounds, I rubbed my other sleeve back to expose the snakebite. Tied-on bark fell away, as I opened and closed those fingers several times. To my surprise, the hand felt much better. Even its color changed during the long night walk. Ugly blackness vanished, replaced by normal skin tone with scattered blotches of red.

She finished her inspection of my arm and removed a water bag from Plutus. She watered him before allowing either of us to drink.

I tried to be tough despite increasing pain in the claw slashes on my back.

"I'll set up a fire," I said.

"No fire. Bad men too close. Eat dry food. Move fast."

She opened a satchel hung off her shoulder and produced my package of Mack's antelope jerky.

"Hey, did you steal that from my grub sack?"

"No," she said indignantly. "Payment for fix stupid white man who get snake bite. You eat? Or, just talk like fool?"

"Whoa!" I thought. *This little woman just put me in my place.*

It was then that I noticed her womanly shape under loose-fitting, animal skin clothes.

She can't weigh more than a twelve-year old boy.

Extraordinarily lean, her muscles rippled with every movement. Her small waist and gentle curves suggested a lady-shape that might dress up nicely in a party gown. In college, my friends liked puffy girls with large breasts and big hips. I always preferred country girls. They knew hard work on farms and had more energy than their city counterparts. I liked their vitality.

"Eat," she ordered. "Cross desert before sun too high."

She handed me three pieces of dried meat and one of the water bags.

"Drink good. Last water, two hours. No more until reach middle of desert. Wait here."

She must have been gone nearly an hour. When she returned, her arms surrounded a large bundle of grass mixed with dry leaves. The grass was for Plutus. She pulverized the leaves on a nearby rock, mixed them with red clay and added water.

My cougar-bitten arm hurt badly.

The Indian smeared her poultice on both my upper and lower puncture wounds. After tearing a strip of cloth from the bottom of my shirt, she wrapped my arm and the poultice with a makeshift bandage. I was astonished how fast the mixture reduced the burning.

Without explanation, she moved behind me, lifted my shirt up over my head and tossed it on the ground. Several ragged tears and large circles of blood marked where the puma's claws cut into my back. The woman wiped my back with fresh water before smearing her medicinal concoction into the wounds. She brushed flies off my shirt and rinsed out the blood.

After untying the fasteners of my shirt, she ordered me to hold my arms behind me. My wet shirt slipped on, and she reached around from the back to pull it closed in front. Her body pressed firmly against my back as she began fastening my shirt from the top down. When she reached my abdomen, her hands slipped under my shirt and grazed muscles made large by many years of sculling practice in college. She paused for a moment as if enjoying what she felt. Her breasts pressed into my back, and although not large, I enjoyed their warm firmness. I dared hope more would come of her interest in my body, but our contact ended abruptly when she walked away angrily without buttoning my shirt all the way.

"We go. Finish your shirt. Follow me. Watch for snakes and desert wasp."

I took the rope lead for Plutus and obeyed.

"When will you tell me your name?" I brought up my earlier question.

We walked for ten minutes without comment.

"Kaga," she called over her shoulder. "My people call me, Kaga Ishta."

Nothing more was said for the next two hours.

We rounded a rocky mound, and I got my first view of the desert. Flat and white, with widely scattered cacti and scrub trees, it looked inhospitable.

"Are we going out there?" I asked.

Chapter 12

Mile after mile of hot sand and cracked clay passed under Kaga's relentless pace. My feet got hot despite protection from heavy boots. I looked at the Indian's thin animal skin moccasins and wondered how the blistering sand must feel to her. Somehow, she did not appear affected by the growing heat. Plutus, on the other hand, hung his head low as the heat grew oppressive.

"Kaga, Plutus needs water."

"Horse fine. Bad heat comes in one hour. Must reach place of my people before high sun. Then, we rest until dark."

"This place have a name?"

"Valley of death."

"How much farther is that valley?" As soon as I asked the question, I realized a more important question. "Hey, why do they call it Valley of Death?"

I was not sure I wanted to hear the answer.

"Home of no-head bugs. One sting, you die," she replied. "We stop at that rise."

Kaga pointed to a rocky ridge ahead. It turned out to be the rim of a long gully cutting across the desert as far as I could see. We ascended the near rim of the gorge where loose sand ended and hard rock made travel easier. Kaga slowed our pace as we followed a narrow trail down a steep cliff to the floor of the cut.

"Come, look." She stopped by a group of small boulders and pointed at the shade between two of the rocks. "No-head bug. Stay away. One sting, you die."

I had seen detailed drawings of scorpions in one of my college biology courses, and I even spotted a few during my trip from Wichita to Tumbleweed. This one ignored us as it consumed a small insect. The creature looked much more menacing up close.

"When are we stopping for water?"

My lips had begun to crack from the dry desert air.

"Soon."

She continued at a slower pace as we crossed the boulder-strewn arroyo.

The far side of the gully had steeper walls, but an ancient trail cut into rock eased the uphill climb.

"Cave of ancestors," Kaga said as she pointed to a series of cave openings further up the ledge. "We rest there until night. Too hot now."

We bypassed two entrances and turned into the third, and largest, cave opening. In the interior shade, I noticed faint rock paintings depicting herd animals like antelope and buffalo with child-like stick figures of primitive hunters surrounding them in a fight to the death. It was cool inside the cave, our first relief from searing heat in over six hours. Even Plutus relaxed.

Kaga dropped the lead rope and began removing my horse's burden. After carefully leaning water bags against the base of the cave wall, she removed a bundle of hay that she had tied to his saddle before we entered the desert.

Plutus wasted no time eating the dry grass. While he ate, Kaga poured a small amount of water into a crude rock bowl carved in the stone wall. My horse almost shoved her aside to get to the liquid. She found his antics amusing, laughing openly for the first time since I met her.

"I give you little water," she gently chastised Plutus. "You get more after cool down."

This strange woman obviously knows how to care for horses, I thought. *She's not bad caring for injured men either.*

Kaga took a long drink from one of the water bags before handing it to me. Water never tasted so good.

She opened one of my saddlebags and tore a large strip of Mack's antelope jerky into two pieces, handing me the larger of the two. Holding jerky in her teeth, she sat cross-legged with her back against the base of the cave wall and untied the straps of her rawhide foot coverings. She wiggled her toes and pushed them deep into the cool sand on the cave floor.

"Take off boots," she said. "Must take good care of feet when cross desert."

Seemed like a good idea, so I took her advice. Cool sand felt wonderful on my hot, sore feet. It was as soothing as a foot massage I got one time in college.

"Must sleep." Kaga said and closed her eyes. "We walk all night."

I had many questions, but the tiring walk across the desert sapped my energy. Sleep came as a welcome relief.

When I awoke, Kaga and Plutus were gone, along with my saddle.

I panicked and ran to the cave entrance. It was late day. Long shadows spanned the entire gulch. In the distance, three horses with riders appeared as dots at the top of the far canyon wall. Even at this distance, I could see the horses suffered. Their heads drooped low as they obviously suffered from severe dehydration. The riders did not seem to care as they cursed their failing animals and started down the cliff trail.

Movement in my peripheral vision caught my attention. It was Kaga and my horse coming up the cliff trail. Plutus was saddled with a fresh bundle of hay tied on.

"We go." She motioned a warning with her head toward the distant riders.

I did not need an explanation. Kaga followed me into the cave as I ran to get my boots.

"Stop!" she called out.

Stop what? I thought as I began to insert my foot into a boot.

Kaga snatched the boot from my hands and turned it upside down. A small amount of sand spilled onto the cave floor. She handed it to me and repeated the action with my other boot. A small scorpion dropped from the interior of the second one and scampered along the base of the cave until it disappeared into a crevice.

"In Valley of Death, must check boots, hats and blankets for no-head bugs." Then, she changed the subject. "Bad men near."

We quickly loaded the rest of our equipment and water bags onto saddle rings. On the way out of the cave, she opened a small bag tied to a rope around her waist and poured a handful of salt into the remaining water in the wall trough. She saw my puzzlement.

"Bad men and horses need water. Salted water poison in desert. They drink, they die."

Without hesitation, she took the lead rope and pulled Plutus behind her. She showed no outward reservations about poisoning the men or animals.

Amazing, I thought. *This woman is a lethal.*

We skirted quietly along our side of the canyon following a well-concealed trail past large boulders. It led to the crest of the ridge and looped away from the canyon, out of sight from our pursuers.

In the distance, a line of gray-blue mountains stretched as far as I could see, but immediately in front of us, oppressive miles of desert presented a daunting barrier. We kept the Indian's familiar hard pace, skirting scrub brush and tumbleweeds that dotted tops of hot sand dunes. As the last of the sun dropped below the horizon, oppressive heat continued to rise from sand.

"Night come soon," Kaga said. "Desert very cold when sun goes down. We have luck tonight. Good moon for travel. Reach mountains before morning."

Chapter 13

It must have been near midnight when Kaga stopped our brutal pace. The full moon rose a little after dark. She was also right about the cold, but she understated how cold it would get. I had not noticed the growing chill before we stopped. Standing still made me shiver.

Kaga unrolled one of my camping blankets and used her knife to cut it into two large halves. She draped her piece over her shoulders and pulled the flaps around her body, tying it in place with a rope from around her waist. I copied her with mine and used my belt to secure it. The added warmth felt good.

We ate and drank water, but she did not say a word. When Plutus finished drinking, she resumed her customary strong pace.

Terrain began to slope upward. I felt my calf muscles burning from the exertion. I prided myself at being in great physical shape from all my years on the rowing team, but this little woman made me feel like a weakling.

"I need to rest."

"No stop. We near trail to mountain. Keep going until light."

What was I going to say?

There's no way I'm letting some little woman make a fool out of me, I thought followed closely by, *"How the hell am I going to keep up with her?"*

I fought exhaustion and forced enough second wind to make it through the last couple of hours. Early vestiges of light on the eastern horizon confirmed my suspicions. Full-sized trees and ground foliage bordered the faint trail. This also meant water.

Kaga slowed noticeably and turned into a small clearing hidden behind thick bushes and shaded by a couple of towering evergreen trees.

"We camp," she said. "I get food. You unpack horse."

"Should we have fire? Won't Zeke and his friends see us?"

Kaga allowed a satisfied smile.

"They not follow. Cannot cross desert with weak horses during heat of day. If drink salt water, they die. We safe."

I rubbed my aching arm. Kaga noticed and removed the dressing revealing wrinkled, dry skin surrounding the teeth wounds. She pulled her knife from its belt sheath and gently scraped away the dead tissue, exposing fresh pink flesh where the punctures had sealed. Residual pain in my rattlesnake bite hand made it stiff, but when I flexed my fingers, I discovered to my relief, that full range of motion and most of my strength had returned.

"One more day," she said while applying a fresh poultice to the cougar wounds. "Unpack horse and make fire. I get food."

Morning chill lifted quickly with the rising sun. I removed the blanket-wrap that Kaga made the night before. The Indian returned with three dead chipmunks for breakfast. When we started to eat, she opened a small sack and poured dozens of soft, dark berries into a crude bowl made from a large piece of bark. The hot meat was good, but the delicious berries provided sweetness as refreshing as any eastern bakery deserts.

Exhausted, I fell to sleep breathing sweet-smelling evergreen and comfortable in the warmth moderated by shade. Kaga jostled me and announced it was time to hit the trail again. I was not ready. Judging by the high sun filtering through tree boughs, I could tell I had slept away most of the morning.

"You talk when sleep," Kaga smiled as she leaned back to lift the saddle onto my horse's back.

"What did I say?" I asked with guarded concern.

"Who Tess?"

"Uhh," I hesitated. "She's an old friend."

"She's friend? Why you fear her?"

"What the hell did I say to make you think that?"

"You say her name . . . three times."

The Indian squaw faced me as if waiting for more of an explanation. Her dark eyes peered deeply into some recess of my being. I felt naked.

"What makes you think I'm afraid of her?" I asked, hoping to diffuse the growing tension from her interrogation.

Kaga looked down to break eye contact.

"You sweat. Not happy when say her name."

I briefly explained my tumultuous breakup with Tess. Kaga frowned, disapproving of some aspect of my former relationship. Plutus nuzzled her, and she rubbed his lower jaw in apparent mutual condemnation of my recent past.

"Food not far. We go." Kaga ended the uncomfortable discussion by leading Plutus onto the trail, again heading uphill toward towering mountains in the distance.

I hurried to catch up, but she set another of her torrid paces.

We must have hiked for five hours without talking when my guide turned off the trail into a clearing carpeted with a thick layer of pine needles. Water gurgled in a small stream at the far side of the area and dense undergrowth cloaked the opposite bank of the brook.

I began unloading Plutus without being told by the Indian. She seemed to approve of my initiative, and I wondered if we were beginning to think alike. Kaga spread the last of the hay bundle in front of my horse and crossed the stream. She vanished into thick vegetation.

"Kaga," I called after her, but she did not reply.

Plutus neighed and seemed perfectly content to eat. I did not tether him. All my belongings rested in a disorganized pile where I dumped them, but something gnawed at me. I sensed Kaga was angry with me, but I could not figure out why.

I kneeled at the edge of the stream. Clear, cold water spilled through my fingers. I drank my fill and washed the dust off my face. When I stood, I called out once again for the Indian woman with no reply.

Distant sounds of water splashing into a pool carried from the woods. It came in the direction Kaga went. I crossed the knee-deep stream and pushed apart chest-high bushes along the stream's far shore. I followed a game trail upstream until I caught glimpses of water cascading from a cliff far above. Multiple tiny waterfalls poured from spaces between boulders and fell out of sight behind ground bushes near me. Thick blackberry bramble obstructed my view of the pool below, but loud splashing left no doubt about deep water nearby.

The impenetrable thorn bushes ended at a thicket of tall, thin reeds. Parting the streamside stalks, I saw a small pond of clear blue water with ripples fanning out from the falling showers. Moist blue-gray stone of the cliff wall shined from moisture, and patches of dark green parasitic plants grew precariously in wet crevices. It was beautiful.

As I enjoyed nature, a shadow moved from behind the largest of the waterfalls. Kaga stepped through the water with her face turned up enjoying its cool embrace. Her hands came through first, followed by her face and breasts. She was completely naked.

"Oh my," I muttered and pulled back.

It was improper for me to watch, so I rushed back to our camp where I busied myself organizing my gear. Mental images of her firm body, glistening in the cool water, persisted despite my effort to be a gentleman and purge them.

Chapter 14

Brush rustled on the side of the clearing away from the stream. I looked up expecting to see Kaga had returned through the woods instead of along the creek.

Five Indian men stepped into view and slowly approached me. Drawings I studied during my college years showed Indians wearing war paint and headbands adorned with bird feathers signifying some kind of rank. None of these displayed such headdress, although the rest of their attire closely matched the pictures. Dark brown, bare chests had a leathery look. Moccasins, like Kaga's, made no sound as they walked across the dry pine needles.

"Hello," I said, hoping to show friendliness. "My name is Cole."

The apparent leader stepped close to me and spoke a language I did not understand. He pointed at my pile of equipment.

I patted my chest trying to tell him it was my property, but he did not react. His stoic face troubled me. I could not read his intentions.

One of the bare-chested men went over to Plutus, spooking my wary horse.

"Hey! Get away from him." I shouted.

The head Indian yelled some kind of order to his man who stepped back obediently.

"Thank you." I nodded, attempting to show appreciation to the Indian leader.

Several bags hung from a rope tied around the leader's waist. He untied one of the smaller sacks and handed it to me. Puckers in the fabric smoothed out when I stretched the opening to look inside. Dozens of blue-green rocks filled the interior. They were beautiful but not of value to me.

Plutus snorted forcefully and began backing up as the nearest Indian began circling him. My horse stomped the ground and kept turning to face the threat.

"Leave him alone!" I shouted.

The warrior grabbed my horse's mane and swung up onto his bare back. Plutus reared up and turned throwing the unwanted rider into the air. The Indian landed on all fours like a cat and grinned as if he enjoyed the challenge posed by the animal.

"Get away from my horse, dammit!"

I stepped toward Plutus to intervene, but the iron grip of a calloused hand seized my upper arm and stopped me cold. The bag of gems, or rocks, or whatever they were, spilled on the ground as I faced my assailant. I did not like to fight, but learned as a boy that the best way to meet aggression was with resolved defiance.

The Indian leader grunted a command and his subordinates began digging through my personal things. One found my rifle and held it up admiringly. I jerked my arm free from the handhold and grabbed for my gun belt lying on the ground near my feet.

A painful kick to the side of my knee collapsed my leg and sent me to the ground in a heap. The leader pointed at the bag of blue-green rocks that spilled on the ground and followed with a sweeping gesture covering my horse and all my stuff. Then, he pulled out a long-bladed knife and pointed it at my face. The warning was clear.

Scrub brush along the far side of the stream parted and Kaga strode across the shallow water into our camp. She walked directly to the leader and spoke to him in an even tone. Her head poised with pride and determination as she stood toe to toe with the warrior. A one-sided diatribe directed at her had no effect on her attitude. At the end of the leader's monologue, he made some kind of disparaging remark and spat on the ground.

My lady-friend ignored the apparent insult. She talked to him in cool, even tones. I do not know what she said, but I recognized the last three words. "Kaga. Kaga . . . Ishta."

All the Indians looked up at the same time when they heard her name. She stared at the man nearest Plutus and spoke directly to him, again in a measured tone. The man looked back and forth between the tiny woman and his muscular leader, obviously conflicted.

Kaga issued her command again, only forcefully this time. The man backed away from my horse. Three others who had been pilfering my packs dropped their booty and moved behind their leader as if seeking protection.

The Indian leader spoke to Kaga, again clearly in anger.

She did not answer. Kaga opened one of several small skin-pouches from a shoulder strap. Black powder with silver flecks poured into the palm of her hand, and she dropped the container on the ground. Three fingers on her opposite hand dabbed the black substance, and she left three diagonal lines across her cheek. The same fingers wiped her forehead leaving a single, thicker smudge.

Kaga began to chant. Her body swayed in rhythm. She twisted like a snake as she went deeper and deeper into a standing trance. I got to my feet behind her.

The Indian leader backed up, actually pushing his men as he did so. Panic showed on their faces. In a wild scramble, all five of the camp raiders vanished back into the woods.

"Kaga, are you okay?"

She continued to sway and did not respond. I touched her shoulder. Her clothes and hair were soaking wet. All tension left her body, and she dropped limp into my arms. I lowered my friend gently to the soft forest carpet and kneeled beside her.

"Kaga?" I asked as I combed wet hair off her face with my fingers.

She moaned and opened her eyes. As soon as she saw my face, she startled and scrambled to her feet.

"They go?" she asked.

"Yes. They're gone. They left everything, even those rocks." I pointed to the spilled bag of stones.

Something made her laugh.

"What happened, Kaga?"

She ignored my question, as she had so many of my questions before. To tell the truth, I was getting a bit annoyed with her secrecy.

Kaga retrieved her bag of black powder, re-tying it to its place on her sash. She waded into the stream and washed the black substance from her face and hands. I could not help noticing that her wet clothes clung to her body silhouetting her shape in remarkable detail. Again, I suppressed sinful thoughts as her sensual figure moved with lithe agility.

"Were they from your tribe, Kaga?"

She busied herself repacking our scattered things without responding.

I took her by the shoulders and turned her to face me despite slight resistance.

"Please, Kaga, stop shutting me out. What happened with those Indians? Why were they afraid of you?"

She opened the black powder pouch and poured a small quantity into her hand.

"Magic powder. Summon demons to kill at my command."

I touched the powder and sniffed it. Common soot smelled the same.

"They believe I call evil spirits. That is why I not return to my people. I am outcast."

"Where did they get that idea? This is just soot."

"Kaga Ishta means Demon Woman. Name they give me when banned from tribe."

"Do you have another name?"

"Little Prairie Dog," she hesitated, "before I killed husband and his two brothers."

I was stunned.

"What happened?" I tried to hide my shock.

"Mother was white. I am half-Indian. Father beat mother and forbid her teach me ways of white men. She want me know, so she teach me English in secret."

Makes sense, I thought. *Now, I understand why this Indian woman speaks my language.*

"You said you killed three men. May I ask what happened?"

"Are you afraid me . . . because I kill them?"

"No." I lied.

Her face grew taut as she related her story.

"Father sold me to young warrior who took me for sex. I only fourteen summers. He demand sons, but I not give child after many moons. Whiskey make Indians crazy, and he drank of the white man's fire water too much."

She turned away from me and continued talking while tying gear to my horse's saddle.

"One night, he came to lodge drunk. Beat me with dog whip for not giving him son. I cried. It make him angry, so he forced sex to me and left when he done. I clean blood from whip cuts, when he return with two brothers, all whiskey-crazy. They took turns on me, and I refuse to cry, so they beat me. I still not cry."

She stopped what she was doing and faced me, looking deep into my eyes. Despite the cold tone of her voice, I saw seeds of tears in the corners of her eyes.

"When they fall asleep, I cut throats and took off their heads."

I knew she was studying me for a reaction. I did not flinch.

"I change clothes and go to sleep until first light of morning. When I scream, warriors rush in and see three dead men with no heads. I told tribal medicine man of dream that a demon came to my teepee, and when I wake, their heads gone. Chief of tribe found heads of the men between their legs under buffalo skin. Medicine man say I evil—I bring demons. My tribe sent me away, afraid of me. I have no home. Indians fear me and white men hate me."

I was not sure what to say. Poor girl was raped unmercifully and fought back. I cannot say I disapproved. And, now she lives in a thin shadow world between Indians and white men.

"Do you miss your mother?" I asked.

"Mother dead. Her warrior beat her for not make boy child. I was five summers when she told me she carry another child. She fear might not be boy, and that she would be beaten or sold to another tribe. She tell me she love me, and next morning, she jump off mountain cliff. Yes. I miss my mother."

Nothing more was said about the Indian incident for the next few days as we traveled higher into the mountains. Despite several attempts to broach the subject, she shook her head rejecting my attempt to discuss the subject each time I brought it up.

The trail wandered generally to the northwest, often taking detours to the southwest as mountains grew larger and blocked our way. Kaga found wild berries, edible roots and occasional small game to provide food during our travel. We stopped at obscure watering holes and camped in gorgeous forest areas that, for the life of me, I could not figure out why settlers had not discovered long ago. I kept running notes about the travel during our infrequent rests. I often wrote for the last half hour each day while Kaga foraged for food.

"What you do?" she asked me after an early dinner. I was dipping my pen into the ink bottle and making notes in my diary.

"I'm documenting our travels."

"What mean documenting?"

"I write stories about our journey for my readers back where I come from."

"Read to me?"

I read that day's notes.

"Why you write things that not important."

I explained to her that life here in the woods was very different from life in the cities.

"City people are interested in how people live in the woods."

"Why?"

"Because, it's so different to them."

"Why?"

"City people do not grow their own food. They do not know how to find roots to eat. They can't skin a rabbit," I explained.

"You lie!" Kaga expressed surprise and amusement at the same time. Her smile brought me a measure of peace. She had been very distant since telling me about her past.

"No lie," I replied. "City people don't know how to survive out here."

"Are you city white man?" she asked almost gently.

"Yes, I was, but I am learning ways of the woods by watching you."

Kaga was pleased by my show of respect for her knowledge, but she turned her face away a bit embarrassed by the compliment.

"Very cold tonight," she said. "Need big fire."

I put away my notes and added more scavenged wood to the fire. We sat together watching the flames grow as the last sunlight faded under heavy cloud cover. This night, I was not tired for the first time since I met this woman. She set blistering paces when we traveled, and I always slept deeply when the opportunities arrived. Not tonight.

"Kaga, were those Indian warriors from your tribe?"

She laughed as if I should have known better.

"No, I Lakota Sioux. My people live north of here. Those Navajo."

"If they are not of your people, why did they react to your name?"

"When stories travel one tribe to another, grow bigger. Apache, Comanche and Navaho think Kaga Ishta is demon woman who fights Great Spirit for control over their spirits. My name is my protection. You saw them run."

"Do Lakota and those other tribes speak the same language?"

"No, but have many words in common. Told them I summon my demon spirits if they did not leave. Navajo not dangerous. Apache warriors more difficult to scare."

"Which Indians are the most dangerous in this area?"

Kaga smiled, "Me."

We did not talk much more, mostly little grunts in answer to my simple questions. She was right about the cold setting in. I added more wood to the fire and grew concerned that our scavenged wood supply might not make it through the night. In the distance, a wolf howled, several coyotes yipped and an owl screeched in its nightly hunt. I loved the sounds of outdoors.

It must have been well after midnight when I added the last of our larger wood to the fire, hoping it would get us through the night. Kaga understood the situation, but did not seem as concerned as I was. When the fire began to burn down, she leaned against me, resting her head against my shoulder. I was happily surprised by her unexpected familiarity.

Chapter 15

It was early morning and still dark. I shivered under my camp blanket and realized we would need heavier bedding for this mountain travel. Firewood burned down an hour earlier, leaving only a red bed of glowing coals. I moved closer to the hot embers. It was not enough.

Kaga whispered, "Open blanket."

I rolled over to see my friend on her knees next to my bedding with her covers draped over her shoulders. Lips had a blue tint, and she trembled visibly. I pulled back the flap of my covering, and she slipped in next to me. Her hands and feet were cold, but her body heat felt wonderful. She pulled her blanket over mine to double our protection against the cold.

My shivers slowly subsided, but a new kind of warmth spread throughout my body as she placed her arm across my chest and a leg across my thighs. Her warm breath felt wonderful on the side of my neck, but a strange, sweet smell greatly excited me. My manhood came to life against my will and pressed into her thigh.

"No," she said with her lips touching my ear. "Just stay warm."

Morning came with a start. Kaga threw back the covers sending a freezing blast of cold air across my body.

"We go. Big storm come. Must get to shelter before night."

I looked at the clear blue sky and strong wind howling through the treetops.

"I don't see a storm. How do you know a storm is coming?"

"Bees. They work extra hard before storm. Watch them yesterday when gather flowers."

She pointed at a small pile of purple flower petals where her blanket had been at the beginning of last evening.

"What are those?"

She picked up a few of the crushed flowers and held them under my nose. The sweet scent matched the wonderful fragrance when she cuddled with me last night.

I smiled at the pleasurable recollection.

Kaga brushed the flower residue lightly across her skin at her neckline and asked, "You like?"

I sniffed close to her neck.

"Yeah. What kind of flower is that?" I wanted to make sure I mentioned that intoxicating scent in my journal entries.

The corners of Kaga's mouth turned up in a sweet smile, but as I had come to learn, she would answer my question in her own good time. She walked away.

My Indian guide set a much faster pace than in recent days. Even Plutus struggled to keep up with this natural woods-woman. We put several mountain peaks behind us by weaving along steep trails through narrow gorges. Late in the day, she led us along a rocky cut between two towering cliff walls. The trail here looked well worn but was only wide enough to handle a single file procession of people and animals. It ended on a terrace overlooking the largest valley I had ever seen.

The east side of the valley rose into snow-capped mountains that extended as far as my eyes could see. The granite monsters vanished into a thick layer of high altitude clouds. In the center of that great valley, ribbons of green water wandered through vast prairies of golden grassland. Even at this distance, I realized dark patches scattered on the grasslands were enormous herds of wild animals.

"My people call this Land of Giant Bear," Kaga announced with reverence.

"Why do they call it that?"

She ignored my question and led us down a steep slope toward the flatland below.

Fast moving storm clouds thickened and darkened as they backed up against the eastern mountain range. In less than two hours, we went from warm sunshine to cold rain and strong winds. Kaga pushed our pace despite slippery footing.

Twilight began to set in under the ominous gray overcast. We passed several areas with large trees that offered partial relief from the storm, but Kaga did not care about them.

"There's a good grove of trees back there. Why don't we backtrack and set up camp?" I asked.

"Almost to shelter," she said and ignored my suggestion.

Kaga walked several hundred feet ahead of Plutus and me, as we simply could not keep up with her on the slippery footing. She skirted around an odd-looking rise in the slope ahead and disappeared. When I reached that spot, I saw two doorways and several windows built into the downhill side of a large dugout shelter promising protection from this storm.

Inside the long cave-like building, the ceiling was high enough that even Plutus had ample clearance. It felt nice to be out of the rain, but it was difficult to see details in the dark interior.

"Build fire. I get food."

Kaga went back into the rain leaving me with the same task I had at every stop. I considered returning to the wooded areas we passed for firewood, but, by now, fallen wood would be wet and impossible to ignite.

"Let's hope somebody left some wood in here for days like this," I spoke to Plutus.

My eyes had gradually adjusted to the darkness, and to my great relief, the back wall had wood stacked the entire length of the dugout. I set about shaving kindling and pried a bullet out of a cartridge. When I fired the gun into the tinder, it caught immediately and we soon had a raging fire in a pit near one of the windows. Whoever built this place knew how to vent smoke.

I removed my shirt, coat, hat and boots, and placed them on wood sticks I pushed into soft soil near the fire. When Kaga returned, I proudly showed her my clothes-drying setup, complete with an empty set of sticks for her benefit.

"Help me clean food," she said and held up several small animals. I admit being a little disappointed that she did not acknowledge my creative drying-rig. Instead, she handed me a knife and headed back out into the rain. "Follow me."

I slipped into my warmed clothes. When I found her half a mile from the shelter, she had already gutted and skinned two baby beavers. We prepped the rest together in the driving rain.

That night, we feasted on fresh meat, and Kaga talked with unusual openness.

"What like to live in city?"

I described metropolitan life to someone who has no conception of such living.

"Do you think I would city?"

"I don't know. You have freedom out here that we don't enjoy in cities. You might find the limitations and social demands uncomfortable."

Kaga sighed. "It not matter. I can never go your cities."

"Sure you can. If you want, I'll take you into Sacramento or San Francisco when we get up there. They aren't as big as eastern cities like Boston, but you'll get a taste of city life."

"You not understand. I am half-breed. Not welcome with Indians or by white man."

She untied her moccasins and adjusted them on a drying stick.

"You not live in west," she said. "Much hate between white man and Indian."

I was not sure how to address this truth. Stories about Indian raids and retaliatory massacres by my own people caught my attention in college. Bitter truths about the West suggested that there was little room for friendship. I chose to avoid those issues when I decided to write about the gold rush. Even the Santa Fe Trail I selected for this journey out west was a southern route to avoid Indian hostility that I had read about, mostly in territories to the north.

"People don't need to know you are half Indian." I offered encouragement. "There are many different kinds of people in the east. People with dark skin, the same as yours, come from places like Portugal, Italy and Turkey. They look similar to Indians. If you want to go to the city, I'll take you. We'll introduce you as my Turkish friend. Nobody will know."

Kaga untied her shirt fasteners and removed her wet top to hang it on a drying stick. She showed no concern about naked breasts. Indian ease about nudity conflicted with my Boston upbringing, but when she removed her pants and hung them on a drying stick, my shock must have been evident.

"You not like my body?" she asked.

"Uh, umm . . ." I stuttered. "Women stay clothed around men where I grew up."

She unrolled a sleeping blanket and wrapped it around her shoulders crossing the ends over the front of her body. After tying a short length of rope around her waist to hold the improvised clothing in place, she held her arms out to the sides and faced me.

"Better?" she asked with a coy smile, almost mocking me.

This time, I did not have an answer.

"Your pants wet," she said. "You should dry them."

Kaga pointed at the empty drying sticks and tossed me a blanket.

"I not look," she said and turned her back to me.

After I hung the last of my clothes between two drying sticks, we huddled on a floor mat made of woven dried reeds. I found it at the back of the shelter. They were quite comfortable.

"I would like to see your city, if you take me."

She took my hand in hers. I could feel her strength, yet I noticed the paradox of a gentle softness. I squeezed her hand, and she responded in kind.

"How far are we from Sacramento?" I asked.

"Three, maybe four days, unless rain make rivers big."

After adding wood for the night fire, she suggested we share blankets again for warmth. Logistics were a bit difficult with both of us naked, so I promised not to look at her while she placed her blanket on the ground and folded one side over her nude body. After she was set, I scooted my way under the flap of her blanket until her body pressed snugly against my back, and I flipped my blanket over both of us.

"Are you okay?" I asked.

She reached over my shoulder holding a rawhide bag that I recognized from the night before. Propping on an elbow, she shook half a dozen tiny purple flower petals onto her palm and crushed them by rolling between her hands. A sweet, perfume-like fragrance came from the flower mash. She reached over me and rubbed the flowers on my neck and cheek. Without looking, I could tell she did the same on her neck and chest.

"Last night, you ask name of flower. My people call it Baby Flower."

"Because they are so small?" I asked.

She did not elaborate, but kissed me behind the ear. Her arm threaded under mine and her fingers explored my chest. I will not lie. It felt good, real good.

"You have strong body, white man."

Kaga's hand explored the front of my abdomen, cresting each line of stomach muscles as if memorizing every contour. Without stopping, she worked her way down to what she wanted. I rolled onto my back, and her head vanished under the covers. Her hot mouth brought a flood of sensations as she explored my manhood. She sensed my growing tension and increased her tempo until I crested despite trying to save my best for what I hoped would happen next.

"I'm sorry," I said, thinking I had failed to control myself.

Her head came out from under the covers, and she hushed me with two fingers across my lips. Pulling fully on top of me, she did not let go of my manhood. Kisses began tenderly and became more passionate while she gently massaged until my masculinity recovered. Her body was taught and muscular, unlike the soft curves of Tess. Heat from her firm breasts piqued physical urgency in me as she guided my love into her moistness.

She was tight and swayed her hips from side to side until I fully penetrated. We enjoyed a mutual rhythm that grew quicker as our pleasure transcended from two people making love into a merger where two become one. Every movement of my body triggered a matching response from her. She had a hunger I wanted to satisfy, a need that seemed to have no end. I thrust hard in the final explosion of our oneness. Kaga whimpered and bit lightly into my earlobe. Tremors rolled up her body, and she stiffened in ecstasy, squeezing me with all her strength.

We collapsed in afterglow, her face resting softly on my chest. Her body melted onto mine, and we made no attempt to disengage. Sleep came with us linked as one.

Heavy rain was beating down outside our shelter when I awoke in the morning. Kaga's relaxed body perfectly meshed with mine. Her contours fit me as if made solely for that purpose. Light was dim. The fire had burned down to a bed of coals.

Kaga usually rose before first light, but not today. Deep, slow breathing against the side of my neck meant she was still fast asleep.

I lifted my covers and tried to get up without sending a chilly draft over her. Kaga's arm tightened, pulling me firmly against her bare chest.

"I'll be right back," I whispered and kissed her cheek. "I have to add wood."

"Hurry, white man. I need you."

She kissed my neck and released me. I added several thin branches over the remaining coals and stacked progressively larger wood over them. They did not ignite immediately, but growing smoke promised a nice fire in a short while. I slipped back under the covers to a wide-awake Kaga. Eager morning sex surpassed any waking moment I had experienced with Tess.

I could spend the rest of my life living like this, I thought.

Chapter 16

Morning on the third day in the hillside lodge brought a cloudless sky and very chilly north winds. Racks of smoked meat promised adequate food for several days, and even Plutus stirred in anticipation of returning to the trail.

"I take you Sacramento," Kaga said with an odd monotone as she busied herself packing food that we had dried over the past few days.

My excitement grew about getting to the hub of gold mining territory.

"We'll stay in Sacramento for a couple days, and then we can take the river boat to San Francisco. It's a bigger city. I hear they have even have big-city comforts like the theatre and opera houses where I grew up."

"I not go city," Kaga said without looking up from cutting meat into smaller strips. "I take you close Sacramento, but you go into city without me."

"What? But . . . but, I promised to show you the city."

"You no need keep promise. I go back to woods where I belong."

"Why are you saying this, Kaga?"

She rose from her squatting position, easily hefting the fifty-pounds of saddlebags. After adjusting them over my horse's back, she led him to a nearby patch of dried grass and dropped his lead rope. It always amazed me that she did not see the need to tie Plutus to a tree. She claimed he would never leave us because he considers us his herd. He never did run off, so I guess she knows horses better than white men do.

I pressed her for why she changed her mind about seeing the city.

"Cole, if I go, there be trouble. You not safe with me."

This was the first time she called me by my name instead of "white man."

"Nobody will bother you. I won't let them."

She smiled and touched my forearm with tenderness.

"White man, you live inside your mind's world. I live in real world. Hatred make men mean, both white man and Indian. I not want you suffer hatred."

"You're wrong, Kaga. Those people are very few. You'll see when we get there."

Kaga took my hand and led me back into our shelter. Inside, she coaxed me to kneel next to the fire, facing her. Opening her small flower bag, she poured more of the dry flower petals onto her palms and cupped them over her mouth. Several deep breaths passed through her fingers adding slight moisture to hydrate the contents. Sweet fragrance released into the air around my head, and the warmth of her breath swaddled my face against a slight nip in the morning air.

The thick carpet of dry Tule-reeds that served as our bed for the past three days spread around us with as much soft appeal as any down-filled bed I had ever known.

My companion rubbed her hands together before massaging the remnants of the flower perfume under loose folds of my shirt. Her hands glided over my chest muscles, and she unfastened the ties holding my shirt in place. Deft fingers folded cloth back until the shirt slipped off my shoulders, dropping to a wrinkled heap.

I can not claim ignorance any more. I knew where this was headed, but when Kaga loosened her own fasteners and allowed her fringed, animal skin blouse to drop away, I was stunned. Never had I seen a more beautiful woman. Our love making had always been during night or twilight. Now, I clearly saw tanned arms framing long, raven-black hair that draped loosely across the contours of her tender breasts. In her jewel-like black eyes, I saw my own reflection. Her lips parted slightly yet nothing was said.

"Kaga, I—" she stopped me with fingertips across my lips.

My Indian lover leaned forward until her full torso pressed seamlessly against me. She bit lightly into my lower lip. My arms folded around her, and I responded the only way I knew, with a kiss through her hair onto her neck behind her ear. Urgency grew as she drew backward pulling me onto the waiting bed. Intoxicated by sweet scent from those magical flowers, and driven by soaring passion, we fell into another place and time where only we existed.

I awoke to a warm noon sun. Plutus pawed the ground outside our shelter.

"You sleep too long, white man," Kaga joked.

Bright blue sky framed the small woman in the entryway. She held my horse's lead rope and rubbed his nose affectionately.

"We must go. Much valley to cross. Put boots on, Cole."

She used my name for the second time. It felt good.

While we were more than casual friends at this point, my Indian guide left no uncertainty about who was in charge. I found myself regulating my breathing to keep up with her pace. At times, she extended our distance by going into a short-stepped trot that she was able to sustain for over an hour before stopping for fluids.

During one water stop, I sat on a large rock studying the land around us. Those large mountains to the east gave a dramatic, ragged edge to the horizon. They protruded from layers of foothills covered in random heavy oak trees, brown scrub brush and fields of golden brown grass. One of the closer hills caught my attention when a dozen dark dots began moving. I pointed and asked Kaga what they were.

"Whites call them elk. My people have name means big deer."

"Big?" I asked. "They don't look that big to me."

Kaga found my ignorance amusing, laughing to herself.

"Come. We get back on trail."

She stretched for a moment before grabbing the horse's lead rope. I couldn't help noticing her fantastic lady shape with her silhouetted against the mountain backdrop.

"What trail?" I asked. "I don't see a trail."

"Look." She dropped to a crouch. "See footprint?"

I did not see any indentations.

"Where?" I asked in a challenge.

She picked up a small stick and drew in the dry dirt. This thing was massive!

"Valley bear." She outlined a large depression with four claw marks pointing in the direction we were headed. "Very big. Bear follows small herd of antelope."

Again, I could not see the evidence of a herd until she showed me small, faint hoof prints. When she had mentioned a trail, I was looking for wagon-wheel marks or human footprints, but we were following a game trail.

"Are you sure following a big bear is a good idea?" I asked.

"Better we follow bear, than bear follow us," she said with a half-smile.

Kaga started walking again but called over her shoulder, "Make long gun ready."

"Do you think we are going to run into that bear?" I asked, genuinely concerned.

"No. We not run into bear. Maybe 'you' run into bear. Have gun ready."

"What? That doesn't make sense. Don't bears attack Indians?"

"Yes, but I run faster than you."

Oh great, I thought. *She's leading us into a disagreement with a damn bear, and she thinks it's a joke.*

Chapter 17

Progress slowed as the sun dropped to the low mountain range in the west. That range was not nearly as towering or impressive as the granite peaks to the east, but it was interesting in different ways. Every morning, fog poured between its peaks, vanishing in long, gray fingers that rolled down into the valley. Green stripes of vegetation marked the moisture deposited by the daily fog drift.

"We stop." Kaga led us under huge branches of the biggest Valley Oak tree I had seen.

"Are you sure?" I asked and pointed at fresh claw marks about three feet higher on the tree trunk than I could reach. "That's a huge bear."

"Bear want natural food, not people. He follow herd until he catch one."

"You've been right, so far." I shrugged despite my reservations.

"Big moon tonight. Bear hunt antelope after sun sleep. We okay, but keep gun close in case bear too old to hunt normal food."

"What does his age have to do with hunting?"

"If bear cannot catch small antelope, he look for easier food."

"Like?" I asked.

"You," Kaga said with a cold certainty.

"What about you?" I shot back.

"No problem for me. You make big, slow meal. Besides, you forget? I faster than you. Help me find wood."

Would she really sacrifice me to save herself? I wondered.

"Is that the Indian way?" I responded sarcastically.

79

"No. It bear's way."

I caught a slight curve of her cheek as she tried to hide a smile, enjoying this verbal joust.

We gathered a lot of wood, plenty for the whole night. My bedroll provided the only soft place to rest under the tree. This night, we remained dressed and cuddled together before the fire as a bright moon illuminated vast areas of California's central valley.

"Why did you tether Plutus tonight," I asked, knowing that was not her way.

"Bear not far. If he come to our camp, horse know first." She leaned tightly against my side and snaked her arm through mine.

On the opposite side, I reached out to confirm the proximity of my handgun. Cold metal gave instant reassurance. Above the gun, my rifle leaned against the tree trunk, positioned upright so my hand would fit perfectly into the grip at first touch.

Fire alone should keep a grizzly away. All these other precautions? Probably overkill.

"Cole, I sleep. You stay awake. When moon high, wake me, and you sleep,"

It did not take any explanation for me to understand her concern about that bear.

Kaga slipped into a deep sleep. Her body became limp under my arm, and her breathing slow and deep. Night owls hooted occasionally, and the ever-present *yip, yip, yip* of coyotes kept me company. I hated to leave Kaga's side, but our fire needed tending, so I lowered her onto the camp blanket and added wood until a large blaze lighted the area under our tree. She wiggled a moment to find a comfortable spot and drifted back to sleep.

It was getting chilly. I folded my side of the blanket over Kaga to keep her warm and leaned against the tree listening to night sounds. A bat fluttered through the firelight, chasing some unseen insect. Moonlight shined on the mountain range casting haunting shadows that did not exist during daylight. It seemed like an entirely different place at night.

Plutus heard it first. Snorting, he began pulling against his rope. He was not as panicked as he had been by the rattlesnake, but something definitely had him on edge.

I strapped on my gun belt, fastened the leg ties and picked up my rifle. With it resting across my arm, I stood guard over Kaga.

"Easy, boy." I tried to settle Plutus. "It's okay, fella. Calm down."

He peered past me into the darkness. Then, I heard it, too. Rustling brush was not real close, but my horse was right to be concerned. Something big made that sound.

I cocked the hammers on both my rifle and handgun and pointed the rifle in the direction of the noise. Rotating my head from side to side, I triangulated the location of the disturbance.

"Howdy," a voice called out from the dark. "Got room at yer fire?"

I did not respond. Kaga startled me when she touched my elbow. I did not even hear her stand up. Forearm muscles rippled with tension as she held a hunting knife in front of her chest.

"Friend, we ain't bad folk, just hunters trailing game. Can we come into your camp?"

"We're armed, so come easy," I shouted

Several men laughed a bit nervously at my answer and called out assurances.

"Thanks, fella. We're coming in slow. Don't get trigger quick."

Three men emerged from chest high grass and entered the fire's glow. Two wore heavy beards, probably not shaved in years, and the third looked to be younger, maybe not yet old enough to grow a manly beard. All of them carried old-style buffalo rifles and wore crudely made animal skin over-clothes.

Kaga stayed behind me, almost completely obscured from their sight.

"Mister, I'd feel a might better if'n you lowered that rifle," the oldest man said.

"Sorry. I didn't know what to expect. Come on in."

My fire was located near an old tree branch that broke from the oak tree many years before. I had positioned the fire there for sitting next to the warmth. The men helped themselves to welcome heat, leaning toward the fire with their hands outstretched, palms facing the flames.

81

As I lowered my rifle barrel toward the ground, I thumbed the hammer and pulled the trigger to un-cock it. I still did not trust these guys, so I slipped the rifle butt under my arm, but kept my hand resting on my side arm. Kaga remained hidden.

"Your kid can come out. We really ain't bad folk, just hunters." The leader tried to reassure Kaga, assuming she was a youngster.

"Mind if we put coffee on your fire?" the other bearded man asked.

"Suit yourself. We don't have any to offer."

The group leader laid his rifle on the ground behind him and opened a satchel he had been carrying in a shoulder harness.

"How about I give ya some of my elk jerky to thank you for your hospitality? Damn good stuff, if I do brag a little."

"Thanks," I said. "Never ate elk before."

I stepped toward the fellow holding out the jerky and inadvertently exposed Kaga to full view. Her knife blade glinted in the firelight as she inserted it back into its sheath.

The hunters stared at her.

"I'm Bradley," the oldest man said without taking his eyes off Kaga. "This here's my brother, Kendall. Skinny kid, who can't grow a beard, that's Kendall's boy, Mica. What's your name?"

I did not want to get familiar with these strangers, so I used the name Mack coined back at the stagecoach station.

"Name's Pete, Texas Pete." I intentionally kept the palm of my hand on my forty-four to suggest that they should not take me lightly. "Thanks for the jerky."

I bit into a piece of the elk. It was surprisingly sweet and tender.

Kaga sat back against the tree while the men, including me, stayed around the fire enjoying more elk jerk-meat than we should have.

I asked how to make elk jerky, and the old hunter explained how he prepared the meat for drying. These men seemed like honest hunters, and I let my guard down.

"So, Texas Pete, you don't look like much of a hunter. What brings you out this way?"

"Heading to Sacramento. Got business to settle."

The older man squinted as he studied my sidearm in the flickering light.

"That kind of business can get you kilt, young fella."

"That's my problem. What are you doing out here in the middle of nowhere at night?"

"Trackin' a bear. Big'ol grizzly called One Eye. Took to killing cattle on the ranchero down by the river."

Kendall, the brother, got excited when talk changed to the bear. He'd been pretty quiet up until now.

"One Eye's been around for over twenty years," Kendall said. "Saw him kill another bear, fighting over a salmon on the San Joaquin River. That's how he lost his eye. Bout two years ago, he changed from hunting wild game to taking domestic stock. Rancher put a bounty on him. We aim to collect it."

He nodded in the direction of Kaga. "That your squaw?"

I did not fully understand why he would ask such a question.

"Squaw? You mean my friend?"

"Yeah. Injun squaw, ain't she?"

"No. She's my friend."

The old hunter glanced a harsh warning to his brother, and tried to break the tension.

"Sorry about Kendall's question, Pete. We don't see many Injun squaws in this area."

Kendall bristled at Bradley's rebuke.

"Don't apologize for me, Brad. Injuns ain't good for nothing, 'cept them squaws."

He looked from Bradley to me.

"How much for the squaw, mister?"

"What?" I had an idea what he meant, but it was so foreign to me that I did not answer.

"How much to buy your squaw? I'll pay you gold or U.S. gov'ment coin. How much?"

The old hunter shook his head and looked at the ground, disgusted by his brother.

"Kaga's not for sale. She's my friend."

"Oh, I get it. You don't wanna sell her. Tell you what, I'll give you twenty dollars, gold, for just one hour with her. That's way higher than the going rate for whores."

"I think your welcome at my fire is over." I stood up. "Why don't you boys move on?"

The eldest hunter jumped to his feet, and shoved his brother backward off his seat.

"You stupid son of a bitch!" he said. "Your boy's sitting right there. What kinda goddamned father are you, asking about a price for sex?"

He turned to the man's son.

"Get your things, boy. Your daddy screwed up our welcome in this camp."

Bradley did not seem to be a bad man like his brother, and the kid looked confused by the whole situation. After emptying their coffee pot into the flames and repacking most of their supplies, the older man approached me, and extended his hand.

"I'm sorry my brother disrespected you and your friend here in your own camp. Don't sit right by me, but let this be a lesson to you. Lotta men in these parts treat Injun women like property. Texas Pete, or whatever your real name is, that sidearm is gonna get a workout if you plan to keep company with a squaw. Problem is, if you kill a white man to protect an Injun, they'll string you up for sure. It ain't considered a justified killing. Be like killing a man over a fried egg, but, from the looks of that gun, you ain't got no problem with killing."

Despite his obvious disapproval of my assumed gunman status, he offered me a handful of elk jerky before guiding his group back into the darkness.

Chapter 18

Night passed slowly. Neither Kaga nor I slept much, but we also did not talk. I tried to start a conversation several times, but she turned away. We huddled under doubled blankets for warmth against a steady, cold breeze coming off the mountains. Plutus got nervous once in the early morning. I got up to check, but whatever bothered him must have passed by pretty fast, and he settled down.

Morning sky lightened above the eastern mountains. Hawks took to the air on strong, frigid winds searching for early morning prey. Magpies squawked about whatever bothers magpies, and those tiny dots of elk herds moved down the hillsides from their night beds. Vast fields of chest-high grass swayed like golden waves under the gusting breeze.

Kaga packed up our camp while I spread the ashes of our fire and covered them with loose soil to prevent wildfire risk. Nearby, Plutus ate grass coated with morning dew. His tail swished gently as he enjoyed the refreshing food.

"Kaga, how far is it to Sacramento?"

"Three days, if walk fast."

"Have you ever been to Sacramento?"

"Yes."

"I thought you never saw a city."

"I not go into city. Only look at city from hills while trade for knife."

She pulled out the unusually large Sheffield-style Bowie knife that she kept in a scabbard tied to her waste. Buffalo hunters used similar knives for rendering their kills. Instead of carved wood or engraved animal bone that most such knives used for handles, Kaga's weapon had layers of tightly wrapped, dried sinew forming high and low ridges that perfectly fit her fingers.

I had seen her skin animals with amazing speed using that tool like an extension of her hand. She always washed the wide blade thoroughly after cleaning an animal. When it dried, she produced a special flat-stone from a pouch hidden and sharpened the edge, often rubbing the blade on the stone for nearly an hour.

"May I?" I held out my hand hoping she would let me examine it.

She handed me the gleaming knife and cautioned, "Careful, very sharp."

Of course, my manly arrogance forced me to test the blade with my thumb. Damn thing cut into me like a barber's straight razor.

"Ow!" I stuck my bleeding thumb in my mouth.

"Stupid white man!" she said with genuine disgust and shook her head.

I mumbled around the thumb in my mouth, "Wow, that's sharp. Where'd you learn that?"

Kaga glared at me. Without answering, she headed out to retrieve Plutus, but stopped about a hundred feet from camp and squatted to study the ground.

"Cole," she called out. "Come, quick!"

As I approached, she pointed at impressions in moist soil. Boot prints left by the hunters were deep and obvious.

"That's just the hunters from last night." I stated the obvious.

"No, look close." Kaga pointed along the drier ground where short grass grew.

"I don't see anything. What's the problem?"

Kaga dropped to her knees and placed both palms on the ground next to each other with fingers spread as wide as possible.

"Bear. Very old."

At first, all I saw was her small hands filling a slight depression at the base of a clump of grass. Then, the overall shape of the indentation became clear. It was enormous. Her hands did not even fill the imprint.

"How do you know it's an old bear?"

"Young bears have small feet and short claws." She pointed to four divots where claws had dug in and turned up the soil. "Long claws make ground break. Straight claws of young bears make mark like this."

She used her knife to scratch a short, straight line in the dirt.

"Looks like the hunters are on the right track," I said.

"No." Kaga stared in the direction of travel shown by the tracks. "Bear hunt white men."

"How do you know that?"

"Here man's boot print. See? Bear foot on top. It tracks men."

Sure enough, once she showed me what to look for, it was obvious. That bear paw covered part of a hunter's boot indentation.

"We'll go east before we turn north to stay clear of the bear."

"Cannot do that," Kaga replied and locked eyes with me. "We must warn hunters."

"They treated you bad last night. We don't owe them anything."

Kaga taught me a lesson in ethics. From this heathen, I saw forgiveness.

"Only one bad man," she said. "Old man and boy did nothing. Must warn them. Then, we go east, away from bear."

"They have buffalo guns. Can't they kill that bear?" I understood her point of view, but I did not feel there was enough threat to those guys for us to take such a risk.

Kaga took my hand in both of hers.

"Old bear dangerous. Very quiet. They get one chance to stop big bear before it kill them. Buffalo rifle very powerful, but only fire one time. Wounded valley bear more dangerous than hungry bear. We must warn the white men."

She was right. I had read stories in college about the brutality and ruthlessness of Indians, especially Great Plains Indians like Kaga, but she defied those stereotypes. I made a mental note to cover this topic in my journalism. I wondered if my publisher would be interested in an expose that contradicted contemporary beliefs of white men about Indians.

Chapter 19

Kaga and I tracked the bear and hunters for hours. I wondered what time of night that animal passed so close to our camp. He had to come by some time after the hunters left and before we freed Plutus to graze at dawn. After I sent the hunters away, I moved him into the firelight of our camp in case the hunters returned to take him. Now, it looked like it was our good fortune that the bear did not detect him as a source of food.

I had been following Kaga now for a couple weeks, but she never moved as slow and deliberate as she did in this stalk. She assigned me to lead Plutus by his tether, and she made me check both my firearms for fresh loads in case the bear doubled back on us. Turkey, deer and a variety of varmints fell to my rifles in the past, but this was the first time I tracked an animal that was capable of hunting me. It was a strange feeling.

Firm soil of the valley grasslands gradually changed to the sticky muck of marshland alongside of a tributary to the San Joaquin River. Fields of grass gave way to thorny brush and thick patches of green reeds extending into the water. Human footprints and massive paw prints sunk deep into the mud, so much so, that even I could read the trail.

It was late afternoon when Kaga abruptly signaled for me to stop.

She whispered, "Wait here. Bear close. Keep rifle ready. I come back soon."

Before I could object, she vanished into a thicket of scrub brush. I looked at the ground with alarm. Deep bear prints were still filling with ground water, providing a vivid idea about the size and proximity of the beast. Plutus pulled on his lead rope. His ears darted and nostrils flared as he sensed danger nearby.

The detonation of a large caliber rifle sounded just ahead. Plutus reared back, startled by the loud sound. A second and third rifle blast sounded in quick succession. I aimed my rifle in the direction of the sounds and scanned bushes for any sign of a grizzly . . . or Kaga.

Something approached with no effort at stealth. I aimed at the sound of snapping twigs and rustling brush, slipping my finger onto the trigger.

Kaga burst out of the brush.

"Come fast. Bear attack hunters."

She turned back, and I followed as fast as I could, but she disappeared. Moccasin prints in wet soil were easy to follow. With my head looking down at her trail, I broke out of thick reeds onto the sandy shore of a narrow riverbank. A huge brown bear stood over the body of one of the hunters while the other two men wielded their rifles as clubs in a futile attempt to stop the savaging of their family member.

Kaga exploded out of reeds near the scene and leaped onto the back of the massive animal. Her sharp knife plunged deep into the side of the beast's neck. It roared and rose upright, trying to dislodge its attacker. Two large, blood covered wounds on its middle abdomen showed where the hunters shot the animal, but pain-rage seemed to override any weakness the bear should have experienced.

With Kaga in danger, my adrenaline surged. I ran toward the bear and aimed at its chest while it spun wildly against her relentless knife assault. I could not fire for fear of hitting my Indian lover. Her legs swung outward from the bear's gyrating body and claws on one of its paws dug into her thigh. In one powerful motion, he ripped her from his back, slamming her to the ground at his feet. The beast's eyes, locked on her.

Rage triggered in me such as I had never felt before. The bear towered over me, but I ran to the bear and pulled the trigger with the muzzle of my rifle shoved against the giant carnivore's chest. The blast ripped into him, stopping his focus on her. Kaga frantically dug her heels into the mud, trying to scramble out from under the massive killer.

I do not know how that animal still lived, but he extended fully upright and stepped toward me. Nearly twice my height, it roared while I backed up and pulled out my forty-four handgun. I fired upward into its chest, hoping for a heart shot. The first bullet rocked the bear, but did not stop it. Holding my powerful handgun with both hands and cocking with my thumb, I emptied my remaining bullets into the same chest area. The beast stopped, swayed several times and collapsed forward, landing dead at my feet.

Kaga wasted no time attending to the mauled hunter. It was the nasty man, Kendall. He lay unconscious with numerous puncture wounds and claw tears. Some bled heavily. His head showed four deep holes from the bear's fangs, and its shape was distorted to one side from a crushing bite.

She applied pressure to the worst of the bleeding and poured dried poultices from her assortment of pouches into several wounds. The old man and boy watched, unable to help. Bleeding stopped almost immediately with the Indian medicine, but he remained unconscious.

Bradley rambled about what happened.

"Never saw that bear. It come out of the bush real fast. Took my brother down 'fore he could aim. He fired into the air, but the boy and me, we hit him with two shots. Ain't never seen a bear take two shots to the chest and keep coming like that."

"Your brother needs a doctor," I said. "Is there one near here?"

"No, but Mary back at the ranchero is good at nursing injured cowboys."

"How far is it to this ranch?"

"Bout a day's walk. He ain't gonna last that long, is he? He can't walk."

Kaga looked up from her first aid efforts.

"Cole, get Plutus. We use horse to carry man."

I hurried to recover my horse and stripped off his load except for the saddle. With help from the injured man's relatives, we loaded him onto Plutus and Kaga sat behind him to hold him up. Mica led the way, keeping a fast pace that the old man could not match. We left Bradley behind and reached the ranchero before midnight.

During the trek, I noticed bleeding on Kaga's leg where the bear clawed her.

The owner of the ranch thanked us for helping his cowboys as well as for killing that bear. Mary, his wife, took over care of the injured man. She also noticed several large blood spots on Kaga's thigh and took my Indian friend into a separate room to clean and dress her wounds.

When things settled down, the rancher fed us and invited us to sleep in real beds in the main house.

"Even the Injun can stay here," he said.

Kaga found the mattress too soft and slept on the floor next to my bed. She and I rose at first light and left while everyone was still sleeping. As I walked past the room where Kendall was put for care, I noticed a white sheet covering him, even over his head. I did not tell Kaga what that meant.

After retracing our trail to the scene of the bear attack, Kaga used her knife to pry both of the bear's upper canine teeth out of its mouth. She rinsed off the blood in the stream and slipped them into a pocket. We crossed the shallow water and headed toward Sacramento, having lost another day of travel.

Kaga's limp became worse, so I insisted she ride Plutus rather than walk. On the second day, she became very hot to the touch. A passing trapper said we were not far from one of the port towns along the San Joaquin River. After Kaga fell asleep, I followed a wagon-rutted trail into town. At the livery, I got directions to the town's doctor, and he agreed to come see Kaga.

Back in my camp, the doctor inspected her leg.

"Bad infection from those claw wounds," he said while shaking his head. "If it gets much worse, we'll have to take that leg."

Kaga drifted in and out of consciousness and did not appear to understand the doctor's concern.

"Keep her wounds clean and watch closely for growing infection. You know where to find me if she gets worse." He hesitated for a moment before adding, "I suggest you keep her out of town. Lot of Indian haters in this place. It's best if she stays out here."

I offered the doctor money, but he refused. After he left, I covered her in both blankets to protect her from the cooling night air.

"Thank you, Cole," Kaga said without opening her eyes. "White man doctor not know Indian medicine. You need fix my leg."

I had personal experience with her natural remedies, so she did not need to convince me.

"Tell me what to do. I'll do it."

Kaga instructed me to mix the dry contents from three bags with a small amount of water producing a thick paste. She pulled her deerskin skirt up revealing three deep claw punctures, each red and inflamed with puss. She handed me her knife.

"Scrape crust off. Open wounds and use knife to push medicine in cut."

As I pulled the flesh apart, she winced in pain but did not cry out. I wanted to stop hurting her, but she insisted that I complete the treatment.

"What about bleeding?" I asked. "Will the blood wash out the medicine?"

"Yes. You must put medicine in again when sun come up. You must do it even if I not conscious."

I promised.

Chapter 20

The next morning, I prepared breakfast and felt my patient's head expecting the fever to be at least as bad as the night before. She felt normal, but awoke from my attention.

"Thank you, Cole, for give medicine last night. I feel better."

She pulled up her skirt, and to my surprise, the redness and swelling was half as bad as the night before. One claw wound still seeped a mixture of blood and puss, but the other two deep wounds closed overnight. Kaga instructed me through the treatment procedure on the remaining infection before I served breakfast.

A buggy approached on the nearby road. I peeked through the brush. It was the doctor.

"Hello there. It's Doc Abbott. May I enter your camp?"

"Come on in, doctor."

"How's your friend doing this morning?" he asked.

"Fever's breaking and wounds are closing."

"Overnight? That's impossible. Yesterday, I was sure she was going to lose that leg. Even brought whiskey and a bone saw with me today. Mind if I check the patient?"

"Okay by me, if it's okay with her."

Doctor Abbott checked Kaga's wounds and expressed astonishment at her recovery.

"What's this stuff on her leg?" he asked me.

"Indian medicine. Kaga told me how to mix and apply it. Powerful stuff."

"Do you know what ingredients are in this?"

"Hell no. I just followed directions."

When the doctor asked her about the contents of her medicine, she refused to tell him, saying, "Tribe shaman make me promise, keep his secrets. I not break promise."

The doctor left, impressed by her knowledge, but frustrated by her silence.

"We'll rest here until you are well enough to travel," I told Kaga.

"I travel now. Do you mind if I ride Plutus until leg heal?"

I took my time breaking camp to give her more rest. By noon, we were following the trail along the large river winding up the central valley.

Kaga marveled when a large paddlewheel riverboat steamed past while we sat on the riverbank eating an evening meal. I explained about steamboats as well as the ocean-crossing sailing ships. She giggled like a child when I explained how large the Atlantic Ocean was. The biggest lakes she ever saw could be walked completely around in a day or two. She expressed skepticism at the notion of a body of water so large that ships took weeks to cross.

We passed through several small towns as we got close to Sacramento. Kaga became quiet and pensive. Something bothered her, but she refused to discuss it. She fiddled constantly with the bear teeth, drilling into them with the tip of her knife.

Most of the towns showed Kaga open hostility. One place was different. Residents had yellow skin and spoke a language I did not understand. I learned later they were from China. Friendly people, even to Kaga, they attempted to communicate using crude hand gestures. We managed to get food and water as well as shelter for a night.

Several women took a liking to Kaga and treated her special, braiding her hair with flowers woven into strands at the hairline. She looked like a princess.

That night, Kaga surprised me. I knew she did not like white-man beds, but she joined me under traditional sheets and blankets. Before going to bed, she applied those purple flowers.

Kaga pushed me back when I rolled toward her, and took full control, as she had many times before. She centered on top of me and positioned my engorged manhood at the center of her passion. To my surprise, soft flesh of her entrance resisted insertion. Gyrating hips slowly to build moisture and lubrication, she worked herself onto the head of my thickness, and without warning, dropped onto me, forcing entry of my full length.

She let out an involuntary gasp. I matched her intensity with powerful lunges.

Our love making took on urgency as she worked her hips to build the deepest possible connection between us. Breathing became ragged, and she moaned gently while rocking from side to side in the love straddle. Climax brought her down hard against my body, breasts smashing on my chest while she kissed my face and neck wildly.

At that moment, I seized control and rolled on top of her, thrusting as hard and fast as I could.

Wrapping her legs around my waist, she dug heels into my back with crossed ankles locked against my buttocks. Arms hooked under mine, and fingertips pressed hard into the muscles of my shoulders. Kaga whimpered through a cascade of spasms, lasting far longer than any before.

Our simultaneous pinnacle answered my own questions about our relationship. I knew in that moment, we were meant to be together, forever.

I rolled onto my side with her arms and legs still locked around me. Her lips continued nibbling in gentle afterglow until we fell asleep.

That night, I decided I would ask her to spend the rest of her life with me.

I awoke slowly. Soft bedding and warm sheets lent a serene peace, unlike any I had ever before experienced. Reaching for Kaga, admittedly with hopes of an early morning repeat of the purple-flower ritual, I felt only a thick comforter and feather pillow. I smiled.

I'm going to surprise her when she comes back upstairs. I hope she has more of those flowers.

My eyes closed, and I drifted back to sleep for a while until I realized she was not back. It took little time that day for me to understand what happened. Kaga was gone.

She left me.

Chapter 21

I sat at the kitchen table wondering what I had done so wrong when an old Chinese woman approached me. Several thin rawhide straps dangled from her fingers and her hands covered something. The old woman spoke in her language and slowly opened her hands. One of the hanging cords threaded through a hole in the base of a giant bear tooth. Another looped in and out through cuts in the top of a small animal skin bag. I loosened the drawstring and looked inside. Dried purple flowers filled the pouch.

During the next week, I hoped Kaga would return. The old Chinese woman brought me soup, rice and bread every day and insisted I eat. It was a mechanical act, and to this day, I do not recall what the food tasted like.

Lonely and confused, I ruminated about why she left. Had I offended her? Perhaps I frightened her, but she acted like she enjoyed our relationship.

Confusion became anger, both at Kaga for leaving, and at me for becoming vulnerable. Girlfriends in college never had this effect on me. Most were fickle and lasted only until they found another man to entertain them. It never bothered me when they moved on. My usual reaction was relief from obligations of a relationship. I had never been ready to settle down.

Tess introduced me to passion like I never believed possible. But, Kaga was different. She was the first woman to touch my core. Without her, my life meant nothing.

I did not shave for a week, and I lost interest in my writing job.

"Mister Colton," a quiet voice addressed me from behind. "Mister Colton, may I speak with you?"

He was thin and very old with deep wrinkles and sun spots on his hands. It surprised me that this Chinese man spoke perfect English.

"How do you know my name?" I asked.

"Your friend, the Indian woman, talked with me after she left our town. I saw her when I was returning from a gold mine in the foothills. She noticed my race and asked me to check on you here in our community."

"Did she say why she left?"

"She did not have to tell me. Her love for you is obvious, but she believes there is no place where a white man and Indian woman can make a home. By leaving, she protects you from the pain of hatred."

"That's ridiculous. I can take her back east where people have open minds."

"Mister Colton, she is wise. My people know of the hatred she fears. Bigotry from white men is not exclusive to her race. She told me you are a good man, not filled with hate like others, and she hopes you will never forget her. That is why she left you the gifts."

I looked carefully at the small oriental man. His grey clothes hung loosely, almost like a dress. Facial hair came to a single point under his chin where a foot-long braid dangled over his chest. His hands folded neatly over the lower section of his tunic, and he was missing several fingers on one hand. Something about this old man did not add up. He looked like a laborer but spoke with pride and a learned manner.

"How did you learn English? Nobody else in this town knows my language."

"You did not ask my name," he replied gently.

Embarrassed by my selfish oversight, I corrected my mistake.

"Please forgive me. My name is Colton. What may I call you?"

"I am Professor Chang Lok. You may call me Lok."

He extended a hand, the one with partial fingers, and we exchanged pleasantries.

"I taught English at a university in Southern China. My country suffered great famine and political unrest, so many of us came to California to seek our fortune in gold."

Momentarily distracted from self-indulgence, I found this man's story fascinating.

"How long have you been here?"

"Almost five years now."

"Do you mine for gold?"

"I did for one year. Panning gold is hard work, much too difficult for a man who came from a soft life of teaching. I lost these fingers while working a gold mining machine before I discovered the truth. Wealth, for me, would come from my ability to speak both Chinese and English, not from personal labor. When white gold miners began hiring Chinese to work their mines, they could not communicate with my people. They need me to translate for them."

Lok lifted a small pouch from under folds of his shirt. It looked heavy.

"This bag of gold is much more than I could ever mine by myself. Owners pay me in gold for my services. Prosperity in the mine fields does not come from hard work, it seems. Wealth goes to those who provide goods or service to miners."

His comment reminded me of things old Mack told me back in the stagecoach relay station.

Lok put a hand on my shoulder and returned the conversation to its original theme.

"Mister Colton, I saw deep love in your Indian friend's eyes. The purple flowers she left for you are to build a new life with a white woman. She wants you to be happy. The bear tooth will keep you from harm. She asks that you wear it always."

I did not say anything. Anger wrestled with confusion and a deep sense of loss.

Lok continued, "I see you love her, too. She will come back to you in her own time. Until then, build a good life, so when she returns, you can provide for her. You must be patient until your paths cross again. I have foreseen that you are destined for each other."

After the old Chinese man left, I picked up my writing quill, opened the ink bottle, and for the first time in many days, I made notes for my next article. My ambition to reach the mining fields returned. I decided to find the untold stories and wait for Kaga to return.

When the ink dried, I saddled Plutus and left for Sacramento, without Kaga.

Chapter 22

I had studied maps of Sacramento before I came west. To tell the truth, I expected more of a city than this. Dirt roads led away from the confluence of the Sacramento and American Rivers in a square grid. Maps warned that floods wiped out parts of the city every few years.

As I entered town from the south, it was raining hard. Streets acted like small streams of muddy water, running fast toward the rivers. I found a livery stable and checked in.

"Howdy stranger," the owner greeted me. "Name's Mike. Got plenty of room for your horse. Like me to wipe him down for you?"

"Sure. How much do you charge for a stall?"

"Four bits a night, cash or gold. Includes hay. Oats cost ya extra."

"Four bits? Isn't that a little steep?"

"Nope. Goin' rate in town. Four bits. Take it or leave it."

I thought about my remaining money. It would not last long at these prices.

"Is there a hotel close—one that's affordable?"

"Cheap ones are down by the river. As you move uptown, prices—"

His train of thought broke when he spotted my gun holster.

"You here on business, mister?" he asked and pointed straight at my forty-four.

"I've come to learn about the gold mines."

"Sure you did." He nodded fake agreement and lifted the wet saddle off Plutus. "Ain't no business of mine, but this town don't put up with killings. You best move on if'n you value your neck."

Plutus shook his mane and snorted in the comfort of having his wet saddle blanket removed. The stable man used a pitchfork to loosen hay from a bale and filled his hay rack.

"Chinese brothel on Second Avenue," he continued. "It's about three blocks due west of here. They got all-night rates or girly rooms by the hour. Can't miss it . . . got a red-painted dragon on the front door. Ugly thing. Red and black with gold highlights. Kind of place you gunfighters like."

"You think I'm a gunman?" I asked, a bit exasperated.

"Sorry, mister. Don't mean nothing personal. Most men wearing guns like that are partial to women and liquor. Just trying to help you out."

He used a large currycomb to lift my horse's hair so it would dry faster.

"My horse's name is Plutus. He's a special—"

"What kinda name's that for a horse?" he interrupted, scrunching his face in a half-sneer.

After explaining the meaning of Plutus, the man lightened up a bit.

"You're different than other gunmen. They don't care about their horses. Can't wait to get to the saloons or brothels. What's your name?"

We exchanged names, and I explained about my fledgling writing career.

"If you're a journalist, why you trying to look like a killer?"

"It's a long story." I patted the forty-four. "This was a mistake. I need to sell this gun and get one that won't cause so much trouble. Where's the best place to do that?"

"Try Big Hank at the Valley Mercantile. Sells guns. Probably fix you right up. He's on the next block. Can't miss his sign."

Pulling my Stetson hat down tight against the rain, I headed into the dark afternoon.

The houses on this street all looked similar. Each had an eight to ten-foot high, aboveground basement with a wide set of stairs leading up to a wraparound porch on the primary floor. I later learned the annual floods that ravaged Sacramento made tall foundations necessary.

I climbed the stairs to the merchant store's entrance, cleaned mud off my boots on a bristle brush mounted upside down on the top step. Inside, several lanterns lit rows of supplies that included everything from sacks of grain to farm equipment, and books to guns. A long hardwood counter spanned the back wall where a heavily bearded man leaned over a catalog, flipping pages almost at random.

"Afternoon, fella," he called out. "What can I do for ya?"

Seems friendly enough.

"Need to replenish my supplies, and I need a map of the gold fields."

The shopkeeper shook his head and spoke under his breath loud enough so I could hear him.

"Here we go again. Another young fool, planning to get rich digging gold."

"No, sir," I responded to his contempt. "I'm a journalist from the east. I'm here to tell the truth about the gold rush we keep reading about back home. Stories about men getting rich just don't make sense. I want to know, where are all these rich miners?"

"Good observation, kid. There's a reason for that. If you're a good—"

The merchant noticed my forty-four and stopped talking.

"Is there a problem?" I asked.

"If you're a journalist, why you wearing that piece?"

"It's a long story. I understand things about this gun now that I didn't know when I bought it. That's another matter for your store. I need to sell this and get another sidearm."

The man still did not trust me and made that clear, so I explained the whole story about getting snookered in Wichita.

"Son of a bitch who sold you that," he muttered, "should be whipped. Coulda got you killed. Do you know who that merchant got it from?"

"He didn't say, and I didn't ask."

The man rubbed his chin, threading his fingers in and out of his facial fur.

"John Barker. That's his gun. Killed twenty men, last I heard."

"How do you know about my gun?"

"Markings and modifications. Barker always shaved off the sight to a flat spot. Said it helped the barrel clear the holster for a faster draw. Let me see it."

He held out his hand, and I place my weapon, butt-first, on his palm.

"See that front sight spot?" he said. "Been filed off completely flat. Yep, that's John's work. He's the only one I know to do that. Most gunfighters leave a smooth nub that clears the holster just as quick, but he swore by that extra filing. Holster leather is also cut at an odd angle. I can spot his style anywhere."

He turned the gun upside down and looked at the bottom of the trigger guard.

"Look here." He pointed at the metal loop surrounding the trigger and held the gun directly in the bright light under his reading lantern.

"See those tiny lines?"

"Yeah. I never noticed them before."

He began counting and ended at twenty-two scratch marks, each spaced exactly the same distance apart.

"Must'a got a couple more after I saw him last. Twenty-two kills. Most guys notch the hand grip. Not him. He scratched into the metal. Said anybody can swap out the grips but the trigger guard makes a permanent record. You say you bought this in Wichita?"

"Got my whole outfit there, even the horse and tack. Came as a package deal."

"Horse? Where's your horse now?"

"At the livery on the next block."

"Come with me. Oh, my name's Clyde, Clyde Hamlin. What's your name, kid?"

"I'm Colton, but the livery hand said your name is Hank."

"Ah shit. Sorry bout that. Got excited about the horse and slipped up. Everybody in town knows me as Hank. I'd appreciate if you keep it that way. I got my reasons."

I agreed.

The shop tender hung his "Be right back" sign in the entry door window, and I followed him into the rain. We walked to the stable under his large umbrella.

"Howdy Hank," the stableman called out.

"Evening Mike, where'd you put this boy's tack? Need to appraise it for a trade."

Clyde's comment surprised me. We had not talked about a trade of any kind.

Clyde, or Hank, whatever he wanted to be called, flipped the damp saddle over on a barrel head to look at the underside. He showed me three initials, C D H, carved on the bottom. The big man giggled like a school girl.

"Son of a bitch. He done it!" Clyde said.

"Who did what?" I asked.

"This here saddle was custom made for me almost twelve years ago. I lost it to Barker in a poker hand just before he went east. Told him I'd get it back someday. Figured I'd have to kill him for it. Never thought it would just walk back into my life. Son of a bitch must'a hung up his gun and started a new life. Said he was gonna do that. I figured he'd get killed by some young fast-draw before that happened."

He hefted the saddle back onto the drying rack.

"Where's King?" he asked the livery owner.

"Who's King?" the stable man asked.

"The horse—horse that goes with this saddle."

Mike got my horse. Plutus obediently followed his lead rope into the yellow light of the large lantern until he saw Clyde. Recognition was instant. My horse surged past the stable man and nudged the shopkeeper affectionately with his nose. It was like old friends embracing.

"King, how the hell are you?"

Plutus tugged on the merchant's shirt pocket.

"Sorry, boy. Ain't got no apples on me. I'll get you some tomorrow."

He grabbed a handful of grain from a large barrel against the wall and hand-fed my horse. His free hand tousled the mane and Plutus nudged the shopkeeper the same way he did me when he was happy. They clearly knew each other. Until now, only Kaga had this effect on him.

"Colton, this is the finest stallion west of the Mississippi. Broke him myself, as a colt. Never should have lost him to John Barker, but I needed money to start that mercantile. John wanted my saddle too, so I made a bad deal. Told him I'd play one hand of poker for his money. If I won, I got the money. If he won, I got the money as a loan that I'd have to pay back, and John got my horse and gear. I lost. Wondered why Barker never returned to collect on that loan. Guess he went straight."

It was an interesting story, and I could tell Clyde cared about Plutus, but as far as I was concerned, my animal was not for sale. I needed him to travel to the gold fields. Besides, I became partial to the big stallion after all we had been through.

"How much for the horse, tack and Barker's gun?" he asked me.

"Sorry, Hank, only the gun is for sale."

"Kid, I don't think you understand. I don't have to buy these things from you. It's just a matter of time until some hothead kills you for wearing that gun. Then, I'll get what I want from the mortician real cheap."

"He's right," the stable keeper chimed in. "There are a gunmen right here in this area. They'll shoot you down on sight when they see that gun you're packing."

"I don't care about the gun," I said, "but I've been through a lot with Plutus and—"

"Plutus!" Clyde yelled. "What kind of dumb-ass name is that, boy?"

I explained the Roman God of Wealth story, and they both laughed at me, unappreciative of my clever intent.

"We'll talk later about this, kid. Truth is that horse knows people. You could only ride him if he trusts you. Let's go back to my store. We need to talk."

As we left the stable, he grinned and asked, "By any chance, kid, do you play poker?"

Chapter 23

Clyde opened the storefront door, but instead of removing the sign from the window, he flipped it over to the "Closed" side.

"So, kid, you're out here to tell the real story of the gold fields."

"Yes sir, and I'm sorry about keeping Plut . . . uh, King."

"That ain't over yet, boy. Like I said, I can buy him from you alive, or I can wait 'til you're dead. Makes no matter to me."

He noticed my grimace.

"Calm down, Colton. I ain't serious about getting you shot to get my horse back. Wouldn't do that. Let's look at my selection of guns, so we can get rid of that invitation to kill you. Course, you'll have to buy the one you like. There's no resale value in that killer iron."

"I understand. What do you think happened to Mr. Barker, your friend?"

Clyde got a curious look. He squinted and tightened his lips in a sneer visible through all that facial hair.

"Let's get this straight, John Barker was no friend. We were, shall we say, business acquaintances. When I said I might have to kill him to get my horse back, I meant it."
I chuckled and stifled a smile. It sounded funny for an aging, overweight shopkeeper to think he could take on a proven killer, a cold-blooded fast draw in his prime.

"Mighty big words for a shopkeeper," I joked. "I mean, maybe you could beat him to death with a shovel, but come on, Clyde, that guy's a gunfighter. What makes you think you could kill him?"

"You got a point there, Colton, but for the wrong reason. John always was faster than me, but he was never confident he could beat me. When you're inside the other guy's mind, you win, every time."

I was getting confused.

"How can a shopkeeper outdraw a gunfighter?"

Clyde thought deeply for a minute before making a carefully considered decision.

"Come with me."

He parted a floor-to-ceiling curtain covering a doorway at the end of the counter. Upon entering the back room, he took a slow-burning incense stick out of a tall glass vase on a shelf and blew across the smoldering tip. It glowed red. Inserting the glowing tip into a lantern sitting on a tall dresser by the door, the lamp's wick caught fire and the room danced in the hard shadows made by the oil lamp.

Clyde lived in this rear room. Several large animal heads graced one wall, each mounted on a wood panel. There were two deer, an elk, and a grizzly bear head but it was not nearly as big as the one Kaga and I killed. I winced for a second as I recalled her wild ride on the back of that huge bear, stabbing it over and over with her knife. I wondered how long it would be until the Chinese professor's prediction would come to pass.

The back wall had a single window completely covered in sackcloth, and a black, wood-burning stove sat in the corner for heat and cooking. Firewood, stacked neatly on either side of the stove, waited for winter months that were rapidly approaching. I imagined how comfortable this room would be on a cold winter night with the potbellied stove burning hot. The nearby wall featured a small bed covered in piles of animal furs laid out by matching pelts. Beaver, bear and deer skins were obvious, but one smaller stack did not look familiar. A square table with two wood-slat chairs filled the middle of the room, standing on a worn bearskin rug. In the corner of the entry wall, dirty dishes filled a wood dry-sink with a large bucket hanging under the spout of a water pump.

"You hungry," Clyde asked.

"Now that you mention it, yeah, I'm real hungry."

"Here, try some of my jerk meat. Don't sell this stuff. It's my private stock."

He tossed a pile of smoked meat on the table. The meat was lighter in color than other jerk-game I had eaten.

"Salmon," he said. "Ever eat smoked salmon?"

"No. Never even heard of the stuff. What is it?"

"Fish. They run up the river every fall to spawn. Indians showed me how to smoke the meat so that it lasts all winter. This run come up the American River last month. It's fresh."

I bit off a small piece of the curled, red-brown meat to test its flavor. It was delicious.

"Kid, I like you. More important, King trusts you."

"Thanks. Means a lot to me that a horse approves of my character," I joked.

By now, I should have learned that sarcasm did not go over well with these westerners.

"Think it's funny, do ya?"

"No, sir." I lied. "I shouldn't joke like that."

"That's okay, kid. Most people can't read animals. So, you want stories about gold mining. I can tell you things about myself and gold miners that your readers might find real interesting. Problem is you've got to keep my secrets until after I'm gone from this area. I'm leaving pretty soon. Think you can do that?"

What was I going to say?

No, Clyde. I'm not going to keep your secrets.

I did what any good journalist would do. I promised to keep quiet about his information while secretly reserving the right to change my mind if the information proved essential to a great story.

Clyde slid out the bottom compartment of his dresser. Dust puffed up from inside.

"Haven't opened that drawer for five years."

He pulled out several folded blankets and tossed them on the floor. Reaching deeper into the drawer with both hands, he brought out something wrapped in thick rawhide rags.

"I put this away when I figured out the truth about gold mining." Seemed odd, seeing such a rough man treating this package like a newborn child. When he folded back the animal skin coverings, I saw a well-worn leather belt with a large, decorative buckle and a holster. He lifted them up and showed them to me with a reverence people usually reserved for family heirlooms.

"Lotta miles on this old belt. You know what you're seeing?"

"Looks like a gun belt to me, sir."

"Stop calling me 'sir.' I don't like most people who go by that word."

"Sorry, sir—I mean, Clyde." I suddenly saw the resemblance. "Is that what I think it is?"

"Yep. Identical to yours. John Barton made it back in the day. He was great with leather."

It was like looking at my holster. Same cutaways. Identical decorative engraving. Even the light brown color of the leather matched perfectly. This could have been cut from the same cured cowhide. Leg ties, hanging at the bottom, were the same color and length as mine, too. I glanced down at my own gun to verify the similarities.

Clyde threaded the wide belt through over-sized slits on the body side of the holster and fastened it around his waist.

"Still fits," he said with satisfaction as the belt buckle hooked onto the most worn hole.

He jiggled his waist until the belt settled into a natural, slightly downward angle across his hips. Clyde tied the leg strings around his lower thigh, making them tighter than I would have expected. His hand hung relaxed a few inches from the place where the handle of the gun would be. He practiced a drawing motion that looked awkward and unnatural.

Clyde's shoulder dropped and his elbow bent slightly, but his hand never lifted the imaginary gun out of the holster. Instead, it moved backward from the leather casing, and his wrist rotated to a position that would turn the gun barrel from vertical to horizontal. While the motion looked strange, it hinted at cold efficiency and practiced perfection.

"That's how it's done, kid."

Chapter 24

Clyde looked at me before repeating the motion, only this time, he added step-by-step narration.

"Contact with the gun handle." His hand snapped inward ever so slightly.

"Rotate." The elbow dropped, wrist shifted and imaginary gun rotated in a single motion.

"Fire." His finger squeezed the fantasy trigger. "Another one meets his maker."

A mixed grin and sneer pressed through his heavy beard as he relived some memory and paused a moment to bask in its glory. He turned to face me.

"Figured it out yet, Cole?"

"I think so. Were you a gunfighter?"

"Yes . . . and no. Real gunfighters live for the next kill. That lifestyle is a never-ending measure of your manhood. Me? I was different. Never wanted to kill nobody. My reputation for being fast kept them coming. Told every swinging dick I did not want to kill him. Warned them all, but dumbasses kept coming. Forced me to stay on the move."

"How did you end up a merchant? Didn't that make it easier for them to find you?"

Clyde picked up a piece of the smoked salmon and ate as he told the rest of his story.

"This store was John Barton's idea. He traveled all over the west playing poker and gun fighting for a living. That man sure enjoyed killing."

He ripped off a large chunk of the dried fish and took a swig from his canteen to soften it.

"About five years ago, he got shot by a young gun. Managed to kill the kid, but it took a mighty big bite outta his confidence. While he was healing, he told me he was scared for the first time in his life."

"Scared of dying?" I asked.

"Nope. Scared'a living. Fool fell in love. Being a gunfighter means you got to keep on the move. Family don't fit in. Any weakness can be exploited by other gunman. If he knows you care about a wife or kid, he'll shake your concentration by telling you what he's going to do to them after he kills you. Heart rate goes up. Nerves get shaky. Concentration slips. Eyes get twitchy. Nothing will get you killed faster than distractions. John knew it, too."

Clyde took off his gun belt and laid it on the table. He talked over his shoulder as he reached deep into the still-open drawer.

"That gun you're wearing, it was his. Custom made. Lighter than a thirty-six and shorter barrel for quicker draw. Gunsmith swapped out the thirty-six barrel and cylinder for a forty-four. Trigger's doctored, too. That gun has some serious kick to it."

I thought back to my surprise when it flew out of my hand in the bar fight with the drunk.

"John left for the east with Betty-Ann. Must have sold all his things in Wichita, including that gun and my horse. Probably living the fat life now. Maybe even sired a young'un."

Clyde laughed at the notion of his killer-friend enjoying gentile society.

"How did he fall in love, if he was always on the move?" I asked. "Don't you gunfighters guard against that?"

Clyde lifted up a heavy object wrapped in burlap and tied securely with three thin cords.

"Got that right, kid. Fast-draw men move a lot. Relationships with women are supposed to cost money and end the next morning. That's just the way it is."

He released the ties and opened the package with great satisfaction. As the last fold of wrapping turned back, I saw MY gun sitting on the burlap—an exact duplicate by the looks of it.

"Only two guns of this kind in the world," he said.

"May I?" I asked, and he nodded.

Immediately looking at the finger guard, I expected to see tiny scratches, one for every man he killed. It was smooth.

"Disappointed?" he asked.

"Surprised. I thought you said you killed a lot of men."

"I did. Stopped counting at thirty-one."

"Where are your marks?"

"Weren't you listening, kid? Told you I didn't kill for pleasure. Kept the number in my head up to thirty-one. Stopped count after that. Don't know why I bothered in the first place."

He held out another chunk of fish that I eagerly accepted.

"After John got shot, he started talking about how to get out of the gun fighting business. Turns out, he and Betty-Ann had the same problem. She owned a bar and a brothel in Nevada City. The bar's where John got shot."

Clyde took the gun out of my hands and slipped it into the holster on the table.

"Betty-Ann taught John and me the secret of wealth in the gold fields. Told you I'd share that with you, but you got to keep it to yourself until I'm gone."

I nodded, again agreeing to keep his secrets.

Clyde leaned close to me as if someone nearby might hear.

"Wealth don't come from hard work. Hell, if it did, them China men would all be rich. Hard workers, them yella skins. Nope, wealth don't come from hard work, Colton."

I found myself leaning closer, mesmerized by this worldly man. He tapped on my forearm for emphasis.

"Eggs, shovels and sex. That's where the money is. Stupid miners work all week for a couple ounces of gold. Then, they pay me way too much for equipment like sluice pans or dry goods. I seen a single egg sell for over a dollar in gold up in foothill towns. Back where you come from, eggs sell two for a cent. Miners find a lot of gold, but they got to eat."

"You said 'sex' in your list. Are you talking about brothels?"

"Yep, but not the whores. They don't make as much money as the madams who own the business. Poor whores get taken just like miners do, only not quite as bad."

I thought about Clyde's comment while he elaborated.

"Up in Grass Valley or Coloma, there's only one woman for every ten men. Betty-Ann, she was one smart businesswoman. Figured that out. She made money off the miners by opening a bar and bringing in dancing girls. After she got the miners drunk, they spent all their gold hooting at legs and tits. One day, she realized she could double her profits by opening a brothel next door. She got rich taking miner gold."

He spit a fish bone onto the table.

"Everybody knew she was collecting more gold than the local banks. Failed miners noticed it, too. Some decided it would be easier to liberate her gold than to work in cold, wet creeks. Her bar got robbed three times in one month. Bartender pulled a shotgun on two men in one robbing, but they shot him dead and walked away with a day's gold collection. Betty-Ann could not find another man tough enough to tend bar. No law in those towns either. She needed protection for both her bar and the whorehouse."

It was not hard for me to put two and two together.

"Did she hire John?"

"Yep. I sent him to her when I heard she needed a good gunman. I was trying my luck with a sluice pan, at the time, and didn't want the job."

"You said he got shot. Did that happen in the bar?"

"Yep, but it weren't no robber. Young buck hoping to make a name for his-self tracked John down. Not even seventeen yet. John warned him, and a couple miners jumped the boy trying to prevent a shooting. Youngster broke free and drew on John. There were only two gunshots. John shot the kid through the heart, but he took a bullet in his left shoulder because he hesitated while he pushed a bar patron out of the line of fire before he could draw."

Clyde folded his gun and holster in the wrapping on the table and retied the strings.

"These things will get you killed, Colton. John got lucky. Betty-Ann nursed him back to health, and they hightailed it outta California. She got rich off the miners and so did John while he worked for her. Son of a bitch took my horse with him when he left. Course, you brought King back to me."

He winked at me.

"I told you, Plutus is not for sale."

"That's still a stupid name, kid. When I get him after the undertaker buries you, I'm gonna tell him he gets his real name back."

I shook my head in mock contempt.

"When did you start this mercantile?"

"About the time John got shot." He leaned back in his chair. "Gunfighters don't get old, boy. They only get beat—once. John got lucky. He got a second chance. I hope they set up a nice little farm in Missouri, maybe even have a couple kids. He must of meant it when he said he was getting a new start, because he sold his tools of the trade. All I really want back is my horse."

Clyde put his gun and belt back in the bottom drawer and parted the doorway curtains to go back into the store's front. I followed.

"Let's get rid of that hip advertisement you're packing. Got a preference for a sidearm?"

"This was my first revolver. I don't know what to look for. What do you suggest?"

"Depends on what you plan to use it for. Can't beat a forty-four for killing critters, especially big ones like bear or big cats. If you plan to use it for men, caliber's less important. Thirty-six caliber bullet in the heart kills a man just as dead as a forty-four."

He opened a showcase with a dozen pistols on display and reached to the back for a beautiful handgun in a decorative engraved holster. Custom bone grips on the handle showed a little wear, but overall it looked new.

"This here's a 1851 Colt Navy Special. Thirty-six caliber. Sweet gun. I test all the guns I buy, and I clean them before they go in the case. This one's my favorite. Whadda you think?"

He withdrew the weapon from the holster and checked the cylinder to make sure it was unloaded before handing it to me.

I did not like it. It felt awkward and unbalanced, not light and natural like my forty-four.

Clyde noticed my reaction.

"You fired John's gun yet?"

"Yeah. Couple of times. Shot a cougar and a Valley bear with it."

I did not tell him about the drunk in the bar.

"No kidding? Shot a grizzly?"

I told him a shortened version of the story.

"Don't compare any of these guns with that one." He pointed at my hip.

"That forty-four's been modified for fast draw. Lighter than any other gun in its class. Got a super sensitive trigger pull, too. Stock guns don't feel the same."

I sighted down the barrel of the Colt Navy and felt the trigger resistance. Sure enough, it was stiff. Even cocking the hammer felt uncomfortable. I never could have cocked and fired this revolver fast enough, to kill that grizzly before getting overrun.

"I don't like it. What if I just keep my gun but switch out the holster so gunfighters don't recognize it as a killer tool?"

Clyde thought about my suggestion.

"That might work. I don't have a holster that will fit that forty-four right now. It requires a custom fit. I can get one made at the leather shop, but it will take a couple months. You can wear this Navy Special until we get the replacement."

"Clyde, I'm going to take your advice to get rid of this gun. I've already seen people mistake me for a gunman just by seeing this thing, but I'm mighty curious about something. You know, as a journalist, would you teach me that fast draw stuff? It looks like fun."

My new friend looked at me as if I was crazy.

"Fun? Haven't you been listening?" It was not a question.

"I'm not planning to draw on anybody. It just looks like it would be fun to see how fast I can draw. I learn real quick. How about it?"

He walked away making no effort to hide his disgust. It was getting dark in the store and rain outside seemed to be getting heavier. Clyde turned up the wick on a couple lanterns before coming back over to me.

"You really killed a grizzly with that thing?"

"Yeah. Had to empty it into the bear before he would go down."

Clyde stroked his beard while he thought.

"Let's make a deal, kid. I need help in this store, and I want King back, the saddle, too. If you work for me for six months, just for room and food, I will teach you how to fast draw," he paused for effect, "and I'll give you this store in exchange for the horse and saddle when I leave. This mercantile is the real story of the gold rush, anyway. All the gold ends up with bankers, water barons or folks, like me, selling stuff. I've made a fortune selling goods for markups at ten times my cost. What do you think, kid? Horse for the business. We got a deal?"

Chapter 25

Three men entered the store together. One approached me as I was working behind the store's counter. His clothes looked like all the other miners I had met while working for Clyde. I loved listening to their stories and adding fresh insights to my articles. I sent my writing to the newspaper with the stagecoach drivers each week.

This man smelled bad. He probably had not bathed in months and a razor could not have touched his face in several years. Despite looking like a miner, he did not act like one.

"Morning," he said. "Rope broke in my mineshaft lift. Block and tackle's fine, but ain't enough rope left to fix it. Can't bring out no ore without that lift. Got any heavy rope for sale?"

Clyde kept large spools of rope in the storage room because they took up too much retail space on the store's floor.

"Sure. How much do you need?"

"Hundred foot," he replied. "How much will that cost?"

I did not know the price Clyde charged for heavy rope, so I called him out from his private quarters in back. He gave the man a price, and the miner was not happy.

"That's robbery! I ain't paying you that much for a damned rope."

"Suit yourself, fella. Nearest heavy rope is in San Francisco. I suppose you can give the captain of the River King steamboat your money, and he can buy it for you cheaper next time he goes there. Believe he makes that run couple times a month. Course, he's also gonna charge you a delivery fee, and you'll be out of production for a few weeks."

"That may be, mister, but your price just ain't fair."

Clyde got mad.

"I bought that goddamned rope two years ago. It sat in my storage room all that time, getting in the way of my business. Why would I do such a stupid thing? I do it so some goddamned miner who doesn't take care of his equipment will be able to get back to mining with as little loss of production as possible. My price compensates me for my troubles. Now, put up money or gold, if you want that rope. If you don't want to pay my price, then get out of my store. I'm sure the next miner who needs heavy rope will be happy to find it so fast."

Something did not feel right. While Clyde argued with the miner, the man's two friends disappeared behind rows of hardware near the front door. A woman started up the stairs from the street, and one of them slipped out the front door. He stopped her halfway up the entrance steps. She listened to him for a minute and looked over his shoulder into the store before returning to her buggy and leaving. He reentered the store, vanishing behind rows piled high with goods.

"Look mister," the miner said with a more conciliatory tone. "I ain't got that kind of money you're wanting. Can't you give me a break on the price?"

I noticed the hat of one of the hiding miners as he made his way behind stacks of grain toward the far end of our counter.

"How much you got?" Clyde asked.

"How much rope can I get for this?" The miner opened a small cloth bag so Clyde could look inside.

"Can't tell how much you got in that bag," Clyde said. "Dump it in this tray so I can get a weight on it. Then, we'll work something out. Cole, get the heavy rope coil."

"Yes, Hank," I said and went into the storeroom where I also slept as part of my room and board arrangement.

"What the hell?" I heard Clyde say. "You best put that away."

I peeked out of the back room through a peephole. The miner held an old Texas Patterson in both hands, aimed at Clyde's face. Its hammer was cocked, and the man's index finger rested on the dropdown trigger. His hands were shaking.

My dad had taught me to shoot targets with one of those old Colts.

At the far end of the counter, the other two miners hurdled over the smooth wood and ran toward Clyde with guns drawn.

The rest is still a blur. As best I recall, my forty-four hung on a peg near the entrance to my room. I grabbed it and peeked through the hole again. All three men screamed at Clyde to open his safe while aiming guns at him. He kept it unlocked during business, so he just stepped back and pointed at its door, already slightly open.

Both men behind the counter shoved Clyde aside and scrambled to get into the safe. My greatest concern was for the gun pointed at my boss's head by the first miner.

I cocked my gun and rolled into view around the doorframe with my gun aimed at the head of the man threatening Clyde. He saw me and began to turn his gun in my direction.

I fired.

The gunman's head snapped back, and his gun fired into the wall above my head. Without hesitation, my next shot was into the nearest robber who crumpled forward on the floor.

Clyde dove backward, away from the third man, giving me a clear line of fire.

I saw his barrel lifting toward me before I could cock my weapon, so I rotated behind cover of the doorframe. He fired, and for the second time in my life, I felt splinters penetrate my flesh from a close bullet impact. I risked a quick look. Another bullet slammed into the wood right where I stuck my head out. He was ready for me. I could not get a shot at him without exposing myself.

Two rapid blasts of a twelve-gauge shotgun ended the threat. The other guy only had a pistol, so I knew by the blasts it was Clyde who fired.

"Come on out, Cole. It's clear."

Two dead men lay in a heap where they fell behind the counter, and the man I shot landed on his back with a small hole under his eye and the back corner of his head missing.

"Fetch the sheriff, Cole. Put the 'Closed' sign up on your way out. Don't want my regulars to see this."

I ran as fast as I could to the town jail.

118

For the next two hours, the sheriff went over details for his report. I was impressed with his thorough questions. He judged the killings as justifiable self-defense and instructed the undertaker to haul away the bodies. During the lawman's evaluation, he dumped the content of the man's gold bag onto the counter. It was mostly pyrite, stuff we called "fool's gold."

"Hank," the sheriff used Clyde's public name. "These guys might be the highwaymen that have been robbing miners and farmers all over the foothills. You can have their guns and horses to compensate for your damages. Afraid there's nothing else of any value in their things."

After the lawman left, Clyde asked me to clean up and reopen the shop. He went back into his private area without saying anything else to me.

I ran the store myself that afternoon. It seemed odd that my boss stayed out of sight for so long. He usually came out every hour to visit with me or talk with regular customers. Some of the patrons heard about the robbery and asked me if he was okay, but he never showed despite easily hearing their voices through the closed curtains.

At dark, I locked the store, closed the safe and cleaned up for dinner. Still, there was no sign of Clyde. I figured he needed to be alone.

After eating, I turned my lantern as bright as it would go, so I could write my daily notes and prepare another article for my eastern employer.

This article was difficult to write. I kept thinking about the men I killed today. It felt right at the time, but I wondered if there was a better way to stop those men, a way without killing. No matter how I replayed the scene, they gave me no other choice. And I wondered what Kaga would think.

Will she lose respect for me? Should I even tell her?

I finished my writing and sealed the envelope containing my article for delivery to the local stagecoach line. It would take a couple weeks to reach my publisher, and I wondered how the editor would react to this one. My other writings entertained readers with things like the drama I experienced in Tumbleweed or survival in the desert, but they did not address subjects of social controversy. This one questioned the white man's attitude toward other races. I shared Kaga's point of view without saying her name. To my readers, she was just some Indian squaw.

This might not get published, I thought and shook my head in contemplation. *I'm okay with that. I wrote the truth. If you guys can't see fit to print the truth, then maybe I need to change publishers. Guess I'll know in a couple months.*

A strange noise came from Clyde's room. Something solid and heavy fell onto another solid surface. I went to Clyde's curtain and listened.

"What's going on it there? Clyde, you okay?"

"Yeah, I'm fine, kid. Just busted my damn finger."

"How'd you do that? What was that noise?"

"Come here, Cole. You might as well know about this."

I parted his curtain but could not see in the dark.

"Fire up the lantern, will ya?" Clyde said.

I grabbed one of his incense sticks and ignited the lantern by the door. Clyde was sitting on the floor, in pain, with his left hand pressed tight against the floorboards.

"What happened?"

"I was coming back in and dropped the trapdoor. Smashed my finger."

He nodded toward his hand on the floor. The table that usually occupied the center of the room rested against the side wall, and the rug was tossed against the table's leg. Clyde sat upright with his small finger wedged in the seam of a partially closed trapdoor.

"Grab that rope and pull up this door. Finger's stuck."

I pulled gently on the rope's knotted end, and the wood hatch moved slightly.

"Ow!" Clyde yelled. "Yank the goddamned thing open. Don't torture me."

I held my breath and made one strong pull. The heavy flooring resisted for a split second before snapping open, almost hitting Clyde in the head as it broke free.

His small finger curved backward at an angle never meant for a human hand. Some skin was scraped off and blood trickled down his forearm.

"Need me to get the doctor?"

He did not answer. Instead, he grabbed his mangled finger in his good hand and stretched it as hard as he could away from his palm. The bend in the baby finger straightened, and having set the bone, he released the finger.

"It'll heal now," he said. "Hand me that bottle of whisky. I got to get rid of this pain."

Clyde poured some over the wound and chugged more than I had ever seen him drink.

"Do me a favor, kid. Put that trapdoor in place, and cover it with the rug and table."

I complied while he got to his feet pushing up with his only good hand.

"I don't get it," I said. "Where have you been, and why sneak in and out of here through a hidden door?"

"Had to take care of business."

"What kind of business? And, why sneak?"

"Kid, there are some things it's better you don't know. What's for dinner?"

"Beans and rice. Wasn't very hungry. There's some left on the stove in my room, and it's still hot. Want me to get you a bowl?"

After getting food for Clyde, we sat at his table while he ate.

"Not hungry, huh?" he asked.

"Yeah, no appetite tonight."

"That happens for the first few."

"First few what?"

"Killin's. You get used to it, after a while."

"Is that supposed to be a good thing? What if I don't want to get used to killing?"

Clyde drank more whisky and shoveled beans and rice into his mouth. When he answered, he talked in a muffled voice through the food.

"Thanks for covering the shop for me."

"I didn't know you left. Where'd you go?"

"Like I said, Colton. Had some business to settle."

That was when I noticed he was wearing his old gunman's rig. The leg straps were tied tight. I pointed at the weapon.

"Why are you gunned up? Thought you quit killing."

He got mad.

"Don't get mouthy with me, boy. I don't answer to you."

"Sorry." I knew I was wrong to press him.

Clyde drank two more long swigs from the bottle, and his facial tension eased.

"Naw, you got nothing to apologize for, Cole. You stood up like a man, today. Covered my tail, right good. Thank you."

He held out the whisky bottle to me.

"Want some? Best damn stuff ever invented by man."

Chapter 26

Two weeks passed with no explanation from Clyde. I used my work in the mercantile to visit with everyone from miners to bankers, always probing for storylines about the realities of the gold rush lifestyle and peculiarities of the west.

Not a day went by that I did not wake up and stroke the bear's tooth beneath my shirt. Every morning began with me wondering where Kaga was. Winter meant heavy snow in the Sierra Nevada Mountains, and I worried about her. For some strange reason, I trusted the old Chinese man's prophecy, but I was beginning to wonder if she would come back.

This day, the sheriff was waiting at the front door when I unlocked.

"Morning, Colton. Hank around?"

"He's not good about rising early. Need me to wake him?"

"Naw, let him sleep. It's not that important. Just following up on the robbers you fellas killed a couple weeks ago."

"I thought that investigation was over. Is there more to it?"

"Hunters found two dead men yesterday in a camp east of town. Both shot through the heart. Forty-four, by the looks of it. Been dead at least a week."

"What's that got to do with Hank?"

"Actually, it's got to do with both of you. From the belongings we recovered in that camp, it looks like those boys you killed were part of a gang of highwaymen that have been causing trouble all over these parts. We figure they had a falling out within their group. Couple got shot, and the rest must have left the area real fast. Left all their belongings behind. Lots of tracks, mostly heading up into the hills. Must be four of five of them."

"How does that affect us?"

"Some folks get real mean when you kill their kin. They might come back here to get even with you boys, or, they might just show up to buy more supplies. You've already seen how they pay for their goods. Just warning you, be on the lookout for them. If you see strangers hanging around, let me know. I'll chase them out of town."

I thanked the lawman and closed the front door behind him. As soon as the door latched, Clyde spoke to me through his curtains.

"Good man, that sheriff, but he's not the brightest lawman I ever met."

"Were you listening?"

"Yeah. Couldn't sleep last night. Weather's turning. My knee hurts like hell when the weather turns. Big storm coming."

Clyde parted the curtains and entered the store holding a cup of fresh coffee.

"You really are missing out in life, Cole. This is the nectar of the gods. Sure you don't want to try some coffee?"

He saluted me with the cup of coffee and took a sip.

"No thanks. I never took a liking to the stuff. Why do you think the sheriff is not smart?"

"He's right about those men we shot. They belong to a family of highway men. Used to be miners but never could get it right. Lots of failed dreams out there in the mine claims. Seen men hang their selves when all their money run out, and they didn't have no gold to show for it. I recognized the leader—the guy you shot in the head—at first sight when they come in the store, but I had to play along with him to prevent bloodshed."

"You knew they were going to rob us?" My mouth hung open in shock.

"Yep. Had everything under control . . . til you shot him."

I was stunned.

"But, he could have killed you," I protested.

"Not a chance. He was scared to death. Would'a grabbed my cash bag from the safe and stayed out of town for years, afraid of getting caught for strong arm robbery if he come back."

"What about your money?"

Clyde swung the unlocked safe door open and removed a heavy bag of gold collected from customers the prior day. He dumped it onto the counter top. Dozens of tiny river pebbles rolled across the wood.

"Rocks. Nothing but little rocks."

"Where's the gold? I've been following your instructions every day. Put thousands of dollars of gold and cash in that bag since I've been here."

"Nope," he said and pulled a small pouch from under his shirt. He emptied it on the counter and a small pile of gold nuggets spread next to the rocks. "I switch out the bags after every purchase with cash or gold. The safe only holds stones from the river. Robbers never check money sacks. Just grab and run. Been robbed six times in the last four years. Never lost a dime."

"But . . . but, he had a gun on you."

"Yeah. About that, you almost got me killed. If you had'a shot him in the chest instead of the head, dead-man reflex would have pulled that trigger. I'd be dead. A shot man usually squeezes the trigger when the bullet hits him, even if he's shot clean through the heart. Head-shots are different. A head-shot man just crumples. Damn lucky you blew his head off."

I did not know what to say.

"I like that you stood up for me, kid. Means a lot to me. You given any more thought to selling me my horse back?"

"I thought that was part of our deal. I work for you for six months, and we trade the business for my horse and tack."

"You're right, Cole, but I might need to leave town sooner than I thought."

"What's going on, Clyde? Something doesn't feel right, and you still haven't taught me to fast draw like we agreed."

Clyde scooped the gold back into his personal pouch and put the rocks back into the safe. He had a cold demeanor, almost as if he was angry with me.

"Put up the closed sign," he said. "Get your gun and take a hundred rounds and caps from the ammo rack. I'll be right back."

An hour later, we reached a stretch of riverbank with no houses or barns in sight. The river ran fast with lots of floating debris, swelled from recent rains. We dismounted and Clyde pulled his gunfighter gear from his saddlebag. He took a moment to rub the nose of my horse before giving me the first lesson in fast draw technique.

"Quick draws begin with familiarity of your weapon. It has to be as personal as your own hand. Let's see how good you can aim."

A large tree floated toward us on the river. Most of it suspended under water, but several small limbs stuck up at different angles.

"Trim the limbs off that tree, Cole."

I tried to aim but the missing gun sight on the tip of the forty-four made it difficult. I missed with my first three shots.

"This is how it's done," Clyde said.

He did not sight along his weapon, firing instead, from the waist. Four shots rang out in rapid succession. The first two splashed close to the log, but the other two hit the base of limbs, and one-inch-thick branches toppled into the water.

I was impressed.

"How do you aim without sights?"

"Close your eyes."

I did.

"Touch your finger to your nose."

Again, I followed instructions.

"How did you find your nose without sights?"

"Huh? That doesn't make sense. I just touch my nose naturally. It's automatic."

"Exactly," Clyde said. "Don't try to aim at the tree limbs. Watch where your bullets splash, and walk your aim up to your target. Pretty soon, you won't be missing, even on the first shot."

I lifted my gun and fired in the direction of the tree. Clyde put his hand on my arm and pressed it down.

"Try it from down here. Fast draw requires firing from the waist."

I pulled the trigger, and my bullet splashed in the middle of the river, well past the target. I lowered my gun barrel and fired the last shot in the cylinder. It kicked up water just short of the log, but much closer. As I reloaded, Clyde started the first of many lectures on gunmanship.

It was approaching noon when we unlocked the shop and opened for business. He laughed at Kaga's joke, the one where she warned that if the bear was chasing us, it was my problem because she could outrun me.

"Sounds like you've got strong feelings for that Injun," Clyde observed.

"Kaga's pretty special. I hope she comes back."

I put wood into Clyde's potbelly stove and started a pot of beans for lunch. Clyde opened a sack of flour and showed me how to make pan biscuits. We ate a bigger than normal lunch and cleaned our guns on his table. He showed me how to disassemble my weapon and cautioned me not to use grease on the internal workings. Said gun grease would make the trigger action stiffer and should only be used to prevent flash-over between cylinders. Instead, he preferred whale oil, the same light oil he burned in his lanterns.

"Whale oil needs to be replaced fairly often," he said, "but it's the price a gunfighter must pay for the fraction of a second in extra speed to stay alive."

While I watched him work, I my thoughts drifted to Kaga. Miners said heavy snow hit the high country this week. I worried about her safety.

Chapter 27

The mercantile door opened forcefully, making the bell ring louder than normal. Clyde grabbed our special guns and slipped them under the counter. I jumped up as the sheriff crossed the floor in long strides toward the counter.

"Hank, fella came into the jail this morning. Claimed you killed two of his friends in cold blood. What's he talking about?"

Clyde stood face to face with the sheriff.

"Those men who tried to rob me, they're part of the same gang. Most of them are family. They come out here from West Virginia, nearest I recall."

"How do you know this?" the sheriff asked.

"Met their whole clan when I was a miner. They come here for gold, but some crook sold em a played-out claim up on the Yuba River. They wasted a whole year of work, and all their money, trying to sift gold out of that barren stretch of river. I felt sorry for em."

"Why didn't you tell me about them when I was investigating the killings?"

"Didn't figure their past mattered after they was dead. What difference would it make?"

The sheriff added more details.

"He claimed the three bodies at the undertaker's place. Got real mad about one being shot in the back with a shotgun. I understand you were protecting the kid, but they kept yelling about a fair fight. I got no problem with any of that, but what can you tell me about these other two killings he claims you did? He said you showed up in their camp and came in firing. Don't make sense to me, even if you did kill one of theirs during a robbery."

Clyde rubbed his beard. I could tell he did not want to discuss this matter.

"Marcus, you've known me since I gave up mining and bought this store. I'm an upstanding member of this community. I've been right here in my store every day since the robbery. Colton can vouch for me. Right, Cole?"

He caught me off guard, but I thought fast.

"Yeah, of course," I said. "Clyde sleeps in the back room, and I sleep in the storage room. We've worked together every day."

"That's good enough for me, boys. This guy and his kin are trouble makers who need to go back to where they come from. I'll chase them out of town next time I see them. You fellas watch your backs for a few days. I don't trust them."

"Thanks, sheriff," I said. "I'll let you know if they show up."

Clyde handed the sheriff a small paper bag that he had been filling with ribbon candy from a countertop candy jar while we were talking.

"Little something for the wife and kids," he said. "Say hello to the misses for me."

Clyde watched until the lawman was completely out of sight.

"Thanks for covering me, Cole. I guess I owe you an explanation. This is the second time that you proved I can trust you."

I followed Clyde back into his room. He added a log to his stove and tipped the mattress off his bed. It had been resting on a wooden framework, housing three, large drawers below the bed. Loose wood slats crossed the framework above the drawers to support the mattress. He removed the slats from the far end of the frame.

Long drawers showed beneath the slats, but the one at the far end of the bed was shorter than the others. Clyde reached into the square, open cavity between its back and the wall. He lifted a heavy canvas bag and set it on the table with a loud clunk sound. Reaching into the space two more times, he lined up three bags on the tabletop.

"Look inside," he told me.

Gold! All three bags bulged with gold. Each one must weigh fifty pounds.

"Why isn't this gold in the bank?" I asked.

"Don't trust banks or bankers. Better that people think I'm just a poor shopkeeper."

"Damn, Clyde, you're rich!"

"Now you see why I want King back? I need a strong, fast horse to carry me and this gold back east where I can settle down under a new name. You can have this store when I go. It will make money for you, just like it done for me. You can write your stories from here, too."

"What about those two dead men?" I asked.

Clyde's shoulders slumped.

"I didn't go to that camp to kill nobody. Hillbillies think different from regular men. I knew they would consider our killing of their family as a blood debt, one they got to settle. It's an eye-for-an-eye land, where they come from, but I hoped to talk some sense into them."

Clyde sipped his coffee.

"That was a mistake. When I entered their camp, they didn't know about the deaths yet. I wanted to tell them myself before rumors started spreading. I apologized for the killings and offered them twenty dollars each, in gold, to leave California and go back where they come from. They agreed and even apologized for the robbery. Said they didn't know their cousins had planned it. That was when a couple hotheads showed up in camp, shouting their mouths off about someone gunning down their brothers. One of them recognized me and drew. I reacted like in the old days. Killed him 'fore he could pull the trigger. The other one dove to the side and fired at me, but he missed. I put him down. The others ran away."

"What now, Clyde? Are you planning to leave soon?"

"When we struck our agreement, I told you I was looking at six months. Not sure I want to deal with this bullshit about two dead inbreeds. Could be a problem, so I might leave sooner."

My friend's decision might impact my plans. I needed some time alone to think.

"I'm going out, Clyde. Will you be okay in the store without me for a while?"

"Sure. We're good—you know, between us—aren't we, Cole?"

This was the first time I ever knew Clyde to need reassurance.

"You've been good to me, old man. Your secrets are good with me. I just need time to think about my future. Looks like your future is pretty well set." I pointed to his bags of gold and joked, "Better put that stuff away before I raise the price for Plutus."

As I turned to leave, Clyde grabbed my arm.

"Take your gun, Cole. There's people out there with a score to settle."

He was right. I did not like the idea, but I strapped on my weapon before walking into a crisp, mid-day breeze, headed for a bar I liked down by the river. I enjoyed spending time there, sitting on a planked deck built over pilings in the water where I watched the river run past. It was a peaceful place.

Chapter 28

The stagecoach pulled to a stop in front of the store as I was coming down the stairs.

"Looking for Colton Minar," driver called out. "Address says he's at this place."

"That'd be me, mister. Who's looking for me?"

The driver set the wheel brake and climbed down from his coach. He flipped up a canvas flap in the back that protected traveler's luggage from rain and dust. A leather pouch, with "Postal Service" stamped on it, hung from a hook. The driver opened the mail pouch and handed me a thick envelope addressed to me in care of the store.

In the bar, I ordered my usual beer and some fresh salmon meat before sitting down at the last table along the deck. I liked this table, because it received the last of the setting sun each evening. This was the first time since I left my publisher's office that they had an address where they could reach me. I sent two articles from that town, Tumbleweed, and one from Mack's stagecoach rest station on the Santa Fe Trail. He promised he would put it on the next stage after I left, but I never had any way to know if my writing actually reached the editor.

Since Mack's place, I sent two stories from Rancheros in the central valley and one from that Chinese settlement, each time hoping they found their way into the stage's mail delivery systems, but I had no guarantees.

Here in Sacramento, I knew the four articles I had sent would get delivered, because I personally handed them to stage drivers.

This envelope meant that at least one of my articles from Sacramento found its way to the intended address. I opened the thick package, choking back the anxiety every writer feels when about to see if his word-smith talent succeeded or failed.

A dozen neatly-folded pages of newsprint fell onto my table. I looked inside the envelope and saw a cover letter stuck against the side. I fished it out and eagerly read the content.

"Master Colton Minar,

I admit personal skepticism at your proposed series, Truth About Gold and the West. Please accept my sincere congratulations on exceeding our paper's greatest expectations. Our readers are embracing your revelations about life in the west. Exposing them to unexpected realities and raw truths rarely seen in civilized society seem to have captured their imaginations.

Sir, you should know that your journalism attracts such a following as to increase our subscription rate by over five percent. For this reason, our board of editors voted to double your compensation per article, to be compensated retroactively. Our bank note is enclosed.

In addition, we would ask that you abstain from writing for other publications, as we have been informed such offers may soon be directed to you from competitors. For exclusivity, we offer the position of Staff Writer and a new contract running from the date we receive the enclosed agreement until one year hence. Please sign the Staff Writer contract herein in presence of a county sheriff or State of California magistrate, and ask them to provide witness by their mark and seal.

Thank you for your steady production of quality articles.

Yours in respect,

Arthur C. Morris, Senior Editor"

I took a heavy gulp of my beer and bit into a large chunk of warm, grilled fish and looked over the newspaper page clippings.

My first two articles expressed the cheap price put on life in that small town where I stopped first. It said a man could be killed for the cost of a whiskey or four bits not left on the barrel-top in a livery stable. These first articles came out on page fourteen in the General Interest section of the paper.

As I read through articles, I noticed my editor had cut some of my words, but much to my satisfaction, he did not make changes to my basic thoughts.

Flipping ahead chronologically to my article about white-man's bigotry, I did not believe that subject would get published. Bigotry was openly condemned in northeastern culture, yet, while unspoken, ugly bias against minorities or anyone of different social class permeated much of society that I knew. I figured editors would see my topic and reject it as too controversial.

Here it was, completely intact. The editor even wrote a personal note on the extract.

"Colton, great article! This is the kind of mirror most readers find uncomfortable when placed before them. It's not easy to face one's own character flaws. I have included our letters-to-the-editor page to show you the sway of your comments. Remember, criticism carries as much importance as compliments. Both mean your words impacted readers. Keep up the good writing, A. C. Morris."

I sat back in great relief to scan the letters to the editor. Reader responses filled an entire newspaper page.

"Shame on your paper for publishing Mr. Minar's scurrilous accusations about white people. Such talk should be banned. Mrs. Tupper, Women's Temperance Society, Boston."

"God bless your paper for the courage to reveal an ugly, hidden truth about our society. Reverend Charles Martin, New Jersey."

"That writer better never show up in our community. We'll show that arrogant, elitist snob how we deal with Injun lovers here in Tennessee. (name not included)"

"One man's bias is another man's social order. While bias does exist, it need not become inflamed to the level of hateful bigotry. There is nothing wrong with segregation of society, so long as each element may live peacefully within their place, Mayor, Huntsburg, South Carolina."

I read comments, marveling at the breadth of emotion festered by my simple writing. Feelings in the west tended to be openly expressed. Back home, bigotry ran just as deep, but stayed cloaked under a false veil of tolerance.

   This package from my publisher gave me a needed boost in spirits. I thought back to the reason I needed this time in the bar. How was I going to reconcile with my readers, or more importantly, with myself, after killing three men in my short time in the west? I came out here to be a writer, not a gunman. I rubbed the grizzly bear tooth under my shirt and wished Kaga was here, so I could share my good fortune.

Chapter 29

The sun dropped in the west, and I sat alone on the bar's deck in growing darkness.

"Cole, I'm closing the bar. You've got to leave pretty quick."

"Sorry, Bart. Got caught in my own thoughts and lost track of time."

I left the bar with my cherished papers tucked inside my shirt. As I approached the store, I noticed a couple horses tethered to our horse rail. That was not unusual, but three men stood down the street next to their horses, each holding a long gun across their arms. The sheriff's warning came back to me. I hoped those idiots were not making trouble.

Instead of continuing into the store, I stayed to dark areas and slipped down the back alley behind the mercantile. A large window in the aboveground basement was propped open with a tree branch. I stepped into the pitch black beneath the mercantile. A powerful forearm slapped across my chest, and a calloused hand covered mouth.

"Shhh," Clyde whispered. "Quiet."

He released his hold on me. Boot sounds clunked on the wood floor above. Somebody was in Clyde's room. We could hear intruders opening drawers and throwing items around. Clyde's sidearm aimed at the bottom of his trap door. I would pity any man who looked through.

Glass shattered against the floor. The only glass in the room, other than a window and Clyde's ceramic mug, was two lanterns. Burning fluid began dripping through tight spaces between flooring boards. Boot sounds made a hasty retreat to the front door. We watched the legs of two men as they ran down the stairs, crossed the narrow wood sidewalk to mount their horses. They left in a hurry, followed by the other three men waiting down the street.

Clyde stepped up the ladder to his trapdoor and pushed the wood up. Fire surrounded the secret entrance. He leaped to the ground.

"Through the front," he yelled. "Grab a bucket and get water from the horse trough."

Clyde pushed the front doors open and ran to his room. He ripped down the burning curtains and a thick black cloud of smoke billowed into the store. I grabbed a bucket from the row of goods near the entrance. After dipping it as full as possible, I reached Clyde's room where he was on his knees smothering fire under his bearskin rug.

"Get the mattress!" he shouted.

I threw water across the burning end of the mattress. Fire vanished in a cloud of steam. Shirts hanging on the wall were burning from the bottom up as did curtains on the lone window.

"I'll get more water," I yelled.

"No," Clyde stopped me. "Throw the curtains and clothes outside."

I ripped down the curtains by the holding rod and grabbed the wad of shirts at the top where fire had not yet reached. I ran through the store and threw the flaming cloth onto the grass between the building and sidewalk. A neighbor saw the smoke and grabbed a bucket to help. When we reentered Clyde's room, acrid smoke rose from smoldering wood, cloth and animal skins. Clyde coughed forcefully from inhaling the fumes. We dumped water on embers.

"I'll get help!" the neighbor shouted and ran from the building.

"Thanks, Cole," Clyde said and stood up. "We stopped it in time. Only minor damage."

"Was that the highwaymen?" I asked.

"Who else?" he replied sarcastically. "I need your help hiding my gold."

He threw the damaged mattress aside and grabbed the gold bags, dropping them through the open trap door. I followed him back into the lower level carrying a lantern as instructed.

"Sheriff will be here real quick. Got to get my gold into this hiding place until he leaves."

He placed the lantern on an old chair in the darkest corner of the basement. In its light, I saw a dark green safe with a faded back logo painted on the front mounted a couple feet above ground in a brick wall. He entered a combination and opened it.

We lifted the heavy bags into the box.

The sheriff galloped up just as we got back to the street. Several residents formed a bucket brigade to help put out the fire. Smoke and steam still drifted out of the open doorway.

"It's under control," Clyde called out to everyone.

"What happened, Hank?" one of the customers asked.

"I was a dumb ass. Set my lantern on the edge of the table and knocked it off. Burning oil dripped through the floor before we could put it out. Splashed onto some clothes and curtains making it look worse than it was. I'd appreciate if you dump some water on those."

He pointed at the smoldering pile of cloth on the grass.

While I fanned the front door to help the smoke clear, Clyde visited with the sheriff and locals. I wondered why he told a lie about the attempted arson.

Later that evening, we retrieved the sacks of gold, and I asked him about it.

"Cole, I killed a lot of men back in my gunfighter days. Townsfolk don't take kindly to gunmen. I only need this place for a few more months, and then I can go east to start a new life. Until then, my real identity needs to stay secret. Those Kentucky boys know my true name and background from before my mining days. I can't take a chance on them breaking my cover story. Trust me, it's better this way. They think they burned me out, and they believe I will tell the sheriff who did it. That should keep them away for a while."

"What if you're wrong?" I asked.

"I'm not," he snapped back and changed the subject.

"You ready to get some more fast-draw training?"

"Yeah. When do you have in mind?"

"Let's go out at first light. We can shoot a couple hundred rounds and still open the store early enough that nobody will know we were gone. You hungry?"

We cleaned up the mess and moved Clyde's personal things into the storage room along with my stuff until we could fix the fire damage. I took several large sacks of rice and made a bed for me, leaving the cot for him. When Clyde settled down for food, I sat with him and shared the good news from my newspaper publisher. He was as happy for me as I was. I handed him one of the newspaper pages.

He looked down at his hands.

"Cole, I got a little confession to make." He extended the paper back to me. "I can't read, but, I'd rightly enjoy hearing some of your writing."

Flattered, and a bit nervous, I wanted his approval, so I read the story about the cheap price of a soul in the west. He shrugged at my story, unimpressed. I read a couple more articles, ending with the one about bigotry.

"Interesting," he said. "Did you know there's a law here in California that coloreds can not legally testify as a witness in our courts? That includes Injuns and mixed bloods. Been in force since 1850. Lot of talk around Sacramento about changing it, but ain't been done yet."

"Really?" I found that surprising. "I thought bigotry in California was limited to men's hearts. You're telling me, it's even written into law?"

"Don't be so quick to judge us, boy. Some folks back east still own slaves."

He made a fair point.

I set my articles on the counter.

"Clyde, I don't want to make you mad, but I'm still worried about those hillbillies."

"Should be, kid. They'll kill you as soon as look at you. Cold-blooded, those people. Why do you think I'm teaching you gun skills?"

Chapter 30

It was still dark in the morning when we reached our shooting place on the river. Cold weather set in with winter. Clyde bought me some heavy clothes for the season and joked that the price for my horse and saddle were getting a might too high for him. He playfully threatened to end our deal and wait for that undertaker sale.

"I know it's cold. Take it off anyway," Clyde said in response to my reluctance to shed my heavy coat. "If a gunman calls you out, he ain't giving you time to remove your heavy coat. You best drop that coat right quick so your gun's free."

Damn, it's cold, I thought. *How the hell am I supposed to draw when I'm shaking with chills?*

Clyde read my mind.

"Don't worry about the shakes. They'll go away after the first couple shots. Here comes a floater. See how many limbs you can cut down."

My first two bullets went way long.

"Good shot," Clyde said.

"Good?" I asked, a bit surprised. "They were nowhere near my target."

"Not true. You had a perfect line on the limb, just went long. That's a good sign. Now, just dial in the range."

It took me another twenty rounds to get my targeting down. After that, every round nicked the target branch or impacted within inches. Aiming from my waist began to feel natural. I went through a hundred shots in half the time of the prior day.

"When do I learn to quick draw?"

"You're already learning it. Aiming fast is the last step in the fast draw. It's also the most important part. I killed lots of guys who were faster than me, but they missed with their first shot. I didn't. That's one of the secrets. Don't ever forget that, Cole. It ain't who's fastest what wins. It's the guy who's still alive after the last shot."

His perspective helped me to value my aiming drills more. On the way back to the store, I mentioned concern for Kaga, considering the winter cold.

"What are you gonna do with your Injun friend, if she comes back?"

"Not sure, why?"

"Indians draw lots of suspicion in the city. Nobody trusts them."

"Figure I'll cross that river when I come to it."

"Hope she shows up before I leave. I'd like to meet the woman who screwed your mind so good."

He laughed. I did, too, although for different reasons.

"I think you'd like her, Clyde. She's mean, like you."

Chapter 31

Winter deepened with a vengeance. Heavy snows closed down all the gold panning, and even hard rock mines closed because they could not get supplies. City poverty camps swelled with itinerants escaping the danger. County fair grounds clogged with tents, and arguments were common between sour-tempered, displaced miners running low on supplies. Most were accustomed to living off the land near their claims, but they could not hunt within city limits. Even when they ventured outside Sacramento, game was scarce due to excessive hunting.

I spent some time visiting the camps for my journalism. Every tent held a story. One man brought his entire family out west hoping to get rich. His youngest, a thin girl with a nasty cough, watched me intensely while her folks told me their story. She was cute. Maybe six years old. Her whole short life had been spent on a sailing ship in servant quarters or living a crude life in a tent by a stream. She clung to a tattered doll that looked to be handmade from old clothes or discarded curtain fabric. With light brown hair, big blue eyes and a tender smile, she leaned out from behind her mother to watch me. Each time we made eye contact, her mouth lifted in a shy smile, and she pulled back out of sight.

"I lost my job in a Pittsburg steel mill," he said. "My hand was crushed under a hot bar-roller, so I could not carry heavy loads after the accident. They let me go. We was living in the company houses and they did me like they do all former employees. I didn't have to pay full rent while I worked for the company, but when they let me go, I found out the excess house cost was carried on their books as a debt. Iron works security officers went through my house and took everything of value against my debt."

With nothing left, the man and his family booked onto a steamship as servants for rich people in exchange for travel to California.

"One rich guy said he appreciated the hard work and good attitude of my wife. He gave her a big tip when we got off in San Francisco."

His wife looked down at the dirt as her husband told that story. I got the impression the tip was for more than hard work. She seemed ashamed.

"We used the money to buy a surplus tent and sluice pans for the gold fields, but there was not enough left to pay for a claim. I went from claim to claim offering to work for a percentage. Didn't look good at first, but then I met Matt Jolin. He had a good claim but got too old to work it, so we agreed to a fifty-fifty deal. Me and my boys worked hard, and he was happy for the gold we found. He also liked my wife's cooking."

His wife made a half-hearted smile at the compliment.

"Everything was getting better until those West Virginia highwaymen came through. Stole our gold, food hunting rifle and all my gunpowder. They shot Matt, too."

His misses sobbed as he told me the story, so I knew it was true. All the while, the boney little girl listened and coughed.

When I got back to the mercantile, I began gathering things.

"Clyde, I need a sack of flower and some fish jerky for a family in the miner camp."

"They paid for it? Get the money first. Those miners ain't trustworthy."

"I got the money. Paid in Liberty Heads, two dollars."

"Where'd they get gold dollars? Lemme see them."

I handed Clyde gold US-mint, dollar-coins that I took out of my bank deposit box on my way back to the store. Clyde would not agree to my plan, so I told him a small lie.

He bit into one of the coins.

"Damn, that's real gold. Wonder where miners got those."

I did not bother to elaborate, as I stacked one bag of flour, one cornmeal, some dried rice and beans by the door.

"Where's that jerk meat?" I asked.

"None left. Sold it all last week."

143

"Let me have some from your personal supply."

Clyde looked up at me from a picture book.

"It ain't for sale."

"Come on, Clyde, family has a sick kid. They need meat to get her better."

"Ain't our problem, Cole. Don't get soft on them miners. They'll head back into the hills when the snows melt. We'll never see them again."

I ignored Clyde's comment and went into his room.

"What are you doing?" he asked more as a challenge than a question.

I opened his cabinet and removed several thick strips of dried salmon.

"Here, since you're so damned worried about yourself," I said, and tossed him another one-dollar coin.

Plutus carried the food sacks tied across his shoulders in front of my saddle as I rode him between tents in the refuge camp. A group of men blocked my passage.

"Mister, are those food sacks?" the leader asked.

"What do you think?" I answered sarcastically knowing they were trying to intimidate.

"We'll take those off your hands. Pay you after we get back to our claims."

"Get out of my way," I said with as much force as possible.

"There's at least ten of us. You best take my offer before these boys decide to take things into their own hands."

I brushed back my coat exposing my forty-four to plain view.

"You can't take all of us with one gun. You're pretty stupid, mister."

"I don't plan to kill all of them. I plan to kill you."

I glanced across the group.

"And, then you! You're the biggest. And, you," I looked into the eyes of a man leaning on a shovel. "You're a dead man, because I'm not letting you take that shovel to my head."

The men I singled out got a frightened look on their faces and backed away, but the rest of the crowd closed in. I used the quick draw training from Clyde to make my point. I drew my gun so fast the closest men winced. It aimed directly at the nearest man's chest. I cocked the hammer.

"Calm down, mister. We didn't mean nothing," he said and backed up.

I panned the gun across the front row of men.

"Who wants to die first for a five-pound sack of flour? I can take out at least six of you before you get me. Come on!" I shouted as if I was entering a rage. "Who's first?"

The men stepped aside and cursed me as I passed.

I walked Plutus beyond the family's tent, not wanting the threatening men to know where I left the food. After riding all the way to the levee, I circled around and quietly approached the family's tent under cover of dusk. Tears flowed when they saw the food.

"I deeply appreciate your help, Mister Colton, but I don't want no charity. Where can I find you to pay you back? I'll get back to gold mining in a month, and I'll make a point to pay."

"I work at the Valley Mercantile on T Street. No hurry on paying me back. You take care of this family."

The little girl went into a heavy coughing spasm.

"You want me to fetch the doctor?"

"We got no way to pay him."

"He owes me a favor. I'll ask him to stop down here."

"Thank you," the mother said. "She's been sick for two weeks. I'm worried."

I went directly to the doctor's home and told him about the small girl. He packed his doctoring bag and headed out immediately.

Over the next few days, heavy rains swelled the American and Sacramento Rivers threatening devastating floods in low-lying areas like the fairgrounds. Some of the indigent miners found work on the new Sacramento Valley Railroad project building a rail line between Sacramento and Granite City.

I checked on the child and her family every few days. The man took a job supervising workers on the railway construction. Sacramento Valley Rail was happy to hire a man who knew how to work with iron and steel, and he was happy to earn money for his family. He offered to pay me back out of his first paycheck, but I refused, suggesting he use the money to move out of the tent and into a real house. Despite the doctor's treatment, the man's daughter got sicker and terribly frail, while her older brothers thrived on the increased food.

One day, I arrived at their tent with good news. A patron of the mercantile owned an empty house and was willing to rent it to their family. I called into the tent asking permission to enter. There was no answer, yet I distinctly heard talking inside. I called again.

The tent flap folded back slowly and the doctor stepped out. His face hung gaunt.

"We lost her," he said to me.

I knew immediately whom he meant. Quiet sobbing emanated from the family in the tent.

The father appeared in the opening.

"Colton, Annabelle is with the Lord. Can you come back in the morning? We need time alone."

I never got to deliver my good news. The next morning, everything was gone. Tent, the family, the little girl's body . . . all gone.

Chapter 32

Business in the mercantile fell off without gold from miners to pay our inflated prices. Clyde assured me there would be a surge in business as soon as the miners panned their first gold in the spring. Some of the newly hired railroad workers began shopping in our store. It helped. I was also thankful for the steady income from my journalism contract. It gave me spending cash during the slow times. I did not tell Clyde about my bank deposits. Figured it was wise for me to have some backup money in case things did not work out the way we agreed.

All winter, I practiced my fast draw techniques. Clyde said I got fast, real fast. More importantly, he was right about shooting from the hip. It became natural. I particularly enjoyed quick draw competitions he created between us. We'd wedge river clam shells in tree bark, ten on each side of the tree. First one to shatter all his shells from forty feet got free lunch at the river café on the other guy's money.

Clyde cheated. He'd start his draw before he yelled "Draw."

It shook him up the first time I beat him to the tenth shell even after he cheated on the start. I could fire six shots, reload and fire another four faster than him. When it was my turn to call the start, I never cheated. It got to where I beat him most times. He took it hard.

During the worst days of winter, I took Plutus on long patrols along the low snow line. Locals told me it was a colder winter than normal, and I worried about Kaga. There was never any sign of her, but I went up to the snow almost every day.

Winter let up early. Snow thaw in the foothills increased local flooding and miners headed back to the foothills to pan for the fresh gold that washed down every winter. My articles became more controversial. I hoped my editor would like them.

The miner whose little girl passed away showed up one morning and gave me four gold dollars in payment of his debt.

"Thank you, Mister Colton. My family will never forget you."

"How are you doing now?"

"I quit the railroad. The old man I was panning for left me his claim, so I sold it for enough to buy a small plot of land up above Old Dry Diggins. We buried Anna on the hillside where she used to play. Built our cabin there, too." He choked up. "Before she died, she told us God sent you in our time of need. She said you are our guardian angel. I believe her."

We talked a couple minutes, and he gave me instructions to his new homestead. He assured me I would always be welcome in his home.

"Cole," Clyde spoke to me after the miner left. "I'm leaving as soon as the high passes clear of snow. You ready to keep our deal?"

This time was inevitable—I knew it. Plutus was more than a ride to me. He'd become a friend and companion. I did not give a hoot about the tack, just the horse.

"I know, Clyde, but that horse has gotten to me. Can't you find another one? I'll buy you two horses instead of him. One can carry you and the other can carry your gold. Wouldn't that be better than one horse?"

"You made a promise, kid. I kept my end of the deal. I want King, uh, Plutus. Two horses mean twice as much food and water. They will also slow me down if I have to run. By the way, I got used to his name. Kind of like it now. I think he'll stay Plutus."

For some strange reason, his decision gave me a small peace of mind.

"I know, I know we made a deal. My word's good. How long do I have before those mountain cuts thaw?"

"Two, maybe three weeks."

A loud crash of shattering glass interrupted our conversation and a rock bounced across the store floor. I was wearing my gun, prepared to do some target practice before opening.

"Clyde!" Someone called through the broken glass from the street. "Clyde Hamlin, you son of a bitch! Get out here and bring your gun. You gonna die today."

I reached the window first and peaked out. A tall thin man with a long mustache hanging like spindly ropes from each side of his mouth stood across the street. He was dressed well, with shiny boots, a string tie over blue plaid shirt and a short jacket that ended just above his sidearm.

"Matthew Sanchez," Clyde said barely audible. "He's good. Real fast."

I realized Clyde was assessing the man, not giving me pointers.

"Matt," Clyde called through the broken window. "You gonna pay for this glass?"

"What do you think old man?" the gunman answered.

"Nice day today, Sanchez. You sure you want to die on a glorious day like this?"

"Five years, I been looking for you. Hiding like a scared little girl behind that merchant disguise. I found you. Now, I'm gonna kill you."

Clyde opened the storefront door and walked slowly down the steps. He stopped two paces into the street.

"You gonna shoot an unarmed man?" Clyde asked. "Word'll spread about you being a coward."

"You got five minutes to get your gun. If you refuse, I'll kill you anyway for taking the life of my little brother. People understand blood debts."

"You know I'm faster than you, Sanchez. Why do you wanna die?"

"You were fast once. You're old now and soft. I picked up seven notches since we last met."

"Only seven? That makes you an amateur. You're not worth the price of a bullet."

Clyde reached down to the street and picked up a round, steaming ball from a fresh horse turd. He threw it at the man across the street.

"What the hell?" the man said as he sidestepped the flying manure.

Clyde grabbed a large handful of the stuff and ran at the gunman throwing turd after turd at the retreating man.

"Stop it. I came here to kill you. Get your damn gun," the man almost pleaded as he ran away from the foul projectiles.

"If you were going to kill me," Clyde said, "you would have done it by now."

"I'll be back at noon," Sanchez yelled and swung onto his horse. "Come out and face me like a man, or I will tell everyone you're washed up. You're a coward."

Clyde washed his hands in one of the horse troughs on the street before coming back inside the store.

"You going to face him?" I asked.

"Depends on him, don't it? If he leaves town, it's over. If he comes back, I got no choice."

"Call the sheriff. He hates gunfighters."

"Can't. This guy knows my real name. If he tells the law who I am, then we could lose everything I've built."

"Take your money and hit the trail."

"He tracked me here. He'll follow me. Even if I take the southern route, he'll follow. Cole, there are some times in life when decisions are made without your approval. Fate dictates, and you simply react. This guy's younger brother pulled on me. I killed him. Sanchez is on a blood quest. There's only one way to end it."

"But—"

"Cole, no more distractions. I'll be in the basement."

Clyde put on his sidearm, filled his coffee mug and went into the basement floor of the store. I heard him practicing his draw, complete with a full trigger pull each time. I never saw him so serious.

Chapter 33

As noon approached, I kept close watch on the street. Foot and buggy traffic was light, and there were no kids playing in nearby yards. Five men in long, black winter coats rode down Fourth Street, the cross street at the end of ours, but I did not recognize the horses. The men's faces could not be seen under wide-brimmed hats. I was not worried about them as they went out of sight.

Sun hit the high point, and Matt Sanchez rode slowly down the center of our street. He dismounted and looped the reins several times around a horse rail across from the store. He rolled a cigarette and removed his travel coat, draping it casually across his saddle.

People must have a sixth sense about gunfights. The street emptied of all pedestrians and riders. Even birds seemed to leave the area. It was the strangest thing I ever saw.

Sanchez walked a couple paces toward the mercantile. Spurs jingled with each step, and his shoulders flowed with trained relaxation. In him, I saw all the lessons Clyde taught me. Ease of movement, economy in his stride, energy saved for that final explosive burst with gun in hand. I worried about my friend.

"Clyde," Sanchez called from forty feet out. "Time to pay for my brother."

There was no reply.

"What's the matter , old man? You a coward?"

Again, no response.

Clyde told me every gunfight hinged on one or two minor details. I remembered his lecture, "Always catch the other gunman by surprise. Everything you do to unsettle him, swings the advantage to you."

"Sanchez!" Clyde shouted from the shade between two buildings down the street.

Matt Sanchez spun on his heels to face the sound. It caught him by surprise. I smiled. Clyde got the jump on him.

"Nicely played," Sanchez said, trying to sound unruffled. "I should have known you would play these childish games."

Clyde walked from the shadows into the street.

"This is your last chance to live, Matt. I don't want to kill you, but I'll do it."

"Big words from a has-been. You can't beat me. We both know it."

It was just as Clyde taught me. He called it "The Dance," where both gunfighters banter trying to undermine each other's confidence. He said some gunfights ended without a shootout, if one man succeeded in destroying the other's confidence.

"Matt, you have a pattern. Did you know that?"

Matt did not speak.

"I watched you go against Sid Novak. He beat you, but you sidestepped to your right."

Sanchez blustered, "Guess you better aim to your left, then."

"I saw you take down Cracker Johns, too, up in Sonoma." Clyde kept it up. "Took you two shots to hit him. You won't get two shots against me."

Sanchez made the sign of the cross on his chest.

"Talk's cheap, Hamlin. I want you, now!" Sanchez spread his legs shoulder width and squared his body to Clyde.

Both men froze, each with a gun-hand poised about two inches from their weapon handle.

Movement caught my eye across the street between the houses. Several men had been hiding behind shrubs. They stepped out and approached the street holding rifles aimed at Clyde.

I opened the door and shouted, "Ambush!"

Clyde did not react to my warning. Sanchez drew. Clyde stepped to his right and drew so fast I did not see his gun move. They fired simultaneously, and Clyde fired a second time within an instant of the first one.

I ran down the stairs slipping my hammer loop off and cocking my gun as I did.

Five men in long black heavy coats raised their weapons. I drew and automatically fired from my hip, hitting the nearest man in the upper chest before he could pull the trigger.

Clyde ran back toward me and the safety of the store. Two shots rang out. He went down, shot in the upper leg. His forty-four tumbled across the ground.

The four remaining gunmen ran toward the street, three aiming at Clyde and one turning toward me. My shell game training with Clyde proved its worth.

I fired my remaining five rounds in less than two seconds. It was just like wiping out the shells on the tree in rapid fire competition, only this time, there would be no break to reload after sending six rounds. Each bullet had to count.

The guy aiming at me fell backward. One round blew his face open and the second exploded his throat. Three others crumpled to the ground, two with fatal heart shots and the last holding his chest at the shoulder. I dropped my empty gun and grabbed Clyde's weapon. He had fired two shots at Sanchez, but I did not know how many shots he used against these other guys. I hoped one more bullet was in the cylinder as I approached the wounded man. His gun lay on the ground two yards away. I recognized this guy. He was one of the West Virginia gang I saw when they burned the store.

"Don't kill me. Please, mister, don't kill me," he begged as I got close and aimed Clyde's forty-four between his eyes.

My bullet had entered his left shoulder below the collarbone shattering his entire shoulder structure. While he leaned on his good arm, blood spurted from the wound quickly turning his blue denim shirt dark red.

As he begged for his life, I ignored him and collected all the guns, including the one Sanchez dropped in the street, and piled them in the road. Sanchez was shot dead-center in the chest and in the lower abdomen. Both shots were lethal, only the gut shot would have been a slower, painful death.

Clyde got to his feet and limped over to me.

"Sheriff will be here in a minute. Get rid of our guns and bring out those Navy Colts that I test fired yesterday. Quick, kid!"

I ran up the steps into the store, spanning three planks at a time, with both our forty-fours. I tossed them onto Clyde's bed and grabbed the Navy Colts that were waiting on his table to be cleaned.

Clyde was across the street talking with the wounded man when I got back to him.

"Put on the gun and don't tie the leg straps. We can't look like gunfighters."

The guns were loaded, so Clyde pushed bullets out to match the total number of shots we made. He put the bullets in his pocket just as the sheriff rounded the corner at a full gallop. The wounded man died about the same time.

Clyde explained that the hillbillies had returned for revenge and brought an expert gunman with them.

"Who took out the professional?" the sheriff asked and nodded toward Sanchez.

"Boy here, he saved my life. Kid's a crack shot. I tried to run from the gunman, but he shot me in the back of my leg. That's when the gunfighter turned on the kid, but Cole was already aiming. Dropped the guy with two shots."

The sheriff took the gun from my holster, sniffed it and checked the cylinders for remaining bullets.

"Fresh fired," he said. "You got real lucky, young man. Professionals don't usually let civilians get the drop on em."

Clyde limped away from the sheriff, headed toward the store. I followed.

"My leg's killing me," he said. "I got to sit down."

He sat on the steps and watched the sheriff check each dead man.

Clyde whispered to me, "If the sheriff asks, I shot the two on the left. You got the other three and Sanchez. That matches the bullet count in our guns.

I nodded.

Sheriff motioned for me to come over there. For the next ten minutes, he questioned me about the sequence of events. I stuck to the simple story Clyde told with no elaboration and sat down with Clyde after the sheriff finished. We watched him pace off distances, supervise removal of the bodies and break up the curious crowd that gathered to see the aftermath.

The law enforcement officer came over to us.

"Stories add up to what I see here. Guess these boys won't be robbing miners anymore. Sorry you had to go through this, but, to tell the truth, I'm glad to be rid of them. I'll see if I can figure out who that gunfighter is. Might be a reward in some other jurisdiction for killing him. If so, I'll see to it you get the money, boy," he said to me.

Clyde's pant leg was soaked in blood all the way around his thigh. Doc took a quick look and offered his buggy to carry the patient back to his office where he had the right equipment to remove the bullet.

Reporters from the local newspaper asked me a bunch of questions.

I cleaned up the broken glass in the store and boarded the window before reopening for business. Funny how something like a killing can be good for business. We must have sold three times as much this afternoon than we did on any other day in the past month. People would browse for a long time just to listen as I answered other folks who asked about the events. Most of the purchases were small. Candy. Bullets. Couple ladies bought cloth and sewing needles and one of them made sure I knew her daughter was of marrying age and a right proper Christian.

As I completed all the small sales, I thought back to a time when I complained about such transactions, saying they were a waste of my time. Clyde pretty near fell off his chair, laughing. When I asked him what was so funny, he said the biggest markups were on the little things. He'd rather sell a whole basket of thread and needles to women than big ticket items like hundred-foot rope coils or surplus army tents. He got me to thinking like a businessman.

Chapter 34

Doc removed the bullet from Clyde's thigh, and I took over the mercantile full time while his leg healed. We both left our modified forty-fours hidden and wore standard Colt Navy pistols in public. The Sacramento Daily Union did a front page article on the gunfight. I was not happy. They made a big deal out of the local boy who shot down a professional gunfighter and three highwaymen.

"How's the leg feeling today, Clyde?" I asked through new curtains he got after throwing away the old ones that smelled something terrible from smoke damage.

He hobbled out of his room balancing a hot mug of coffee and trying to keep weight off his bad leg with a homemade crutch. Half his coffee sloshed onto the floor when he stumbled.

"Dammit," he said. "Stop laughing. You know how much I love my coffee."

I apologized and offered to refill it for him, but before I could do so, the front door bell caught my attention. It was the sheriff.

"Howdy, boys. Got some good news for you, Colton. Turns out the gunman you killed was Matt Sanchez. Wanted dead or alive for murdering two cowboys in Utah Territory. Fifty dollars coming to you in a couple weeks."

"Sounds good, sheriff. Thank you."

"Colton, you've got some explaining to do, or you'll have to leave town, permanently."

I was stunned.

"Why? What did I do?"

"You're lying to me. Those men you shot . . . doc pulled out forty-four slugs from all those bodies, every one of them. Navy Colt fires a thirty-six. Two rounds in Sanchez. Two rounds in one of the five men and one shot in each of the other four. No thirty-six caliber slugs. Mind explaining that to me?"

Clyde put his hand on my shoulder and addressed the lawman.

"Weren't the boy's doing, sheriff. It's my fault. I killed Sanchez and two of those other boys. Used one of the forty-fours from my gunfight'n days."

"Hank, I don't know what you're trying to say, but neither of your stories make sense. One man cannot gun down a professional and five highwaymen with eight bullets from a single six-shot revolver. Why don't you stop this bullshit and get straight with me."

"It's true, sheriff. When I came here almost five years ago, I wanted to give up my past and start a new life as a decent member of a community. My real name ain't Hank. It's Clyde, Clyde Hamlin. I was a gunman, but I never killed for pleasure or profit, only in self-defense. Check the papers. I'm not wanted anywhere."

"Hank . . . or Clyde, that doesn't explain how one man killed six men in a gunfight."

"Told you the truth about this kid's shooting skill. Sanchez has been looking for me for over five years. He drew on me. It was a fair draw. I put two slugs in him at the same time. Didn't know he hooked up with those West Virginia boys. They come charging out of the shade shooting wild. Got me in the leg. The kid grabbed my other forty-four and come to help."

"It's true, sheriff," I said. "When Clyde and Sanchez squared off, I saw those other men moving up. I yelled to him just as they drew on each other and grabbed my gun to protect him."

"One of those boys talked before he died," Clyde told the sheriff. "Said they hired Sanchez and hung around to see the job done. If I killed Sanchez, they planned to come out firing. Kid here, saved my ass. He used my backup gun, another forty-four, and got a couple of them. I got the rest."

Clyde seemed relieved to end his secret life and false identity.

"Sheriff, we didn't go looking for a fight," Clyde said quietly. "They come to us. I'm trying to become a good citizen. If you want me to leave, I will, but let the kid take over the store. He's innocent of anything but trying to protect me."

"Where are those forty-fours?" the sheriff asked.

"Cole, go get both of my forty-fours."

He emphasized "my," so I would understand that he was taking full responsibility for the highly modified firearms.

I went into each back room and collected the weapons and holsters.

The sheriff examined the guns closely. He emptied the chambers and tested the trigger pull and balance.

"My God, that's a light trigger, and the weight of this gun, it's not right. Why is the barrel gun sight filed down?"

Clyde showed the sheriff some of the modifications and explained a gun fighter's ways.

"Hank, you've been a good citizen up until now. Thank you for coming clean with me."

The law officer slipped Clyde's gun back into the holster and laid it on the countertop.

"This changes things, Hank. I figured the boy must be a professional gunman to kill so many people like that. Turns out, it was you." The sheriff shook his head in disbelief. "Never would have guessed you for a killer."

"I'm not, sheriff. I never killed a man without giving him a chance to leave. I never drew on a man for money or in anger, only in self-defense. The boy, here, he's a writer for a newspaper back in Boston. He works in my store as cover for his journalism."

"Problem, Hank, is your kind attracts more of your kind. Word gets out, and every hothead within a hundred miles will come looking to make a reputation. Even if I'm willing to give you a second chance, the decision won't be up to me. Mayor and city council might ask you to close this store and leave town."

"Marcus, the kid didn't do anything but save my life, twice. I'll give him the store, if they will let him stay. He needs a break. Send me out of town, but not the kid."

"I'll see what I can do. Until then, don't go killing any more people, and for God's sake, keep those gunfighter revolvers hidden."

The sheriff looked me in the eye.

"You're a writer, huh?"

"Yes sir. I've even won some awards for my articles about the west."

"No kidding. I never would have known. I better not be in any of those stories!"

"No sir. You're not interesting enough."

It took a second for the sheriff to figure out I was joshing him.

Chapter 35

The sheriff was a good man. Mayor Smith called a closed meeting of the city council. They asked me and Clyde to present our point of view. Couple of them were understanding and recognized Clyde's contribution to the community over the past five years. The sheriff even rounded up a group of local citizens who received credit from Clyde during hard times to testify on his behalf.

One, a widow with four teenage boys, told about her oldest son taking up with some drifters. They got him to drinking and beating up his brothers.

"When I picked up a bag of soup beans from Hank," she said to the council, "he saw my blackened eye and asked how it happened. I was mighty ashamed and refused to tell him. He figured it out. I'd already complained about how William was treating his brothers. Next thing I know, my boy come to me and apologized. Said he got a job in the stables and was going to pay off my debt to the mercantile. Both his eyes were blackened, and he walked with a limp, but he refused to tell me what happened. I figure Hank had something to do with it. When I thanked the blacksmith at the stable for giving my boy a job, he told me it was a favor for Hank."

She sobbed and said, "All my boys are finishing school and getting to be good people, thanks to Hank. My husband, God rest his soul, would thank that man with all his heart for looking after our boys."

Clyde looked down at his hands while she talked. Several more locals testified about the good citizen he had been in the time since he hung up his gun. He never looked up. Clyde helped people his own way, quietly and asking nothing in return. This public display must have torn him up inside.

We left with the council promising to make a decision by week's end. They would have the sheriff inform us at that time.

Back at the store, Clyde put into motion the plan he always knew was coming.

"Cole, it don't matter what I done for this community, they've got to ask me to leave. Gunfighters are still looking for me. Everybody knows, they will show up here sooner or later, and you've already seen what can happen. If it was my decision, I'd ask me to leave. It's the only way they can protect the honest citizens against gunfights in the streets. I always knew this was coming. Store's yours. I'm not waiting for their decision. I'm taking Plutus tonight. Good luck."

"You sure this is necessary? Wait and see what they say."

"It's time for me to go. East of the Mississippi River, I'm just another face in the crowd. I can build a new identity and maybe die an old man instead of eating horse shit in the street with a bullet in my chest."

He left for the stable limping along with a newfound peace.

Plutus did not like the extra weight of the gold sacks, but he easily handled Clyde and the load. I noticed Clyde divided the gold into six smaller sacks to spread the load easier on the horse's back.

It was getting late in the day and reports had come in for a week that the summit cut was passable. Timing for Clyde could not have been better. We promised to meet again someday, both knowing it wasn't going to happen, and I watched him head east out of town. Figured that was the last time I would ever see him.

I was wrong.

Chapter 36

Friday morning, the sheriff was waiting on the front porch of the store when I opened for business.

"Morning Colton. I know it's a bit early for your buddy to rise, but I've got news from the council. Mind waking him?"

"Can't sheriff. Clyde's gone. Left on Tuesday."

"What? I've been fighting for him all week. When's he coming back?"

"He's not."

The sheriff tipped his hat back on his head.

"Hmm . . . I guess he knew what was coming. Guess it doesn't mean much now, but the council split on their vote. Mayor had to break the tie, and he voted to ask Hank . . . uh, Clyde, to leave town. In appreciation for all he did during his time here, they offered him a month to sell or liquidate his business. They also said if he settled in another town nearby, he would still be welcome to visit our city for brief periods. He isn't banned altogether."

I choked back sarcasm, understanding that the sheriff was only the messenger, but I let some sentiment squeak though.

"Tell them, I said their magnanimous gesture befits the image of politicians as scurrilous purveyors of cowardice and indecency."

"What? I don't even know some of those words, but I think I get your meaning. Mind if I simplify it to my own terms?"

I let out a deep breath and tried to control my anger.

"You better not," I said, recanting my outburst. "I'm sure they would not hesitate to find another sheriff if you step on their egos."

"Not that easy for them, Colton. People elect me. I'm not appointed by those egotistical, blowhards in government."

I began to understand this lawman. He served and protected his community with noble creed and fairness, not political expediency and personal bias.

Clyde's right, I thought. *Sheriff's a good man.*

"By the way, Colton, they discussed you as well. Not happy about the killings. You accounted for four dead men in just six months since you've been here, two during the armed robbery, and two, defending Hank in the gunfight. Damn it, I've got to stop calling him Hank. Anyway, couple of the councilmen worried that once a man tastes blood, it becomes a way of life. They agreed to let you run the store and stay in town, for now, but they are watching you. Son, be careful. I'd like to see you become part of our community. Don't give them politicians any excuse to run you off."

"Thank you, sheriff. I'm sure that's good advice."

"What are you doing for dinner tomorrow?" the lawman asked.

It caught me off guard. I was not expecting such a question from him.

"Taking a ride down river to China town in the morning. Why?"

"My clan's roasting a pig at my place. More than enough for you, too. The missus and I would like to have you join us, if you're willing."

"Thank you, sheriff, I'd—"

"Please, Colton, call me Marcus."

"Thanks, Marcus, and I go by Cole. That pig roast sounds great."

We settled a time and he gave me directions to his spread just east of town.

As he reached the door to leave, he turned to me and asked, "Why are you going to that Chinese camp? They don't much like white men."

"Sold them some canvas and heavy thread for making tents. They may not like white men, but I've been selling them supplies since I got here, and they've never failed to pay."

"Hope you know what you're doing. They can be a crafty lot. Watch yourself."

Okay, so the sheriff is not quite as noble as he seems, I thought to myself.

That night, I loaded my delivery wagon with sheets of canvas and a couple small wood boxes filled with strong thread and heavy metal needles. I left it at the livery and went back to the store for a good night's rest.

For the first time since I arrived in Sacramento, I was alone. I sat at my writing table, in what used to be Clyde's room, and reviewed my notes. Not just notes over the last couple weeks, but I went back to my thoughts when Kaga and I traveled together. I missed the adventure. I missed the friendship. I missed her, but it had been quite a while since she left.

Only a fool would think she will return. I thought. *I've waited long enough.*

Chapter 37

The wagon creaked along, following a well-worn route along the Sacramento River until a small, fallen tree spanned the road. I reined in the two large horses of my hitch, more suited for pulling stumps or working a row plow, than for pulling a light buckboard with supplies. They were good animals, even-tempered and obedient, but they lacked the spirit I had come to love in Plutus. I set the wheel brake and attended to the fallen tree, lifting one end to remove it from the roadway.

Three Chinese men rushed from the nearby wild-grape vines. One grabbed the reins of the nearest horse while the other two men took me to the ground. I fought back, but they were unusually strong and locked my arms and legs in a strange kind of hold that I could not break.

"Money," one man said with a heavy accent.

"I don't have any money on me," I croaked out through pressure of a forearm pressing across my throat.

"Money!" He yelled again.

This time, his chokehold made it so hard to breathe that I could not answer.

The assailant demanding money spoke to his accomplices in a language I had heard while in the Chinese camp. He held me down while two men climbed into my buckboard and began pushing supplies onto the ground. One stuck his finger on a needle in the wood box of sewing supplies. He yelled what I could only assume was a curse and sucked on the puncture. They finished going through all my goods and did not like what they found.

"Gold!" the man holding me demanded. He loosened the arm across my throat.

"No gold," I replied, hoping they would understand.

He released his hold on me and the other two jerked me to my feet. At six foot two, I was a head taller than any of them, but I had no doubt about their strength and fighting skills. The tallest of the three wore a sheath holding a carved, dragon handle attached to a diagonal strap across his chest. He withdrew the weapon and displayed a short knife with a curved blade. I had seen the polished sheen of Kaga's knife, and this metal carried that same sharpened threat.

The Chinese man put the blade to my throat, touching ever so lightly. I pulled back as far as possible. He lifted the blade in front of my eyes, smiling at the result. A single drop of blood ran down the blade toward the dragon handle.

Nearby, a bush rustled.

The man with the blade screamed at me in his language, and kept repeating two words in English, gold and money. I had neither.

A strong voice called out from the bushes in my assailants' language.

My three attackers let go and faced the undergrowth, all brandishing similar curved-blade knives. Out stepped the old Chinese professor I had come to know in the camp.

"Lok!" I yelled. "Tell them I have no money or gold."

He did not respond. Instead, he took short steps toward the three men, always putting the same foot forward. The old man seemed to pay no attention to their weapons as he continued to press forward in rapid half steps.

The young men shouted at Lok as if attempting to intimidate him. His lack of reply made them more frantic. One nervous attacker lunged at Lok slashing wildly as he did.

The old man's hand made a circular motion passing around the assailant's arm and pinning the knife-holding forearm against the man's chest.

With little apparent effort, the old man sent his opponent tumbling backward. The man tripped over the tree limb that still crossed the road and rolled several feet. When he got back to his feet, he ran into the woods.

Lok pressed his slow-motion attack toward the man who had cut me. With no warning, he abruptly surged forward, ignoring the second attacker. I wish I could describe his hand movements, but they were a blur. I saw the robber's knife fly to one side, and he screamed when Lok thrust a three-fingered strike deep into the man's eye socket. The third man thrust his knife at Lok, but the old man turned the body of the blinded man, using him as a shield. The blade penetrated the back of the blind man all the way to its hilt, dropping him to the ground, wheezing with a sucking lung puncture.

Lok spoke sternly to both the young Chinese men for the first time. The uninjured man helped the other to his feet, and they left as fast as they could travel.

"I apologize, Mister Colton, for the inhospitality of my people. Hatred from white men has a tendency to breed hatred in return. It is a most sad state of affairs. Let me look at that."

The professor pulled at the cut on my throat.

"Not deep. You will be fine."

"Thank you for helping me."

I grabbed the tree, swung it to the side of the dirt road and began stacking the supplies back in the wagon. Lok helped me, and we rode together into China Camp.

He spoke in a commanding tone to several men who greeted us. They scurried away to carry out his directions.

"Men who attacked you will be punished," he said.

"I'm okay, Lok. That's not necessary. I think you already hurt them enough, especially that one guy."

"Punishment is not for your benefit, my friend. They disobey my rules. Our community laws must be respected for the good of all. Come with me. We have more important matters to discuss."

Lok showed me into one of the larger residences in the heart of town. On the way, I noticed the place had grown both in population and number of buildings.

Industrious people, I thought. *A lot like the people who founded my country who left their homes, many with only the clothes on their backs. Why? To make a better life. I don't understand this hatred toward the Chinese.*

Lok spoke to several men sitting at tables. All stood up and left the room.

"They will unload your wagon and water your horses. I will pay you shortly."

"There's no hurry, professor." I showed respect by using his title from time to time.

"Your Indian friend, Kaga, is back," he said.

My heart raced. I sat upright. "Where is she? When did you see her?"

"She came to me two weeks ago to ask if I know how you are doing."

"Where is she now?" I looked around as if she might walk into the room at any second.

"She is not here, but I told her about your store, and how you come here every month with supplies for us. She is pleased for you. She wants you to be happy."

"When will she be back? I want to see her."

"Your Indian friend does not tell us when she will visit. She shows up at times of her choosing. We feed her, and she leaves as soon as the food is gone."

"Do you know where she lives? Is there a way for me to reach her?"

"Kaga does not want to see you. She would be angry with me if she found out I told you about her visit."

"But, I—"

"You must be patient, Mister Colton. I know she loves you, and the time is near that she will seek you out. Trust me."

Like I have a choice.

After our discussion, I found my rig out front with horses freshened and ready to go. They even cleaned mud off the wheels so I would not get splattered, at least not too badly, on my trip home.

"Lok, you wouldn't have a rifle I could borrow for the ride home. I'll bring it back on my next trip. Next time I get bushwhacked, somebody is going to get shot."

"You don't need a firearm," I have sent word that you are to be welcomed in our community as one of our own.

My mind raced on the trip home. Kaga could not be far away if she stopped at the Chinese camp a couple weeks ago.

She's probably living in the foothills where there's plenty of game and water. I thought.

Chapter 38

"What did you name your new horse, Colton?" the stable tender asked when I swapped the delivery wagon for my new ride.

"I named him Thor, for the Norse God of Thunder."

"You're gonna piss off them Christian Temperance women if you keep coming up with all them heathen-god names for your horses. Why not pick something right, you know, like Buck or Trigger? I got it, call him Rowdy. He's a hard one to get along with."

"What makes you say that?"

The livery worker pulled up his sleeve. A big bruise in the heart-shape of a horse bite spanned his forearm.

"Watch your toes with that one. He'll come around and nip your feet if he thinks he can get away with it."

I had left a note on the storefront saying I was going to be gone all day, so I headed straight out to the sheriff's spread for his pig roast. It was closer to town than I expected. He said it was for family, but I counted eleven buckboards out front. One of them was the doc's rig.

I tied the reins of my new horse to the rope rail, and he bit into my upper shoulder something fierce. Instinctively, I spun around and punched him straight in the middle of his jaw. Nearly broke my hand.

Man, you have a hard head, I thought while shaking the pain from my hand.

His legs wobbled, and he pulled back from me when I tried to rub his nose where I had just popped him, but he made no attempt to nip me, so I guess he got the message.

One of the nearby buggies had a feed bucket hanging under the nose of a young mare. She was fat, so I figured she would not miss a meal. I removed it and offered a handful of prime oats to Thor. He nipped at my hand. I pulled back and slapped him across the nose. This behavior repeated a couple times, until he ate the oats without testing my patience.

For the next twenty minutes, I hand fed my horse, and he behaved on every bite. We finally settled that issue.

"That's the way it works, Thor," I said to the horse. "You be good, we'll get along fine. You bite me, and you're going to feel my wrath. It's your choice, boy."

He pushed me with his nose, more of a friendly nuzzle than anything aggressive.

I hung the oat bag back on the fat filly and walked around back to where I heard a ruckus and smelled the roast pig. Must have been forty people attending. I recognized a couple of city councilmen. I remembered them as the nice ones. A fiddler and guitar player entertained a few folks who danced on a large wood deck.

"Colton," the sheriff called out. "Glad you could make it. How was the trip down the river?"

"Uneventful." I lied. "Just delivered some tent makings and got paid."

The sheriff took me around to meet his relatives and friends. His roast pork was the best I ever had, and everyone asked why Hank did not come to the event. I told the simple truth that he was out of town.

A sheriff deputy approached the top lawman and informed him of an arrest downtown.

"Cole, I'll be right back," the sheriff said. "Got some police business to address. Make yourself at home."

I scanned the crowd for a friendly person.

"Mister Colton, I presume?" a familiar woman's voice asked from behind.

On turning, I saw Tess, yes, Tess from Tumbleweed.

"Wha . . . what are you doing here?"

"I might ask you the same thing, Colton. Last I heard, you were lost in the desert with some Indian squaw."

She hated me, yet she seemed almost glad to see me. It did not make sense.

"We survived. What brought you to Sacramento?"

"Unfinished business," she said with cryptic intent and a slight upturn of one eyebrow.

Chapter 39

"Good to see you, again Missus Grumman," the sheriff joined us. "I see you've met Colton."

Missus Grumman? I thought sarcastically. *That was fast.*

"I'm afraid Mrs. Grumman was recently widowed. Husband fell off his horse, landing on his gun. One of those odd happenings a man just can't anticipate, and they were preparing to go back east for their honeymoon. You have my deepest condolences, madam "

The sheriff tipped his hat.

"You have been so thoughtful welcoming me to Sacramento, sheriff. I could not bear another minute on our ranch in New Mexico after losing my husband, Hardy."

"That farmland you bought by the Cosumnes River produces some of the best crop yields in the county. Great bottomland. It gets replenished every winter by floods. I'm sure your husband would have loved such land."

"Thank you, sir. I think you're right. Hardy always did value a beautiful place to plant his plow."

Did she really say that? I thought as I understood the double entendre.

Her coy smile and nod to me answered that question.

"Colton, perhaps you could introduce the widow Grumman to other folks here."

"Okay, sheriff. Be my pleasure."

Like hell it will, but what else can I say?

I wanted to scream out, "Tess Grumman is really a hooker who screwed her way to wealth. Oh, and Hardy Grumman was not the kind of man to get shot accidentally."

Tess whispered to me as she slipped her arm though mine.

"My name is Nelly, Nelly Grumman. Do not call me Tess."

Tess carried herself like a proper widow as we visited with town leaders and kin of the sheriff. She was in her element, charming foolish men who got willowy-legged when she batted her eyelashes. Got to give her credit, though, that woman does know men.

The sheriff called out to us.

"Colton, Missus Grumman, I'd like you to meet my niece, Isabel. She'll be leaving for Boston soon to attend university. Isn't that where your family lives Cole?"

I used the greeting as an excuse to remove my arm from the clutches of Tess and extended my hand to acknowledge the introduction.

Isabel blended country-girl ruggedness with the innocent naivety of a pretty girl on the cusp of full womanhood. Long blonde hair, gathered by a wide yellow bow into a thick ponytail, hung over her shoulder where it draped from her ample endowment.

"Yes, I grew up near Boston," I answered. "I'll be happy to tell you about the area if you have any questions."

Isabel's fingertips lingered in my hand far longer than required for a proper greeting.

"Good to meet you, Mrs. Grumman," she replied to Tess without breaking eye contact with me. "Would you mind if I borrow this young gentleman to enquire about life in the big city?"

Tess's eyes widened. She glared at the attractive young woman in front of me. I never saw that look on Tess before. She was always the belle of the ball in her brothel.

"Of course, dear." Tess stayed in her role. "Just don't keep him too long."

Tess traced a single finger along my forearm in some kind of subtle girl-to-girl message.

Isabel flagrantly ignored Tess and inserted her arm through where Tess previously had me trapped. As she turned to lead me away, she pulled my arm tight against the side of her breast and half-led, half-pushed me toward a picnic bench on the outer fringe of the area.

172

I heard the sheriff joke with Tess, "Cute couple, don't you think? I'd be honored to take over Colton's introductions."

I glanced back as the sheriff took Tess's arm in his and guided her toward Mr. Carter, president of the largest bank in town. Tess looked over her shoulder at me walking away with Isabel. If looks could kill, I'm not sure if it would have been me or Isabel who dropped dead.

For the next hour, I answered the young lady's questions about my home city. She held both my hands in hers as we talked. I'm not sure, but when she removed her ponytail bow and tossed her head about to loosen the strands, I got the impression it served some other agenda, one I found fetching, but not with enough confidence to act on any hint.

"Are you hungry?" Isabel asked, but did not wait for an answer. "I'll be right back."

She returned with a big plate of pulled pork, beans, fresh bread and two drinks.

"I got you beer. Is that okay? Daddy says it isn't proper for a lady to drink beer, so I brought lemonade for me."

"Beer's good, and thanks for the food."

"Don't tell anybody, but I like beer, too. Just can't drink it when daddy's around."

Feisty too, I thought. *Great girl.*

There was only one plate and one fork, so I was not sure how to react.

"Open up," she said with a large chunk of pork impaled on the fork in front of my mouth.

She gently fed me the bite and stabbed another piece that she took between her lips. Instead of eating it, she rolled the meat on her tongue playfully. I tried with minimal success to suppress my manly urges. This went on for a while—a bite for me, and an invitation from her. Even I finally understood her actions were by intent, not some enticing accident.

"Have you noticed me before?" she asked.

I thought back. She did look familiar.

"Was that you with your dad picking up grain last summer?"

"Yep. Every time daddy went to buy supplies, I came along. He made me stay in the wagon, but I watched you load the grain."

I did recall her. Even though she had been dressed for working on the range or in a barn, I always enjoyed seeing her. She looked younger then. Now, she looks womanly.

"You didn't wear a shirt when you loaded the sacks last summer."

"I'm sorry. That was rude of me."

"Don't be. I loved seeing your body. Where did you get big muscles like that?"

I explained about my rowing club in college and how it works a man's upper body.

"Do you like horses?" she asked.

"Yeah. Worked my way through college in the racing stables. I love horses."

"Come with me. I want you to meet my roan, Buster. You'll love him."

We entered the sheriff's barn hand in hand. I was impressed. It had ten stalls and a huge tack wall with racks of western and English style equipment. One of the saddles caught my attention with its jewels, decorative silver and fancy engraving, obviously for parades.

I ran my hand along the buckskin on that set up, admiring the texture and leather smell.

Isabel placed her hand on top of my wrist as my fingers passed down the seat onto the stirrup fender. She guided my hand downward onto her waist. I turned slightly to face her, and she pressed her body tightly against mine. As she did, she moved my hand under the waistband of her skirt. She was hot to the touch.

"I've been waiting for you, Colton," she said and pressed her lips to mine, "waiting for a long time."

My lips parted slightly as she kissed with growing passion. She pulled me around the corner of the tack wall and pushed me backward into a half-filled hay bin. It was soft, but annoying little sprigs poked through my shirt. I didn't care. She settled on top of me and began moving in provocative ways that a proper gentleman should reject.

"This is my first time," she whispered. "Be gentle."

First time for what? Kissing a boy in a hay bin. I wondered.

Isabel unfastened my pants, gradually exposing my growing interest. She pulled her skirt up and straddled my hips. To my surprise, she wore

174

no undergarments. When my passion came in contact with her soft warmth, I couldn't help but think of Kaga.

I shouldn't do this, I thought.

A momentary flash of anger passed over me as I recalled that Kaga abandoned me, and gave me no choice in the matter. It was time for me to move on with my life.

Isabel pressed against me and winced when we joined. I thought I hurt her, but she thrust harder against me with an eagerness that contradicted any notion of discomfort. My growing desire blinded me to any other consideration. I rolled on top of her, and she wrapped her legs around me.

Minutes felt like hours, and for the first time since Kaga left, I enjoyed the intimacy of a woman. I felt a bit awkward, knowing this willing young lady might never take Kaga's place in my heart, but her eager thrusts brought me to physical bliss, marked only by ragged breaths and matching rhythm.

Isabel tightened her legs around my waist and groaned in ecstasy when my seed exploded deep within her.

As we lay in afterglow, Isabel played with the bear's tooth hanging from my neck.

"Where'd you get this? Did you kill a bear?" she asked, excited by the prospect.

"Yeah. Big grizzly. Couple days ride south of here."

I told her how I fired my rifle and then emptied my forty-four into its chest before it died at my feet. I left the part about Kaga.

Something about killing that bear excited Isabel. She rubbed my chest and entwined a leg with mine as she did. Pressing her pelvis against my thigh, her lips nibbled my ear lobe, and her hand stroked across my abdomen before slipping lower to massage my manhood.

"Thanks for coming to my pig roast," the sheriff's voice rang into the barn entrance.

Isabel and I scrambled to get dressed. Bits of straw hung in her hair, and her long straight ponytail was now clumped in uneven bunches, desperately needing a brush.

As soon as our clothes were fastened, she saw a small virginal spot of blood in our makeshift straw bed and spread a clump of hay on top of it. She took my hand and led me, nonchalantly, out of the hay bin as if nothing happened.

The sheriff and a friend scanned both of us and grinned. The sheriff was not amused.

"Hi, Uncle Marcus. I just showed Cole my roan. He says it's a great horse. He also loves your parade saddle. If it ever gets stolen, I know where you should look first."

She had no shame, joking with her uncle like nothing happened. As we turned the corner and passed out of sight along the backside of the barn, she threw her arms around me and pinned me against the siding. We kissed in tight embrace, and she thrust her hips against me as if she wanted more of what we had enjoyed.

"I think I love you, Colton. Maybe daddy can send me to college in San Francisco, so we can see each other on weekends and holidays."

Oh my Lord, I thought. *I didn't give any thought to this possibility when we got together. How am I going to get out of this?*

Isabel found a horse's currycomb on a fence and dragged it through her hair a couple times to remove random bits of straw and realign her long straight strands. She giggled as she ran the comb through my hair, catching a couple pieces of straw in her hand that fell off.

"Fix your shirt before we rejoin the party," she said and began unbuttoning my fasteners.

I looked down. My buttons were out of sequence making my shirt hang unevenly. I hoped the sheriff had not noticed.

We strolled among the guests, Isabel clinging to my arm as we did. Tess saw us and quickly looked away.

It was getting dark, so I told Isabel I had to leave. She walked me to my horse, and using Thor as a privacy shield, she kissed me deep and passionately one last time.

"I leave for college in a week unless daddy changes his mind. Can I come see you at the store?"

"Sure. Any time," I said, despite knowing this could lead to trouble.

Chapter 40

I did not go home. Kaga was on my mind. I had to resolve our relationship, one way or the other Professor Lok would tell me where to find her.

The full moon provided plenty of light to travel the river road back to the China Camp. I stopped once to remove irritating hay from my drawers. When I entered the crudely constructed city, only a few street lanterns provided areas of light. Nightly returning Delta fog cast an eerie glow around each lamp. Streets were usually deserted at this time of night, but not tonight.

Chinese did not drink or play poker like white men did, so I was surprised to see several men huddled in the cold outside the front door of the professor's house. There were no horse hitches in this town. Chinamen tended to walk everywhere or pull light carts using human power.

I tied Thor's reins to a support pole for the awning over a wooden sidewalk.

"Evening," I directed to the group of men. "Any of you speak English?"

Most looked down at the sidewalk, but one man came out of the crowd. He wore a large, black eye patch, and his face was deeply bruised on the cheek below. The lump of a bandage wrapped around his chest bulged under his shirt. This was the leader of the bandits.

After leaving the pig roast, I had stopped at the store to get my gun. I promised the sheriff I would not wear it in town, but I'll be damned if I was going to get robbed when out of town. I slipped the hammer loop off my gun and rested my hand on the handle, being intentionally conspicuous with my movement.

The man bowed slightly, an action I knew as respect, but I found it odd coming from him. I removed my hand from the gun.

He spoke to me in his language. I did not understand a thing he said, until I heard the professor's name.

"Where is Chang Lok?" I asked.

He motioned for me to follow him, and he entered the house.

Inside, I recognized several of the Chinese ladies who took care of Kaga and me when we first entered their world. The old woman who gave me the gifts from Kaga immediately rose and hurried out of the house. Another woman pulled out a chair for me at the table and motioned for me to sit. A teapot adorned with elaborate vine paintings and a set of matching small cups sat on the table. She pointed at it.

"For me?" I asked, not wanting to presume.

She motioned for me to pour a cup of tea, and when I did not immediately respond, she did it for me. The tea smelled wonderful, not at all what I expected. I sipped the hot beverage and felt its warmth all the way to my core.

Ten minutes passed sitting in silence with half a dozen women all concentrating on needlework in their laps. I was about to leave when the front door creaked open, and the familiar old woman returned with a man who looked as old as Lok, but was not my friend.

"Mister Colton, my name is Yip Jing. I was a friend of Chang Lok. He spoke highly of you and told me you are a friend to the Chinese people."

I stood and shook the hand of this stranger.

"Where is Lok?" I asked.

"Our friend is dead. He died this afternoon with no warning."

My heart sank. The only connection I had with Kaga ended in that moment.

"I . . . I'm sorry for your loss. He meant a lot to me, too. What happened?"

"Please sit, Mister Colton. I know why you are here."

I followed his instructions with a numb obedience born of exhaustion and sense of loss.

The old man placed a hand on mine.

"Before Professor Chang died, he told me of your Indian friend. He said you love her, and she loves you, but he cautioned your future must unfold in its own time. He made me promise not to interfere with destiny. She must make her own decision in her own time."

I jumped at knowing this man might be able to take me to Kaga.

"Where is she? I need to talk with her."

"I promised my teacher to respect his teaching. In his death, I must honor his request."

My first impulse was to lift the small man off the ground and threaten to beat him to death, if he refused to give up her location. I had learned about the Chinese people from Lok. He taught me how they held personal ethics and integrity in as high esteem as righteous white men did for their religious beliefs. I forced my internal shaking under control and tried to reason with this man.

"Mister Yip," that was another thing I learned about the Chinese. Their family name came first, followed by their given name. "Can you take a message to Kaga for me?"

That was about the best I could hope for.

"I cannot do that. It would interfere with her natural choice. Trust me. She will make her decision very soon."

I played the only card I had.

"I'm not happy about this. I have been a friend to the Chinese. Never once, have I refused to meet any request for supplies or equipment that you asked, and I never overcharged you like those river-shippers do. Why can't you make an exception for me, this one time?"

Yip Jing looked down at his hands, wrestling internally with conflict about my request. He looked up slowly and sighed deeply before responding.

"Mister Colton. It is true. You have been a good friend to my people. I thank you for that. I do want to help you, but I fear Professor Chang is right. If I grant your request, the natural course of life may be circumvented. Bad fortune always follows such choices."

"But, you'll do it?" I interrupted him in anticipation of a positive answer.

"I will do what I can. I can not give her your message, but I will tell her you expressed your concern. Then, I will answer her questions about you. What should I tell her if she asks?"

I spent the next half hour telling him about my work at the mercantile and how I now owned it. He seemed to enjoy hearing about my journalism articles, including the two stories about the Chinese existence in California. At one point, he asked questions about how his people might be accepted in the east. When we finished, I knew I had done all possible to reconnect with Kaga. The rest would be up to her.

She's in charge again, I thought and smiled. *Just the way she always was.*

"Thank you for helping my people, Colton."

During our conversation, I had asked him to call me by my given name.

"I'm sorry for your loss, Mister Yip. If there is any way I can help, please let me know."

Yip Jing thought for a moment, "I was not going to ask you, but our friend's death came suddenly. In our culture, a coffin and preparation for death begin with someone's lingering illness. We were not prepared for the death of Professor Chang. There is no coffin, and it will take many weeks to obtain one from our people in San Francisco. You could purchase one in Sacramento for us, as long as they do not know it is for a Chinese man."

"Consider it done. I'll bring it to you tomorrow. Anything else?"

"Your help is a welcome relief. I know the professor would be honored if you could attend the funeral as part of his family. He has only a sister here, and she asked me to invite you to represent his family in China."

"I don't know what to do, but if you'll guide me, it will be my privilege to participate."

My ride home seemed faster than normal. I thought about Kaga all the way. She doesn't want me. Why do I keep trying? Sleep came quickly once in bed. It had been a long day.

The next morning, I went to the local undertaker to pick up a coffin for a "miner up in the hills." We loaded it before nine in the morning, and I headed for the Chinese town. I just reached the river bend at Clarksburg when I heard a horse approaching at a gallop.

"Colton!" a girl's voice called from behind my wagon. "Pull up, Cole."

Isabel reined in her roan next to me.

"Hi, Isabel, is something wrong?"

"Heck, yes, I dare say something's quite wrong. I went by your store last night, and you weren't there. I waited near to midnight. Almost got caught by papa, sneaking back into the house."

"I didn't get home until late," I said, a bit perturbed by her interruption in my travel.

"Where were you?" she asked while looking at the casket. "Who's that for?"

"I'm taking this to the family of a miner, and—"

"Why are you taking the river trail? Miners are up in the hills."

Nosey little lady.

"Chinamen are taking it up there for me. I've got to get going. They're waiting for this."

She showed no concern about my delivery pressure.

"Chinamen? Daddy says they're heathens. Don't believe in God. Can't be trusted. Aren't you afraid they won't deliver that thing to the miner's family?"

"Your daddy's wrong. They're people, just like us."

"Please don't go there. They might hurt you. I would die if they hurt you."

"I've been doing business with them for months. There's never been a problem."

I did not say anything about the attack yesterday morning.

"So, answer my question. Where were you last night?" she persisted.

None of your damn business, I thought.

"Is that important?" I asked more in self-defense than expecting an answer.

181

Isabel huffed indignantly.

"After yesterday, I figured you and me, well, you know. We're in a serious relationship, so I've got a right to know where you're spending your time."

Last time I let a lover down, she sent men to kill me. If I did not learn from that, then I'm not as smart as that college degree implied.

"Isabel, yesterday caught me by surprise. It was wonderful, but it also scared me to no end. I don't handle feelings good. Can we talk about this after I get back?"

"It's her, isn't it?" Isabel slapped her reins against the neck of her horse, making it spin around in a tight turn.

"What are you talking about?"

"It's the widow Grumman. She's real pretty. You've been with her, haven't you?"

"Where the hell did you get a notion like that?"

"Don't tell me you didn't see the way she looked at you, and she couldn't keep her hands off you."

She inhaled deeply and yelled, "Were you with her last night?"

It was not a question, more of an accusation.

"I don't see where it's your place to demand an accounting for where I spend my time. Besides, I was at the dead man's home talking with his widow. I resent your allegation."

Isabel blushed.

"I . . . I'm sorry. I didn't know. I just thought. Please, forgive me."

Finally, I thought. *I'm learning how to handle women.*

Chapter 41

I entered the Chinese town expecting to see the usual quiet locals going about their daily business, but the streets were deserted. When I turned onto the main street leading to the professor's home, dozens of men milled in the street outside his place. Decorative strips of bright cloth adorned posts and hung from roof edges.

The crowd parted to make room for my wagon. Without comment, half a dozen Chinese men removed the back gate and carried the coffin inside.

Yip Jing came outside as soon as the casket disappeared from sight.

"Colton, that was fast. Thank you so much on behalf of Chang Lok and our community. Do you have time to join us?"

My new Chinese friend introduced me to several of the professor's friends and students while explaining their cultural funeral rituals.

"After two years," he said, "Lok's bones will be exhumed, cleaned and sent back to China for his final burial. It was his wish to be returned to our homeland someday when he died. None of us thought it would be so soon."

He offered me food from a beautiful silver tray. I declined.

"There is the professor's sister," he said. "I believe you already know her."

We approached the old woman who had been so nice to me many months ago. Jing translated as she formally requested for me to represent the professor's male members of the family at the funeral. I agreed, not having a clue what responsibilities would follow.

Jing explained everything to me, and I promised to do my best. He told me not to worry about the ritual coins to place in the four corners of the coffin or the ceremonial food offerings, as he would provide them.

It was noon when I got back to the store. Several town folks were waiting outside.

"This place always opened on time when Hank ran it," one said sarcastically.

"I am so sorry. I had a death in the family and had to make funeral arrangements."

"Bradley, aren't you embarrassed?" A woman patron chastised the man who complained. "This poor young man was taking care of his family, not ignoring business like you said."

"Sorry, Colton. I assumed that—"

"Shut up, Bradley," the woman said. "Tell him what you need, so we can get home. I have a list of chores for you to complete."

The henpecked man shrugged and asked me for nails, a hammer and a saw. As he paid for the goods, he cringed each time she called for him to hurry up.

Is this the blessing of marriage? I wondered. *I'll bet this is Isabel's idea of wedded bliss.*

After I met the needs of the shoppers, I hung the out-for-lunch sign and went into the back room for a much needed nap.

Knocking on the storefront door brought me out of my slumber. From the bright noonday sun outside, I could not have slept more than an hour.

"Hi Cole," Isabel said, pushing open the door as soon as the lock clicked. "I brought you lunch. I want to make up for my insensitivity this morning."

She noticed my un-tucked and partially fastened shirt.

"Oh my, couldn't wait to see me?" she joked.

"I was sleeping."

"Are you hungry?" she asked without paying any mind to my comment.

Isabel opened the wicker picnic basket and began arranging food on the counter. Despite my exhaustion, fried chicken, navy bean soup and fresh baked bread smelled great. She held a spoonful of the beans to my mouth. For an instant, I found it sexy, but then my first encounter with Tess flooded my memory.

Not again! I thought in a panic and choked on the soup, spilling it down my shirt.

"I'm sorry," I said. "I'll get a clean shirt."

I went into my room to change shirts. Isabel's presence could be a disaster, and I thought momentarily about sneaking out through Clyde's trap door, but that would be mean. I would just have to be a man, and tell her our brief relationship was a mistake.

With my clean shirt hanging open, I peaked through the spy hole to see what she was doing. She was at the front of the store, locking the front door.

I walked out through my curtains resolved to put an end to this charade of a relationship.

"What are you doing?" I asked just as she reached the end of the counter.

"I told you," she said. "I brought you lunch."

Before I started the inevitable conversation about our non-relationship, she snaked both her arms under my shirt flaps and pulled tight against my body. Her lips parted and hungrily searched mine demanding reciprocal passion. I tried to talk, but she pushed me backward through the curtains and peeled my shirt off, all in the same motion. My heels hit the bedframe, and I fell backward onto my bed with her landing fully on top of me.

"You're never going to forget this lunch," she said.

My manhood responded involuntarily. I did want to ravage that hot young body, but her wild excitement frightened me.

185

I tried to talk, but she used my open mouth to probe with her darting tongue. At the same time, she managed to remove her blouse and unbutton my pants. Naked breasts pressed into my chest, and she rubbed my manhood bringing me to a fever pitch. Her hand seized my passion, sending a shock through my body. I protested until I felt her skirt pull up.

Isabel pressed against my manhood. She was in complete control, and I will not lie, I liked it. Moments later, she took my engorged manhood deep into a hot, moist sheath of sensation. Wild plunges with her sitting upright and leaning backward, drove me to a frenzied release, but despite feeling the hot fluid inside her, she did not slow pace. We finished together and she collapsed onto my torso, with face against my neck. Her slow, deep breathing gave me a sense of peace. I began to think it might be enjoyable to have her as a regular part of my life.

We lay together in silence for a long while after the lovemaking.

"Do you feel better, now?" she asked.

"Better? I didn't feel bad."

"You said you were taking a nap. I thought you were tired."

I rolled her off me onto the bed at my side with her leg draped across my thigh.

"You sure do know how to fix men's lunch." I joked.

She took offense.

"I haven't been with other men! I told you that yesterday. Don't you believe me?"

"That's not a suggestion about other men. I'm just saying a lunch like this is fantastic."

Isabel kissed me softly on the cheek, her warm breath bathing my ear when she whispered, "Am I as good as her?"

"Who?"

"You know . . . the widow Grumman."

"What makes you think I ever made love with Tess?"

"Tess? I thought her name is Nelly."

186

"She used to go by Tess," I admitted.

"I was right! You have made love with her. Am I better?"

What the hell's going on? I thought. *Why does she want to compare with Tess?*

"Why are you so sure I've been with her before? How do you know that?"

"Girls know. We can tell at a glance if a man has been with another woman."

"You said I am your first. What basis do you have for such a comparison?"

Isabel looked away from me like an embarrassing past haunted her.

"Colton. I told you the truth. You are the only man I've ever been with, but," she hesitated, "there was another boy I thought I loved. We did not go all the way, but I would have, if he wanted to. I thought we would get married some day—until he met Emma Hoover. He looked at me different after that. I knew they had become intimate. He finally admitted it."

"I'm sorry you went through that. It must have been awful."

She began to tear up.

"It wasn't the fact that they made love that hurt me. It was that he lied to me. Don't ever lie to me. Please."

This young woman was more complex than I first thought.

"You're better than the widow Grumman," I said softly.

She inhaled deeply and propped up on one elbow.

"You DID have sex with her! I knew it. Is it over?"

"It was over a long time ago. I want nothing to do with her, now."

"That's not how she feels. She still wants you. It's obvious."

"Doesn't matter what she wants. She's crazy. You should stay away from her, too."

Isabel liked my answer. She laid her head on my chest and hugged me, while I wondered how I was going to deal with this situation.

"Colton, can we talk about our future?"

"Our future?"

"You know I am leaving for school back east. I really want to stay here to be with you. Last night, I talked with my daddy about transferring to a school in San Francisco. He refused to consider it. I'll be leaving in a week. Cole, I don't want to be away from you."

Thank God, I thought. *My problem is solved by daddy to the rescue.*

Then, it dawned on me. This female excitement would no longer be available, just when I was beginning to enjoy her attention.

Chapter 42

I could not nap after that lunch. I kissed Isabel goodbye, and we agreed to get together as much as possible in the week until she had to leave. My life finally seemed to be getting better. I owned a successful store. My writing was lauded back east, and my love life dramatically improved. I secretly hoped Kaga might come back into my life, but I had no control over her behavior. Hell, I could not even talk to her.

Isabel and I got together several more times before she left. She even introduced me to her father as her boyfriend. He grilled me about my education and could not understand why I would run a lowly mercantile when I had a college degree. I explained how the store provides me with believable cover for interviews with miners and key players building the west. Clandestine activities of my operation excited him. He began offering his own ideas.

"Cole, how would you like to meet Theodore Judah?" he asked. "Theodore is the Chief Engineer on the Sacramento Valley Railroad. It's the first real railroad west of the Mississippi and began construction last year. It'll run twenty-six miles from Granite City to Sacramento. Should take a full day off shipments of gold into our city."

I had heard talk about the railway construction. It provided jobs for a lot of out of work miners and might even make a good story about the rapid growth of infrastructure out here.

"Thank you, sir. He sounds like a great interview."

"Mark my word, son, Theodore is going places. Did you know he published a plan for a transcontinental railroad? When it's done, a man can ride trains all the way from Boston to Sacramento. No long clipper ship passages to Panama. No more hot train rides across the Isthmus and no more muggy voyages across the Caribbean and up the east coast. This young fella's got vision."

My last time with Isabel, she told her father that she and her best girlfriend were traveling to San Francisco for the weekend before she leaves to college. She lied. I closed the store for three days, and we enjoyed each other so many times I lost count. I told her I was worried about her getting pregnant.

"Don't worry about that. Momma got me special sponges from the Mediterranean that prevent babies."

"Did you tell your mother about us?" I was mortified.

"No, silly. She thinks I am saving them for college, you know, in case I meet the right man. She wants me to complete my education before marrying. Daddy doesn't know. He would not approve."

I was surprised but relieved.

"Your momma doesn't care if you are a virgin when you get married?"

Isabel rolled on top of me.

"You sure are naïve for such a beautiful man. I don't know a single girlfriend who is still a virgin, but all our daddies think we are. How old were you when you had your first sex?"

"Sixteen," I lied.

"How old was she?"

"I don't remember." Another half-lie. In truth, I really did not know Tess's age.

"Bull. Everybody remembers their first. I'll never forget my first time with you."

I did not say anything as she wiggled to absorb my manhood, yet again.

"It was the widow Grumman, huh?" she asked and kissed my ear before whispering, "Am I as good as her?"

She moved sensuously against my body as if to provide a basis for comparison.

"Nobody compares to you, Isabel," I said, knowing that was what she wanted to hear. It triggered a frantic surge of passion from her.

When she left at the end of those three days, I found myself thinking about her.

Is this a woman I can settle down with, or is our attraction purely physical? Do I even want to settle down?

The next day I joined my Chinese friends for Lok's funeral service and placed the coins in all four corners of his coffin as I was instructed. They are supposed to ward off evil spirits. I was amazed to learn Chinese funeral rites would go on for another month and a half after he was buried. Yip Jing told me I did right by the professor's family and thanked me. When I asked about Kaga, he told me he relayed my concerns, but said she would not talk to him about me. As far as I was concerned, my relationship with her was over.

This had been a whirlwind week. Clyde left for his new life. I was attacked. I found out that Kaga had been around but refused to talk to me. My Chinese friend died. Tess showed up. I bedded a passionate woman. I interviewed a fascinating visionary of railway development. Isabel left. Now, I could look forward to simple times, writing and not thinking about women.

Chapter 43

Isabel had left my bed before first light on a Monday morning. I did not expect to see her again for four years, although she promised to write often and stay faithful to our relationship. She asked me to make a similar promise. As horny as that girl gets, I figured she'd find some new guy at college, and I'd never hear from her again, so I agreed to her request.

No customers came in all morning. I used the time to oil leather holsters in my gun display. Just before lunch, I heard shouting out front. A young man dressed in nice clothes stood next to his horse across the street shouting. I went outside to see what was going on.

He yelled, "Maker of angels. I want the maker of angels!"

"Don't know who you're talking about," I said. "Never heard of this maker of angels."

"His name is Colton. Newspaper calls him Maker of Angels. I want him. Who are you?"

"My name's Hank." I thought quickly. "Don't know anyone named Colton. If I meet him, who should I tell was calling?"

"Call me Snake. Guy's supposed to be a gun fighter. Tell him, I'll be back to kill him."

He swung onto his horse and rode away.

I locked the store and went to find the sheriff, following the lawman's instructions to avoid trouble. I described this guy and left the matter in his hands. The rest of my afternoon entailed final edits on two articles in preparation to mail them with the stage coach driver.

Heavy rains turned city roads muddy but gave a nice respite from recently worsening street dust. A new hardware store opened on K Street and might have taken away some of my business, but Clyde built strong community ties, so I was not too concerned about competition.

Rain let up at closing time. I pulled the window shades down and locked up, but nothing in my larder appealed to me for dinner, so I headed to my favorite eating place by the river. I wore old trail boots, because I knew they would be muddy and wet when I returned. The café sat on the river next to the bar I liked. Figured I'd eat a good dinner and stop in the bar for a beer before turning in for the night.

I sat at my usual table overlooking the Sacramento River. The diner did not have any better luck today with customers than I did. I was the only patron waiting for a meal. It was so quiet I could hear my steak sizzling in the kitchen as they cooked it.

"Shame you're eating alone," a female voice said. "May I join you?"

It was Tess. Wearing a high fashion dress with four cascading layers of smart fabric, each tipped with embroidered fringe, she looked beautiful. Long, red curls tumbled onto her chest from under a tasteful bonnet with ribbon ties that came together in a pretty bow at the side of her chin. She looked every bit the cultured woman of wealth.

Amazing how nice a scorpion can dress up.

I stifled an evil smile.

"Suit yourself, Tess."

"That doesn't sound very friendly, and I told you, it's Nelly."

"I save friendship for folks who don't try to kill me."

She sat in the chair directly across from me, intentionally obstructing my view of the passing river.

"I understand your feelings, Cole. I would feel that way, too. Can you accept my apology? When you left, it broke my heart, and I reacted as any scorned woman might."

I tipped my hat back in astonishment.

"You think it's normal to send a killer to gun down your ex-lovers?"

I laughed in contempt.

"No," she said. "That was extreme, and I regret it. I'd like to make it up to you."

I'll bet you would, but I've seen what a black widow spider does to her mate.

Being a gentleman, I did not want to eat in front of her, so I called the waiter over and offered to buy her dinner.

"Thank you," she said. "I'm happy to see that you don't hate me."

"A lot has happened since we were together last year."

"Are you talking about that cowgirl, Jezebel?"

"Her name is Isabel, and you know it. Besides, you got married since then."

"Colton, you know why I had to marry Hardy."

I snickered openly, "Yeah, you wanted to settle down, knit sweaters and have kids."

I saw a momentary flash of her infamous rage in those eyes. She quickly brought it under control, but I knew the real monster still lurked inside that sweet seductress.

"Sorry," I said. "I shouldn't have been snide. You might have really cared for him."

Although, I'll bet my store, it was just for his money.

"In my own way," she said, "I liked Hardy Grumman. Sweet man. He was going to take me to New York for a honeymoon. There was nothing he would not do for me."

"What about the Empty Nest?"

"I gave it to Emma James. The men loved her, and she has a little boy to provide for. She doubled her income this way."

I can't believe it. The black widow knows compassion.

Our server arrived with food. I enjoyed my steak and rice, and kept my mouth full to minimize conversation. One thing about Tess, though, she learned proper etiquette somewhere in her life. She ate delicately, spoke only when her mouth was empty and used her napkin to keep her lips properly wiped at all times. Coupled with that fetching outfit, she was damned near as attractive as the first time I met her at the Empty Nest.

Maybe she's telling the truth, I thought. *She IS a beautiful woman. Isabel's raw passion pleases me to know end, but Tess? This woman can bring any man to his knees in the bedroom.*

"Colton, I've heard great things about you in this community. The sheriff told me you are also a feature writer for a Boston newspaper. Is that right?"

"Yeah. I told you that when we first met. I'm a journalist out here to expose the truths about the California gold mining. That's why I had to leave that dust town."

Tess smiled, almost too politely.

"I understand that now. At the time, I felt it was personal, like you took advantage of me and then threw me aside like a worn out brush."

What! You're a damn prostitute. All men use you and leave. I'm not buying that line of horse shit.

"I'm sorry you felt that way," I said feigning a conciliatory tone. "My contract required me to meet deadlines. I had no choice."

She cocked her head aside for a second and tapped one of her long fingernails on the tablecloth while contemplating my comment.

"You were embarrassed by me, weren't you?"

"Why would I be embarrassed by you? Every man within a hundred miles was in love with you."

"It's the brothel, isn't it? I told you I was not one of the working girls."

I avoided the subject.

"You think I was a prostitute, don't you? Well, let me set you straight. I bought that place when it was a rundown whorehouse where working girls met the needs of cowpokes and drifters. Ladies got beat up as frequently as they got paid. When I took over, I banned the men who hurt my women, even shot one in the groin for giving one of my girls a black eye. Those girls were protected by me, and the local men learned to treat them with respect. Even if they're whores, they're also human beings."

Tess impressed me. This spirited woman actually had a heart.

"When Hardy Grumman took a liking to me," her tone softened, "it was because he respected how well I ran the business, not because of sex. In fact, I never had relations with the man until the day we got married."

"But, I thought—"

"I know what you thought!" she snapped. "You figured I was just one of the working girls who took a fancy to you. Well, it's true that I took a liking to you. In fact, I fell deep for you, but I never, not even once, bedded a man for money. I ran a business that catered to men's needs. I took care of their bellies with the best damn food in the territory, and my girls took care of their manly needs."

I felt bad for my behavior and assumptions. Yes, I did believe prostitution was her calling. What else was I to believe?

"Tess, I'm truly sorry how things turned out. I guess I'm good with the written word but pretty poor at talking."

She reached across the table and took my hand.

"Cole, I still have feelings for you. Will you give me a second chance?"

My luck with woman left a lot to be desired.

Tess tried to kill me. Kaga abandoned me, and this new girl, Isabel, smothers me with controlling demands.

"No promises, but I'm willing to keep in touch. We'll see how things go."

"Keep in touch?" she said in a flash of anger. "I bare my soul to you and all you can say is we should 'keep in touch.' What the hell is that supposed to mean?"

"Don't get riled. I just want to take our relationship slow. Lest you forgot, you sent men to kill me once."

She crossed her arms on her chest, and I could hear her foot tapping fast on the wood below the table.

"It's her, isn't it? That little cowgirl with the big tits. Did you screw her? Never mind, I know you did, a woman can tell. Was she as good as me?"

What the hell is with women? I wondered. *Why do they want to compare themselves with each other?*

"Isabel is a nice girl. She left yesterday for college and won't be back for four or five years. My relationship with her has nothing to do with us."

Oh crap, I thought. *I made a big mistake when I used the word "us."*

Tess broke into a wide smile.

"You did have sex with her! I knew it. I sure hope her daddy doesn't find out. Did you know she has two older sisters who both got married . . . uh, real fast? Their babies were both premature. Not sure how an eight pound newborn is premature, but that's not my concern. I hear Isabel's daddy has a bad temper when it comes to his baby girl. He told me at the sheriff's pig roasting that she's the one who will make him proud."

"How do you know all this?"

"While you were soiling his baby girl in the barn, I got to know her daddy, just in case I ever need to speak with him about, shall we say, sensitive matters. I found him to be a very good listener, that is, when he wasn't staring at my breasts. You boys really should get a hold on that bad habit."

Every time I began to believe Tess had changed, not so subtle hints told me otherwise. The claws were starting to show.

I paid our tab and we rose to leave.

Chapter 44

Tess assumed familiarity, looping her arm in mine as we walked out of the restaurant.

"May I offer you a ride home?" she asked as I lifted her from the wood-plank sidewalk over the mud to her single-horse buggy. I hopped in, clicking my boots together outside the carriage to knock off the mud.

"Here, you take the reins," she said and handed them to me.

Sun dropped low on the horizon during dinner, and dusk would soon set in as we pulled up to my store.

"Thank you, for dinner, Colt. Is this your business?"

"Yes, ma'am. I live in the back. Thank you for the ride."

"Are you going to invite me in?"

"There's really not much to see. Just dry goods, hardware and such."

"A gentleman would at least make the offer so a lady could politely decline."

Games. Why do women always play these annoying games?

I issued the polite invitation.

"Why thank you, Colton. I would love to see your store."

Wait a minute! You said you were going to decline.

I tethered the buggy's horse and opened my store, hoping she would be brief.

"Nice store," she said pretending to be genuinely impressed. "You have more goods than I expected."

"Business has been slow with all the recent rain and competition from that new hardware store over on K Street. My inventory stacks up until the miners come down for supplies. Hell, this store will be half empty in a month or two."

"Is there good money in this business?"

I hesitated to tell her about the huge markups Clyde used to get rich.

"Plenty of money and it gives me lots of time for writing articles."

Tess stepped uncomfortably close to me. Perfume gave her a sweet smell, almost as rich and stimulating as Kaga's purple flowers.

"Cole, do I have to make my interest any clearer?"

Finally, she stopped beating around the subject.

"Look Tess, you smell great and look beautiful, but we have history that makes me afraid to get close to you."

She ran her hand along the buttons on my shirt, deftly flicking each open from the top to my belt. I struggled with this important moment of decision. Her violent side could still be there, but I vividly recalled things she did that drove a man crazy. Logic wrestled with libido.

"Colton Minar!" It was the gunman from the morning. I had hoped the sheriff ran him out of town.

"Ignore him, Cole," Tess said with genuine concern. "He'll kill you if you go outside."

"How do you know that?" I asked.

"I know him from my Texas days. Goes by Snake. His real name is Julio Cantini."

"You know all this by the sound of a man's voice?"

Tess self-consciously folded one of her hands into the other and looked down.

"I hired him. He's been stalking you for months. That's how I found out where you live. I hated you. Wanted to see him kill you. That was why I came here. Cole, let me send him away."

I pushed Tess aside and went into my back room. I returned with my forty-four and tied the leg strap while Tess begged me not to go outside.

"Cole, he's real fast. I read about your Maker of Angels reputation in the newspaper, but those men you killed were ordinary. Snake is a professional killer. You can't beat him. Please stay in here while I order him away."

"Don't go out there, Tess. There's no telling what that man will do."

"I hired him. I can get rid of him."

Tess turned sharply and ran out of the store. I raced to catch her. She burst from my entry onto the wraparound porch and stopped half way down the steps.

"Snake," she called out. "It's over. You did your job. Now, leave."

"Get out of the way Miss Nelly," he said. "I got a job to do."

"No. I don't want the money back. Keep it. Just leave."

Snake walked in short deliberate steps to one side. He was clearing Tess from the field of fire between him and me. With his gun-hand poised an inch above an ivory handle, he squared up, keeping close watch on my elbow the whole time. Clyde was right. He said real killers draw on the first sign of movement at the elbow. Snake knew this too.

He must be good.

Clyde's words rang in my head.

You've got to get inside the other man's mind. If he's faster than you, sidestep right to protect your gun arm. Make sure your first shot kills him dead. You won't get a second chance.

Tess kept babbling something to Snake, but neither of us listened to her. We both got tunnel vision, each watching the other man's arm movements as our sole focus.

I ran though my checklist. Hammer loop aside. Yes, I did that inside the store. Hammer cocked. Done. Holster slipped more forward than normal. Done.

I walked along my porch away from Tess. Snake mirrored my position from the street below. The porch railing was right at gun height. I adjusted my plan. I would have to lift the gun more than normal to clear the wood or fire under the railing. We both stopped.

Tess continued yelling at the hired gun that he should leave. I got the break I needed when he answered her.

"I got a reputation to keep, you whore. You paid for a killing. I aim to deliver. Future employers will shy away from my services, if I don't finish the job. You ready, Minar?"

"Who's going to pay for your coffin, Snake?" I replied.

He laughed.

"Big words from a peddler."

"Can you read, or did your momma give up teaching you cuz you were too stupid?"

"Is that the best you can do with insults and distractions?"

He was right. A professional like him would not fall for such attempts.

"You ever heard of Clyde Hamlin?"

He looked surprised.

"Everybody knows Clyde. Why?"

"This gun is his. I took it off him."

He looked under the railing at my holster.

I won!

"Think you can take it off me?"

He hesitated before saying, "We'll find out, now, won't we?"

There was a hint of uncertainty in his voice. He thought I killed Clyde for this gun, and he recognized the distinctive weapon.

Snake's elbow moved. I half-stepped to my right, rolled the weapon out of my holster and dropped slightly to fire under the railing.

He was faster by an instant. I saw his muzzle flash, and at the same time, felt the hard kick of my forty-four. Glass in the window behind where I had been standing exploded as I fanned my left palm across my hammer three more times with the trigger full-pulled.

Snake fell forward. My first bullet entered his neck and severed his spine. The rest of my shots weren't needed, just extra holes lined down his chest. That was another Clyde lesson. Finish the job.

Tess ran to me and hugged me as tight as she could.

On the street, residents came out, attracted by the showdown and their morbid curiosity. They stared at the dead man while his blood began pooling in muddy hoof prints.

Tess whispered to me, "Please, Cole, don't tell the sheriff about his connection to me. I tried to stop him. I'm so sorry."

I told the sheriff a selective version of the truth. About how the man was looking for the gunfighter dubbed the Maker of Angels by the local newspaper. I told him that the widow Grumman begged him to leave, and that I worked my way down the porch to get her clear of any conflict. Figured nothing more needed to be said.

The sheriff instructed the undertaker to haul away the body and bury him in a pauper's grave under the only name the sheriff knew, Snake.

"You okay, Mrs. Grumman?" The sheriff asked. "I'm sorry you had to witness such a terrible act of violence. Let's hope other gunmen will forget about that label in the paper. Colton, here, has been a model citizen, since I asked him to put away that gun. I will admit I'm glad he had it today, or we might be planning his funeral."

He turned to me.

"You done good, boy. Now, put that damn thing away."

As I climbed the steps to go into the store, Tess grabbed my hands.

Chapter 45

Spots of blood dotted my hands. I vaguely recalled glass shards from the window spraying past my gun as I rapid-fired those extra rounds into Snake.

"You're hurt, Cole," Tess said and led me into the store.

"I'll be fine. There's fresh water in a pitcher by the stove in my back room. Would you mind getting it for me? Clean towels are on the shelf above it."

Tess was downright sweet. Washed and dried my hands and removed my shirt to rinse out the blood. She hung the wet shirt near the wood stove and stoked the fire.

When I first met Tess, I admit to being an inexperienced young man. I'd come close before with a woman, but Tess was my first. Like Isabel said, you never forget your first. How often does a man get to rekindle the magic of that first encounter?

"Where are you staying in town, Tess? It's getting dark outside."

"I'm afraid I missed my chance to get home quite a while ago. I'm staying in the new Sloughhouse Inn down by my new property along the Cosumnes River. It's over an hour's ride, so I'll have to find a hotel in town. Do you have any recommendations?"

"Good hotels are downtown. Let's take a ride down there, and I'll show them to you."

I was sitting on my bed, shaking wrinkles out of a fresh shirt, when Tess sat next to me.

"Colton, are you really so naive that I have to spell it out for you?"

She touched a finger to her mouth in thought.

er>SAULT4

"You know, now that I think about it, you were this way the first time we met."

She took the shirt from my hands and tossed it expertly onto the back of the chair. Her own hat and jacket quickly followed.

"I want you, Colton, and I intend to have you, right now."

Oh, good. I thought. *No more guessing. I hate trying to understand women.*

Tess made quick work of my pants and her own layers of clothes. It felt like old times with her in control. I followed her lead, but could not help comparing Isabel's crude, but intense, lovemaking to Tess's drawn out patience. She took just the right amount of time with every step in her seduction. Instructing me on what she wanted for her pleasure made lovemaking with her easy.

"I like that, Colton. Use your tongue in small circles around my nipples. Yes, like that."

I did everything she asked.

"Slow down, big boy," she said, as I got excited. "We're not in a race. Slow and easy."

When she approached her own finish, she squeezed me between her legs and bit lightly into my shoulder.

"Now!" she demanded with a hoarse voice. "Now!"

I used all my strength to thrust as deep into her as possible. We both shuddered under the intensity of the final moment. This was the Tess I remembered.

It must have been close to midnight when she pressed tight against me and whispered.

"Bet she didn't do that."

"Who?" I asked.

"Isadora, the skinny cowgirl." She poked me as if I was supposed to have read her mind.

"Her name is Isabel, and she's not skinny. Got every bit as much womanhood up front as you do."

"Perhaps, but does she know how to use it like I do?"

204

I had to give Tess credit. None of the women in my life could hold a candle to her physical love-making talent.

When Tess asked if she could spend the rest of the night in my place, I agreed despite thinking this might be a huge mistake.

"You should leave at first light," I said, "to protect your reputation as a recent widow."

Before I fell asleep, Tess made sure I had one more experience to compare with the memories of Isabel. She reminded me of that before finally closing her eyes. For once, I was actually happy when she faded out. I honestly do not think I could have done it again.

Chapter 46

Pounding on the front door of the store woke me with a start. It was still dark, so I yelled that I would be right there, fired up a lantern and slipped into my clothes. Tess woke, too, and said she would wait in my bedroom until I knew what was going on.

"Open up, Cole. Hurry."

It was Clyde. Despite the cool night, he was dripping in sweat. He barged in.

"You gotta come with me. I got the doc outside. Where's the wagon?"

"At the livery. What's going on?"

Tess peeked out through the curtains from my dark quarters.

"Sorry miss," Clyde nodded respectfully to her. "Emergency."

Clyde looked me in the eye, "I found your friend, Kaga. Needs a doctor and transport back here to the hospital. She's real sick."

"Can you watch the store until I get back?" I asked Tess.

She agreed, and I followed Clyde to the doctor's waiting buggy. Plutus was badly winded. I'd only seen him that exhausted one time before.

Must have been a long run. Where are the gold bags?

None of Clyde's travel bags were there, just a naked saddle.

Clyde spurred Plutus to a dead gallop. The doctor whipped his mare to keep up. Light in weight, the medical buggy was built for speed, not for carrying weight. It slid sideways on each corner, spraying mud away from us. I was impressed with the doc's skill in handling his rig.

When we pulled to a stop at the livery, Clyde asked, "Get me your new horse? Plutus is spent."

Mike, the stable keeper heard the commotion and came out to see what caused the fuss. Clyde put him to work rigging my wagon horses into their dual hitch while I saddled Thor. He filled me in while I snugged the front cinch.

"I think I found your Injun friend. She's half dead. Kept calling your name. Didn't figure no other Injun squaw would know your name. Hadda be her."

"Where is she? What's wrong?"

"I just made the crest on the Truckee Trail when I seen this small woman in the brush. Thought she was just a girl until I seen her up close. Couldn't eat or take water, kept throwing up."

"Where is she now?" I asked, knowing the Donner Crest on that trail was over three days ride.

"Nevada City. Tied her to me, and Plutus carried us down the mountain to the nearest town with a medicine man. Damn near killed him carrying so much weight. Hadda stash my gold and supplies, so we could make better time. Medical man in Nevada City said he ain't a for-real doc and sent me to Sacramento to fetch one."

I thought aloud. "Nevada City. That's a two-day ride."

Clyde corrected me.

"Not for Plutus. We left this morning, little over fifteen hours ago. Finest horse I ever had. Might take a little longer going back. I'm sending the doc ahead of us on your horse, so he can get there first. We'll follow with the wagon to bring her back to the hospital."

Thor bucked once under the unfamiliar feel of a new rider. I started to tell the doc how to handle that spirited animal, but he leaned flat against Thor's neck, easily adjusting to the horse's attempt to dislodge a rider.

"I've got him, Cole," he called down from horseback. "Did rodeo before medical school. Good animal. Lots of spirit. He's going to need it on this run."

The doctor slapped Thor's neck with reins, and the huge stallion launched into darkness under the faint light of a late-rising sliver moon.

We followed within minutes. I flicked the reins on the backs of my thick-necked geldings. Wagon wheels bounced completely airborne a couple times as we rushed out of town.

Morning light found us climbing elevation toward Auburn. Horses panted heavily under the quick pace and uphill trail. I bought them for their strong builds. Despite tiring, these horses leaned into the rigging and used their body weight to overcome resistance from ruts and bumps.

Clyde rocked from side to side as he slept sitting upright on the seat next to me. The heavily worn trail was easy for the large wagon wheels to handle. When we reached Auburn, I watered and rested the horses.

"Have you seen a well-dressed man," I asked the stableman, "on a big butterscotch stallion come through here?"

"You mean the doctor?"

"That's him. When did he come through?"

"Pretty near four hours ago. Said he was headed for Nevada City. That's a fine horse he's riding. On that animal, he might make it there 'fore dark. You boys followin' him?"

We chatted briefly and ate salted meat while my team rested. I cut their oats short because I did not want them over-eating before the hard, steep pull ahead. My team perked up in less than half an hour of limited water and with a good wipe-down by the stable man.

Our trip ran all day and into the night. I smelled smoke from Nevada City long before rounding a bend and seeing lights. It was after dark, but some people were still on the streets and gave us directions to the town's only medical clinic.

Thor stood patiently tied to a hitch post outside the small building. Still glistening in sweat, he had been ridden hard and not rubbed down. I made a mental note to take care of him as soon as I finished assessing the situation inside.

The entrance door was propped open with a wicker chair and a single lantern in the center of the far wall burned with a low, flickering flame. Shadows danced in the corners from the faltering wick burn. An old man slouched back in another old chair, his head leaning to one side and propped against the high back of the seat. He snorted and rubbed his eyes when Clyde nudged him awake.

"Back already?" he said to Clyde. "That was fast."

He groaned as he pushed up to his feet.

"How's she doing?" Clyde asked.

"Doc give her some medicine that settled her down. Got water into her and a couple bites of bread. She's real weak. Don't know about the baby."

"Where is she?" I asked with some urgency. "Wait! What baby?"

"Doc says nobody can see her right now. Can't handle the stress."

"Can I talk with the doctor?" I asked, not as a question but as a demand.

"Hang on, I'll ask him if he can spare a couple minutes."

He left the front room of the two-story house converted into a medical clinic.

I paced in anger and anxiety.

"Local medic is John Putnam," Clyde said, trying to help me pass the moments. "They tell me he was a medical corpsman in the Army. Fought in the Texas War of Independence and the Mexican-American War. Lots of miners suffer broken bones and amputations, so his skill with a bone saw and setting splints has been real helpful around here."

To tell the truth, I did not give a damn about that military medic. My only concern was Kaga's situation. I began to obsess on what little information I had.

"Clyde, what's he talking about? A baby?"

"She's pregnant, Colton."

"How'd she get pregnant?"

"You really want me to explain that to you?" Clyde asked and shook his head at the stupidity of my question.

Things did not add up.

If she's pregnant, why would Lok and Jing keep such an important fact from me?

The doctor stepped into the room. He looked worn out, shirt untucked and light beard beginning to show after a day of travel and treating the patient.

"Colton, the Indian woman is delirious. She mentions your name but does not respond to my questions. I don't think she speaks English. Do you have a way to communicate with her?"

"Take me to her, doc. She'll talk to me."

He considered my request before replying, "Okay, but don't get her upset. She almost lost the baby until I got her labor to stop. She's resting now, but I need information."

"What do you want me to ask her?"

"Most important, I need to know how far along she is in her pregnancy. She's probably lost a lot of weight, and I need to know how big the baby should be."

As the doctor led me through a long hall, he could not know how much I wanted the answer to that same question.

Chapter 47

Light flooded into the hall from a partially opened door at the far end. I shaded my eyes against the brightness of four lanterns, strategically placed to create uniform lighting throughout the whole treatment room. Kaga was on her side with the rest of her body covered by a white sheet. Her mid-section bulged where it should have outlined her thin waist. I ran my hand across her forehead, brushing several locks of hair back behind her ear. Her skin was cool and unusually moist.

"Kaga," I whispered. "Kaga, I'm here."

Her eyelids flicked but did not open.

"It's me. It's Cole. Can you hear me?"

Again, her eyelids moved but did not open.

I kissed her on the cheek and tucked another strand of hair behind her ear. A tear squeezed from her eye, ran across the bridge of her nose and dripped onto her pillow.

Hope grew that she could hear me, at least subconsciously. I leaned close to her ear.

"Kaga, I'll be here as long as you need. Just get better. And, if you need anything, I—"

She abruptly pulled the top sheet over her face.

"You talk too much, Colton," she said.

Doc pushed close to me.

"You speak English?" he asked.

"Go away," she replied. "You also talk too much, like Colton. Why do white men ask too many questions?"

I could not have been more pleased to hear her sarcastic barbs.

"Kaga!" I said without tenderness this time. "Stop acting like a child. The doctor is trying to help you."

The white sheet snapped back from her face, and she struggled to sit up on the elevated treatment table. Her legs dangled a foot short of the floor. Fire in her eyes suggested she must be feeling better.

"Do not call me child!" she said. "I saved your life. A child does not do that."

The doctor was amazed by her command of our language.

"Is your name Kaga?" he asked.

She ignored him, so I answered the question.

"Yeah, doc. She goes by Kaga Ishta."

"Miss Ishta, you came in here severely dehydrated and unconscious. I'm worried about your baby."

She placed her hand on the abdominal bulge where her lap should have been.

"Baby fine. I go."

She attempted to scoot off the bed, but I caught her under the arms. As I held her above the floor, our eyes met and locked. I could not help myself. I kissed her.

At first, she did not react to my kiss, but her guarded stoicism quickly cracked, and she responded with a passionate embrace.

"I guess she knows you," the doctor joked. "At least, I hope so. May I interrupt this family reunion to examine my patient?"

I lifted Kaga back onto the examination bed, and she began to cooperate. The doctor asked me to leave the room, but Kaga insisted I stay.

He checked her vital functions and pressed for information about the history of her recent illness.

"How long have you been pregnant?" he asked.

"Ask him. Baby his," she replied matter of fact.

"Congratulations, Mister Minar. You will soon be a father. Can you supply an accurate time frame for your child's conception?"

I thought back to our first encounter. It was nearly eight months ago. Our last intimacy would have been less than a month later before she left the Chinese town. I gave the doctor both timeframes.

Kaga ate the rest of her meal and drank lots of water. I left to care for Thor and boarded him in the stable before settling down to sleep in the big wicker chair near the door. Despite the late hour when I got to sleep, I woke before dawn. Kaga waddled into the front room. This was the first time I saw her standing with the distended belly of pregnancy. She walked with one hand pressed into her lower back as it to provide support.

My God, I thought. *She's huge!*

"Are you angry with me," she asked.

"No, I'm confused. Why did you leave me?"

She stood in front of me with her other hand rubbing slow circles on her abdomen.

"I try to protect you from white-man's hate."

"I thought we talked about that. It was not a concern to me."

"Colton, you not live like my people. You cannot know truth that we face. If I bring half-Indian child into your world, you and child will suffer. There was no other way. I left."

"I wish we could have talked."

"Nothing to talk about. We can never live together. You should find white woman who can make you happy and give you sons. I will go into forest. Teach my child Indian ways."

I thought about the widespread death and suffering inflicted on the Modoc Indians around Sacramento. It had been the subject in one of my articles. Disgruntled miners formed vigilante groups that raided Modoc camps for food and just plain meanness. White man diseases also ravaged Indian populations. Those who were lucky enough to avoid angry miners, starved to death when hungry gold seekers decimated local wildlife populations for food.

She raised a valid concern. Maybe we could not live among white society.

"If you're right, Kaga, why can't we live together in the mountains?"

Before she could answer, her eyes rolled back in her head, she swayed and her legs collapsed. I lunged forward and caught her.

"Doc!" I called for help and scooped her into my arms.

The doctor, Army medic and Clyde ran into the waiting area. We carried her back into the treatment room where the doctor and medic checked her vitals and waved smelling salts under her nose.

Kaga coughed against the terrible odor and awakened.

"You should not be walking yet," the doctor said. "Your body is still recovering. You need rest. Why did you get up?"

Kaga avoided his question. It made me feel good to know I was not the only man she regularly ignored.

"She wanted to talk with me," I said.

"If we get some food and water into you today," the doctor said to her, "you'll be strong enough to move to the hospital in Sacramento."

She pulled covers tight to her throat.

"No," she said emphatically. "I not go to white man's city. They hate Indians."

"Where did you get a notion like that?" the doctor asked. "Staff in my hospital treat all people, including Indians. You'll be fine."

Kaga leaped off the table and took a few steps toward the door. I cut her off and wrapped my arms around her.

"Kaga," I said. "Doc's right. You need more medical care in a proper facility. I promise you'll be safe."

"I won't go. As soon as I can, I run away. You will never see me again." She meant it.

"Doc, does she need to be in the hospital?"

"Well, no, but I need her in town, so I can check on her a couple times each day. She went into labor twice, and we got it stopped. She could have the baby prematurely at any time. I know a great midwife in Sacramento who can deliver the child."

I lifted Kaga in my arms and set her gently back onto the treatment table.

"Kaga, you can stay with me in my home. You won't have to go outside. Nobody will know you are there. After our child is born, I will sell the store, and we can move into the mountains. I know a couple beautiful places you might like where no white men come."

She smiled for the first time since I was back with her. It reminded me of the happy moments when we were first getting to know each other. The day passed with me cooking for everyone except Clyde. He agreed to take Thor back to Sacramento to relieve Tess at my store. Doc wanted to ride back with me and Kaga in the wagon in case she had difficulty with the trip.

People in Nevada City seemed friendlier than those in Sacramento. Several women bathed Kaga and dressed her in comfortable, white-woman clothes for the trip to the big city. She looked cute in a lady dress made wider for women with child. One lady's husband built a bed into the back of the wagon to protect Kaga from the rough ride of the heavy suspension.

The return trip took two full days with breaks for food, rest and bodily needs. I never knew pregnant women needed piddle-breaks so often, and when she said she needed to stop, she made it damn clear I only had seconds, not minutes to pull over. Doc told me this was normal, but it sure did not seem natural to me.

We arrived at my store just after dark. To tell the truth, I slowed our travel intentionally to avoid Kaga being exposed to curious locals who might frighten her with unwanted attention.

During the trip, Doc warned me that Kaga's concerns might not be without justification. In 1850, he reminded me of something Clyde told me before. California's government made discrimination against Indians and coloreds part of law. They passed a statute stripping those minorities of their right of testimony in criminal matters. Initially, it was only criminal cases, but since it passed, it had been expanded to civil law. Testimony of these people could not be heard in any court of law. Indian hatred became codified by the California government.

Clyde hurried down the stairs to help us get Kaga and her things into her temporary home. We settled her on my bed in the back room, and the doctor did one last check up before leaving for the hospital to check his other patients. I was happy that Tess's buggy was gone.

Tess, I thought. *What the hell am I going to tell Tess?*

Chapter 48

I settled Kaga while Clyde counted money from the past few days' sales.

"Store business is slow," he said.

"I lost some sales to a new hardware store on K Street. It'll pick up when the miners start coming to town for supplies."

Something was eating at Clyde. I'd been around him enough to read his moods.

"Your friend," he said, "the widow Grumman, she did a good job running the store while you were gone. Asked me a lot of questions about where you went. I acted dumb. Told her you'd be back in a day or two. She said for me to tell you she's looking forward to seeing you again."

"Thanks for keeping her in the dark. She can be pretty pushy."

"Nelly ain't her real name, you know." he said.

"How'd you know that?" I asked.

"Her real name is Tess, Tess Winslow. That name mean anything to you?"

I was embarrassed by getting caught for having spent a couple weeks living in a brothel, but Clyde was my friend, so I came clean. Told him everything.

He laughed, one of those full, belly laughs of his.

"You stupid son of a bitch. That ain't no brothel owner. Tess Winslow is the fastest lady gunfighter in the country. She's wanted for three murders in Texas."

"Naw." I did not believe him.

"Boy, you best put some distance between you and that she-wolf. She's cold blooded."

"But, I never saw any—"

"Colton, you've got to trust me on this. Tess Winslow is about as mean-spirited a woman as I ever seen. Watched her out-draw a man in a fair gun fight in El Paso."

"Fair fight? How's that make her mean-spirited?"

"Weren't the draw that was the problem. She won, fair enough. Gut shot that feller with a Baby Dragoon, only thirty-one caliber. Woman swings a pocket pistol. Lot lighter than a Navy or full Dragoon. It don't weigh nothing. That's how she beats men on the draw. She dropped this guy into the dirt, screaming in pain with her slug in his belly. She walked up to him, real casual like, and shot him between the eyes. Even after he was dead, she bent down and put another round behind his ear. Cold blooded murder."

"Why didn't they hang her for that?"

"She would have swung, but she disappeared. Your story tells me where she went. Small dust town. One local lawman. Pretty woman running a brothel. Not much chance anyone would figure out what kind of woman she really was. She shoulda stayed there."

"How did you come across her in that gunfight?"

"She was my mark. I was looking for her."

"What do you mean?"

"I told you she was wanted for three murders. One of them was my uncle. Tess shot him when he asked her to leave his farm. She was staying in their bunkhouse and wore out her welcome. Lizzie, that's my uncle's wife, said he just got back from hunting birds and had his shotgun across his arms. Tess was out back practicing her fast draw, and he confronted her about leaving. They argued."

"And she killed him?" I asked.

"Lizzie and Tess told different stories to the law. Tess said he turned his shotgun on her, and she killed in self-defense. Lizzie saw him stepping backward away from her with his shotgun pointed at the sky when she drew on him. Done the same thing to my uncle that she done to that gunman in El Paso. Shot him in the face after he was gut shot and laying on the ground.

"Tess had a fast horse and got away while the marshal was looking over the scene of the killing. Lizzie sent me a message, and I went looking for my uncle's killer. Tracked her to El Paso just as she took on that other guy. Tell you the truth, Cole, if he wasn't there, I'd be dead. She's that fast."

"If she's wanted for murder, maybe we should tell the sheriff."

"Nope. This is a blood debt between me and her. Hope you don't have no feelings for her, cause I'm going to set things straight for my uncle."

"But, you said she's faster than you. Won't she kill you?"

"She's got a weakness, Cole. That thirty-one caliber Pocket Colt is her strength, but it has a shortened barrel and small caliber. Every man she killed was gut shot first and murdered on the ground. The secret to killing her is don't give her a second shot."

He went to the candy bin and selected a piece of hard candy and returned holding a folded piece of paper.

"Cole, here's a map to where I stashed my gold and equipment. If I don't make it, it's yours."

He handed me the map.

"Hope you don't mind that I used your story-writing paper and pen to draw that. How do you keep that damn ink from running all over? Took me three tries to draw this stinking map."

Clyde got unusually serious.

"If I get killed, promise me you'll leave, right away. She's here to kill you, Cole. I tracked her all over Texas while she killed gunmen, gamblers . . . and lovers."

"Let her go, Clyde. Killing her won't bring back your uncle. You're a month away from being an old, rich man back east, just like you planned."

Clyde bit into the hard candy with a loud crunch. He winced like it hurt his tooth.

"I'd take your advice if it wasn't a blood debt. She's got to pay for killing my uncle."

Chapter 49

Mike from the livery burst into my store.

"Colton, two gunmen checked in at the livery last night. They talked about which one of them was gonna kill the Maker of Angels. Knew your real name, too, and asked me where they could find you. I told em you was out of town on business."

"Do you know where they're staying? I'll tell the sheriff."

"They're bedding down in my stable—big hay bin in the back. They tried to stop me from leaving, until I told them how bad I needed to piss. I headed toward the outhouse and run away as soon as I was out of sight. I ain't going back 'til they're gone. Mean looking men."

"Thanks for the warning. I'll find the sheriff, and he'll get them out of town. You stay here until they're gone. There's fresh coffee in the back room. Clyde, can you get him a cup while I fetch the sheriff?"

Plutus made quick work of the blocks to the jail.

"Hi Randy. Where's the sheriff? Got some trouble down at the South Town Livery."

"He's not here, Colton. What's the problem?"

"Damn. When will he get back?"

"Not until tomorrow. Took the riverboat down to Stockton. They caught Junior Jenkins, and they're holding him in jail for us. I'm deputized. Can I help?"

This young man served the sheriff most days, but I questioned if he would be able to handle these skilled killers. I took a chance and explained the problem. He said he would tell them to leave town right away and suggested I keep a low profile until they were gone.

When I entered my store, Clyde stood in front of the counter tying the leg strings of his forty-four.

"What the hell are you doing?" I pointed at his sidearm.

"Got a problem. Them two boys at the stable, they're the Macon brothers. Jeff and Jethro. Got no regard for the law," he said and put on his hat as he headed out the door. "Sheriff's going to need back up."

He was gone before I could tell him that the sheriff was not coming, and the lawman would just be a wet-behind-the-ears kid. I ran into my room and grabbed my gun.

Outside, I saw that Clyde took Plutus, so I yelled to my neighbor that I had an emergency and needed to borrow his horse. As I approached the stable, I heard two quick gunshots.

I leaped off my neighbor's horse just as Clyde was dragging the deputy out the barn entrance. He laid the boy behind protection of the heavy wood livery door. I could not tell if the deputy was alive or dead. His heels had left two ruts in the dirt, and he was clearly unconscious.

I ran to Clyde's side with my gun cocked.

"Clyde, what happened?"

"Ballsy kid ordered them to leave town. When they laughed at him, he tried to put them under arrest. One of them shot him twice before I could get involved. Boy staggered to me, and I dragged him out here."

Kid looked real bad. Close range shot to the left chest and another in his lower abdomen, both bleeding badly.

"Cover me," Clyde said and leaned up against the stable entrance.

"Jeff!" he called inside. "I know Jethro's too stupid to understand what you boys just done. That was a deputy sheriff he shot."

A voice inside called back.

"Who the hell are you? How do you know our names?"

"We go way back, fellas. Clyde Hamlin."

"Gunfighter Hamlin?"

"That be me. You boys are in a heap of trouble. Better hope this kid don't die."

"He tried to grab me," a different voice said.

The first voice reacted to his brother. "You stupid idiot! I told you your temper was gonna get us hanged some day."

"Nobody arrests me," the second man said.

Clyde called in, "Jeff, you don't have to hang for Jethro's killing. Why don't you come out here so we can talk?"

"Got nothing to talk about, Clyde. He's stupid, but he's my brother. Stand away, and we'll ride out of here. Besides, the guy we're looking for ain't even in town."

Clyde surprised me.

"Sorry Jeff. He's going to jail. If you try to stop me, you'll go with him."

"When did you start siding with the law, Clyde?" Jeff asked.

"Ain't got no love for the law, but this is my town, and you shot one of my people."

I could hear some rustling inside and subdued talking.

"We're coming out, guns holstered. You ain't no lawman, Hamlin. If you shoot us, you'll hang. If you try to stop us, it'll be the last thing you do. Everybody knows Jethro's faster'n you."

Clyde leaned back to speak to me so they could not hear him.

"They'll draw on us. Jethro is fast and left-handed. I'll take him. Jeff will draw while he's talking, trying to catch you listening. Go on his elbow, like I taught you, even if he's talking. Put your gun away, or they'll start firing before they clear the horses."

He shoved his Colt into its holster, slipping it in and out a couple times to make sure it was loose. I copied him.

"We're holstered. Don't ride out. Walk your horses, and keep you gun hands in sight."

"Coming out."

I stepped away from Clyde to spread their targets.

Neither man looked like talented gunmen. Both wore dirty clothes, heavy beards and strange hats that looked more like rags tied on their heads than shade providers.

I knew instantly which man was which by the right and left-handed holsters.

"Always knew it might come down to this, Clyde," Jethro said. "Hate to kill you. You best back away while you can. Who's your friend?"

He nodded to me.

"They call him the Maker of Angels. He's faster than I ever hoped to be. And, he's faster than you, Jethro. Drop your holster real easy and turn around."

"Yeah right," Jeff said. "So, you can shoot us in the back?"

"You know I ain't never shot a man in the back, Jeff. Watch out for him, Cole. He always draws when he's talking. Now, boys, use your non-gun hands and remove your weapons."

"Ain't going to happen," Jeff said. "You should—"

In mid-sentence, Jeff's elbow bent.

I stepped a half-step right and sent my first shot into Jeff's left chest, a perfect heart shot. His bullet pounded the ground a few feet in front of me as my second bullet entered the side of his neck spinning his head around farther than a human neck is supposed to turn.

Simultaneous gunshots from Clyde and his opponent rang out, but Jethro must have been slightly faster, and he knew the sidestep trick. Clyde's round blew a hole between the gunman's sleeve and shirt, but did not take him down. Jethro aimed his second shot at Clyde just as I was about to fire my third bullet in a rapid sequence into Jeff. Instead, I jerked my gun at Jethro just as my palm released the hammer. I hit him high on his right chest. His bullet puffed up dirt in front of Clyde, and I unloaded the rest of my rounds into his body as he fell forward.

"Cole, I'm hit."

Clyde pressed his gun-hand against his right thigh. Blood gushed between his fingers.

"How bad is it, Clyde?"

"Ain't shot too bad, but damn bullet hit the same thigh where I just healed up from that argument with Sanchez. Son of a bitch, it hurts more this time. Mighta got bone."

People had been watching from safe vantages, attracted by the first shots when the deputy was hit. After they saw the second gunmen collapse, they ran to our aid. The young lawman was loaded into a small buckboard and rushed to the hospital. Several men tended to Clyde.

Chapter 50

Next day, the sheriff came to the store to speak with us. Eyewitness accounts said Clyde saved the deputy's life, and that we tried to take the shooters into custody.

"Dave's going to survive," he said, "thanks to you, Hank. Yeah, I know your real name is Clyde, but to this community you're Hank, so why don't we keep it that way? The boy's alive because of you. I don't care about what you were before you came here. You're welcome to stay as far as I'm concerned, that is if you want to. I'm sure I can get the politicians to agree. Dave is the son of one of the councilmen."

He shook Clyde's hand and turned to me.

"Colton, I like you son, but I've got a problem. Found this in the saddlebag of one of the dead men."

He handed me a folded sheet of cheap paper with printing that rubbed off on my fingers. It was an article torn from the local newspaper. The title read, *Maker of Angels*. It extolled the speed and deadliness of a local gun fighter named Colton Minar. Said he killed as many as five men in one showdown, but it failed to give credit to anyone else, like Clyde, or to mention shooting in self-defense. It made me look like a hardened gunfighter.

"We talked about this before," the sheriff said. "You knew hotheads might track you down trying to make a name for themselves. This is a real problem for the community."

I did not know what to say.

"Wasn't the boy's fault," Clyde said in my defense. "If your damn reporters did not hang that nickname on Cole, nobody would be looking for him."

"I know, Clyde. I'm on the boy's side, but his reputation is out now. Even the witnesses to that stable shooting are spreading wild rumors about his speed. Heard them talking about it this morning. A barber on Front Street said Colton fired six shots, reloaded and fired four more before the first guy hit the ground."

"That's ridiculous," Clyde said. "Cole shot a full load, six rounds in all."

"Don't you think I know that?" the sheriff responded. "I counted the damn holes. Darn good aim, too. Every shot was lethal. You're good, Cole, but you're attracting killers to our city. I think you know what that means."

"No, sheriff, why don't you say what's on your mind?" I asked in anger.

"Colton, you can't live here. Too much risk for this community."

I hated to hear what I knew was coming next.

"Sell your store and disappear, boy. I'll break it to Isabel in a letter. She was real sweet on you. Course, I suppose you already know that."

I almost laughed aloud. Isabel was the least of my concerns.

"What if I buy the store from him, sheriff?" Clyde asked.

"Like I said, Clyde, you're in good stead with city leaders. They'll accept you back. Already talked it over with the ones who control the council. They agreed with me, although, we all think you should keep 'Hank' as your name. No sense in inviting more gunfights to town."

Clyde rubbed his sore leg.

"Sheriff, what if this Maker of Angels got killed? Some unknown kid, or maybe a drifter, gets caught up in the spectacle of taking down a big name gunfighter and bushwhacked him?"

"What are you getting at?"

"Put up a marker in the cemetery, here lies Colton Minar, gunfighter called Maker of Angels. Get one of your writer friends in the newspaper to plant a story about some kid who shot Cole in the back and vamoosed out of town. Didn't even get his name."

The sheriff tipped his hat back and rubbed his forehead.

"You know, Clyde, that just might work. What will you do for a living Cole? If you lose the mercantile, you're going to need some way to support yourself."

Clyde chuckled, "Don't worry about that. He gets money every month from his publisher in the east for stories he writes."

"That's right. I forgot you're a writer. Don't know if the local paper is looking to hire another journalist, but maybe I can get them to give you some work. You'll need a new name and a life story."

The sheriff thought about that last issue.

"Then, again," he said, "if you're as good a writer as Clyde says you are, you won't have any trouble crafting that background bullshit."

"By God, this could work," he said and left abruptly.

Chapter 51

Clyde limped along behind the sheriff. He put up the Closed-for-Lunch sign and locked the door. Then, he grabbed a chunk of taffy, and sat on a bench on customer side of the counter.

"Why'd you close up? Lunch isn't for another two hours."

"I know, but we need to talk."

I'd never known Clyde to be so serious.

"Cole, what are you going to to about Tess? I'm in no condition to deal with her right now."

I had not given thought to Tess since I left to get Kaga. Even after Clyde's revelation about Tess's real persona, I had more on my mind than her.

I replied truthfully.

"I know how she handled it the last time I ended our relationship. I'm hoping she'll be different this time, now that she has all that money from Grumman."

"Why do you think the money will make a difference?"

"I don't know. She's got more to lose now. If she gets caught hiring killers or attempting to hurt me herself, she risks being hanged. Besides, there are lots of young men she could have."

"You don't get it, do you, Cole?"

"I guess not. What do you think she'll do?"

"Ego drives that woman. It drives all cold-blooded killers. She's no different than Jeff and Jethro, just a lot prettier. Gunfighters think they can kill and get away with it. If you deny her what she wants, you're dead."

Clyde pulled out his gun and turned the cylinder checking each chamber to make sure it was fully loaded.

"What about you, Clyde? Did she recognize you when you relieved her?"

"Naw. She still don't know I was ever stalking her. Hell, she thought I was going to steal from you when I come back and took over the store. She warned me that she counted all the money, and if I didn't give you exactly the right amount, she would report me to the sheriff."

We both laughed.

"Funny, huh?" Clyde added. "Bitch is a killer, wanted for three murders, and she threatens me like she's a fine, upstanding citizen."

I forced a stern face.

"You didn't steal from me, did you?"

"Wha . . .?" He took me seriously for a second, then said, "Yeah, stole you blind. Asshole!"

We did not know it, but Kaga was listening to our conversation. She parted the curtains and stepped into view while lifting her large abdomen with one hand.

"Colton," she said in a quiet voice. "You must stop killing. If want me and our child stay with you, you put away gun."

I put my arm around her and guided her to the stool behind the counter. She was too short to hop onto it, so I lifted her up and gently placed her on the cushion.

"I understand, Kaga. Clyde and I worked out a deal with the sheriff to give me a new identity. These gunmen will stop looking for me if they think I am dead."

"Who Tess?" she asked.

I reminded her of the men she helped me escape by crossing the desert and explained their relationship to Tess. She thought for a minute.

"You love her?"

That caught me off guard.

"No, of course not."

"You love with her, recently. In that room."

She pointed to the curtained entrance.

I exhaled long and hard.

"Yes, I did," I told the truth. She obviously figured it out, although, I will be damned if I knew how.

"Smell white woman in bed. Wear sweet smell."

I did not say anything, uncertain which woman's scent she detected.

Kaga leaned forward and wrapped both arms around her abdomen in pain.

"Baby, not happy," she said.

I scooped her into my arms and carried her to bed. She rolled on her side and relaxed.

"Better now. Thank you."

I leaned down and kissed her on the cheek.

"Cole," she said almost in a whisper. "Do you want white woman?"

"Huh? What do you mean?"

She took my hand and placed it on her breast, holding it tight with both her hands.

"You make baby with her. I never give you white baby."

"I hope my child is just like you, Kaga."

What the hell is it with women? I thought. *This insecurity thing is even cross-cultural.*

As I left the room, Kaga called to me.

"Colton. Leave gun here. It bring trouble for you."

I removed my gun belt and hung it on the peg above my dresser by the door.

She smiled contentedly and rested her head on my pillow.

Chapter 52

Clyde had waited patiently while I finished dealing with Kaga.

"Where's your gun?" he asked.

"Hanging on the wall. She asked me to give up killing. I'm not sure she understands that I don't go looking for trouble. It's been coming to me."

"Probably not a good idea to stop carrying until after we get that new identity set."

"I know, Clyde, but I made a promise. I've got to keep it, or I could lose Kaga again. I can't let that happen."

"You ain't gonna do her, or that kid, no good if you're dead."

We sat there in silence for a few minutes while I contemplated his words. My thoughts broke when the doctor peeked through the glass and knocked at the front door. I unlocked the entrance, and he came in accompanied by a middle-aged woman wearing a full-length, black dress with a high-neck collar and puffy sleeves. She had a formality about her.

"Colton, this is Mrs. Miller. She is the most experienced midwife at the hospital. I asked her to accompany me to meet Kaga. I explained the situation. She understands Kaga's fear of the white man's world. When it comes time to deliver the baby, Mrs. Miller provides a level of expertise that will help assure a healthy mother and child."

After I exchanged pleasantries with the midwife, the doctor took a minute to bring Clyde and me up to date on the recovery of the deputy sheriff. The boy was going to make it.

Kaga did not like Mrs. Miller. She refused to talk to the woman and slapped the midwife's hand away when she attempted to lift Kaga's covers to feel the baby through her abdomen. No reassurance from me or the doctor assuaged her distrust of the midwife.

"Well, I guess I'll have to handle your delivery myself," the doctor said to Kaga. "At least premature labor stopped. The baby will arrive within the month if everything goes well."

Clyde was waiting when we came out of the back room.

"Hey doc," he asked. "Do you think it's safe for Cole to leave for a few days?"

"Of course. The baby is still a ways off. Why do you ask?"

"I need Cole to go pick up some things for me that I left up the mountain. They're a couple days' ride from here, and I can't go with this bad leg."

Clyde explained after the doctor left.

"I'm kind of nervous about the gold I stashed on the mountain. Can't travel with my leg like this," he patted the thick bandage on his thigh. "Would you mind taking that map and getting my stuff for me? I'll watch the store, and doc will be here twice a day to check on Kaga."

I agreed and explained to Kaga what we were doing. She was comfortable with Clyde, so I grabbed my gun belt and prepared to leave.

"You promise. No gun." Kaga frowned.

"You're right," I said and replaced the weapon on the peg.

She smiled, and I left almost immediately, traveling light so I could move fast.

It was an easy trip. I gave Plutus his head and let him set the pace, especially during the long uphill grades. Clyde hid the gold and his travel gear behind a couple large boulders with thick brush between them. I recognized the location by the detailed drawing he made. It was amazingly accurate.

Clyde missed his calling, I thought. *Should have been an artist.*

Despite easily recognizing the location, he had shoved the gear so far under the bushes that I could not see it, even up close.

The last time I reached blind under a bush, a rattlesnake bit me. I shoved my rifle under the brush and wiggled it before reaching for the gold bags. Plutus handled the weight of the gold with little trouble. Going downhill for eighty miles was a lot easier, even with the extra weight, than our uphill trip.

Plutus and I rested as needed and slept at night until the moon came out, making the trail safe to ride. I approached Sacramento in less than four days for the round trip. It was nice to see the city in the distance from the Auburn Ridge. In a few hours, I could give Clyde his money and I would see Kaga again.

My spirits soared and Plutus seemed to share my eagerness as he increased his pace noticeably. I let him run in the rolling grassland east of the city. Plutus loved the wind in his face. His head extended as far forward as he could reach while the power of his chest and shoulder muscles rippled against my thighs. Wind blew his blonde mane in my face, and I imagined us leading the big annual horse race in Saratoga Springs. What a magnificent beast.

We slowed upon entering the city, but he acted restless, like he wanted more of that unconstrained feeling. I patted him on the neck.

"Be patient, my friend. I'll make sure we take more runs like that real soon."

People noticed Plutus. He stood out, walking with pride and high-stepping naturally. He belonged at the head of parades, dressed in fine linens, decorative head mask and bejeweled saddle. I thought about offering the sheriff a good payment for that fancy saddle I saw in his barn. It would be perfect.

We rounded the final corner onto my store's street when I saw an unwanted sight. Tess's buggy, parked at my mercantile. I was not sure what to expect, knowing Clyde's feelings about the woman.

Tess came out of the business just as Plutus and I stopped. Clyde hobbled behind her on his crutch. Neither of them seemed upset.

"Hi Cole," she called out and waved. "It's so good to see you. Hank told me you were on a business trip and not expected back for another day."

I wished now that Plutus and I had been a bit slower crossing that grassland. This chance meeting might have been avoided.

Tess reached to stroke my horse's nose, but he reared up and snorted, front hooves slashing the air in front of her.

"Whoa, boy." I yanked his reins, backing him away from Tess.

She let out a fragile yelp of fear and cowered as she stepped back.

Plutus spun in a circle, stamping the ground, and let out several hard blows. I tightened his reins forcing a submissive posture. He settled down but kept turning to look at Tess.

"That animal is dangerous!" she shouted. "He should be put down."

"He's never done that before," I said in his defense. "Maybe he doesn't like you."

Damn good judge of character, I thought.

"If you and I are going to spend time together, that beast better stay in the stable, and if it ever attacks me again, I'll shoot him myself."

I was tempted to set her straight, right then and there, but I knew she might get crazy again. Besides, I promised Clyde I would try to keep things quiet until he healed.

"You don't have to shoot my horse, Tess. I'll keep him away from you."

Tess got really angry.

"I told you to call me Nelly. How many times do I have to repeat it?"

"Sorry, Nelly. I'll keep Plutus away from you."

"Good," she said with a satisfied tone and started back up the stairs to the store.

"Where are you going?" I asked, knowing I had to prevent her from meeting Kaga.

"I want to spend time with you. You ARE coming inside, aren't you?"

"No. I'm on the way to the bank to pay off a note. Then, I'm picking up supplies." I lied.

"Clyde, can you fetch the money for the last four days? I'll put it in the bank while I'm there."

Clyde motioned a salute to me and disappeared into the store.

"Can't it wait?" Tess demanded.

"No. Ever since I killed robbers a few months ago, I have an agreement with the sheriff to keep our cash locked at the bank. Don't want to attract more trouble to the city."

"That's nonsense," she blustered and started back down the stairs. "I'll talk with the sheriff about it. He should not be telling you how to run your business."

"Maybe it's a little overkill, but if I want to remain in this town, I have to play by their rules. You should know how that works, Tess . . . uh, Nelly."

Clyde clomped down the stairs swinging a canvas bag of fake money from his crutch handle while Tess climbed into her buggy and released the wheel lock. He swung the bag of river rocks up to me, and I hung it from my saddle horn.

"Good day to you, Mrs. Grumman," I said, knowing the formality would annoy her.

Plutus trotted around the corner toward downtown. We did not get one full block when Tess's buggy raced by and cut us off.

"I'll be back in the morning," she shouted. "We're going to talk. You'd better be there."

Tess whipped her poor horse unmercifully and rushed out of sight around the next corner.

My fake trip to the bank was no longer needed, having served its purpose, so I turned around. I tied Plutus behind the mercantile. Clyde had built a small water trough and hitch pole out back so he had options for leaving a get-away horse close to his trap door.

"How long was she here?" I asked when I entered the store.

"Not long," Clyde said. "She wanted to wait for you in the back room, but I told her you wouldn't be back for a couple days. Bad timing, you showing up when you did. I think she's on to something."

I made a couple trips out back to get all of Clyde's gold sacks, then we sat at the counter on the tall stools.

"Clyde, why do women get so bossy when you get familiar with them? Sweet as pie until you get close, then it's like they become a stranger."

"Wish I knew, Cole. Wish I knew."

Chapter 53

"She beautiful," Kaga said as she stepped through the curtains.

I hopped off my stool and lifted Kaga onto it.

"Lakota call woman like her 'wee yahn oo zee zee dkah.' It mean 'woman rose'. Very pretty flower, but when red petals drop, nothing but ugly thorns left."

It amazed me how intuitive Kaga could be.

"I'm afraid you're right, Kaga."

I slipped my arms around her from behind. Not seeing much benefit to talking about Tess, I changed the subject.

"How are you feeling?"

She lifted her blouse enough for me to see the baby's movement and reached for my hand. I was amazed at the activity I felt through her bare skin.

"You feel baby?"

My jaw dropped as my child pushed against my hand. I swear Kaga's skin stretched two inches outward, and the outline of the baby's foot was as clear as day. Each tiny toe showed as a light dot on the stretched skin. Kaga affectionately rubbed her hand on top of mine.

Clyde was watching and said, "Purty real now, ain't it Cole?"

This was the first time I really felt excited about my approaching parenthood. I was not prepared for it. It carried an oppressive weight, but feeling my child move inside Kaga made it all very real.

"She come soon," Kaga said.

"What? You called the baby 'she.' What if it's a boy?"

"Not boy. You not happy for girl?"

"How do you know it's a girl?"

"Baby ride high. That mean girl. Boy-baby stay low and drop early."

I did not have any idea what she was talking about. Pretty sure, I did not want to know.

"Cole, you want that white woman?" Kaga asked.

"No, of course not. I told you that before."

"She give you life I cannot."

"Kaga, I don't want the life she offers. Not now, not ever."

"Then, why did you have love with her recently?"

It was a fair question, one I had been asking myself.

"I wanted a life with you, but you left me. I had nobody. I was lonely."

She leaned back in my arms and said, "I never leave you, again."

Chapter 54

Tess did not come back the next day as she said. I did not mind. Putting off the ugly scene I expected, gave me time to prepare my new name and identity.

I decided to go by my childhood nickname. It came from my middle name, Jon. I was a tall, skinny kid and playmates made jokes out of Cole, things like "Cole the bean pole." So, I started telling people my name was Jon and all the teasing stopped.

My best friend's last name was Childs.

Jon Childs, I thought. *That'll be my new name.*

My fictitious persona grew up in Rhode Island, outside Providence. I knew that area well and could hold my own if anyone familiar with the area asked questions. Journalism would remain my occupation, because people in the west did not know me that way. Figured my publisher would have no problem with my new "pen name" because of all the death threats that came after my article about white man's bigotry.

Things were starting to look good. I explained to Kaga why I would need to change my identity. She thought it was silly, but agreed to play along.

Clyde's leg got a bad infection, and the doctor had to cut out some festering tissue. When it still did not improve, Kaga offered to use one of her Indian poultices. I told him about her bear claw wounds, and how the doctor's remedies failed, but her herbal treatment worked. He accepted her offer.

Kaga removed his bandages and carefully scraped away dead tissue with her knife. After exposing the pink skin of the healing site, she removed the doctor's stitches and parted the incision with her knife. It smelled terrible.

Herbs from several pouches mixed with water to form a thick red-brown paste that she worked as deep as possible into the wound. It hurt like hell, but Clyde bit down on a thick towel to prevent screaming. When she was done, she washed off the outside area and wrapped his thigh tightly in rolled strips of clean burlap. He helped himself to several long swigs of whiskey.

I helped Clyde into bed in the storage room. Kaga was exhausted from her effort on his behalf, and she quickly fell asleep in my bed.

Several hours passed while I tended store and added content to my latest newspaper article. Within a week, I would leave this store forever, and become a new person. It was all set. The sheriff confirmed the arrangement. Everybody was on board with the plan.

Then, Tess showed up.

She entered the store in her finest gown, billowing full under multiple layers of petticoats. Make-up powder around her eyes added pleasant cheek shadows. If I did not know the truth about her, I would have been instantly smitten with this beautiful lady.

"Did you miss me?" she asked quietly.

"Not really," I answered bluntly.

"I needed time to think about our future. Cole, I want to try one last time to make amends to you. I'm sorry I threatened to shoot your horse. I understand how close a man can get to his horse. I was just angry. Will you forgive me?"

She walked toward me in a casual, yet intentionally seductive, way.

"Tess, there's nothing to forgive."

"Oh good, I thought—"

"That's the problem, Tess. You never think. You just react. There's no way I could live with a person who I never know if she's going to love me or have me killed."

"I'm a passionate person, Cole. You, of all people, should know that about me . . . and I'm passionate about you. Life with me will never be dull. I promise."

I took in a deep breath and decided this must be the time.

"Tess, any relationship we had is over. I'm not interested in anything you have to say."

Here it comes, I thought. *At least, there's no China here for her to throw, and she can't heft fifty pound sacks of grain . . . at least, I hope she can't!*

Tess's face flushed. Her eyes opened wide, and her breathing increased forcing her breasts to swell in the uplift of her corset. Veins on her neck protruded.

"It's that little bitch, isn't it? Is she here? Damn it, she is here, isn't she?"

Tess stepped around me and ran through the curtains into my room.

Kaga had a blanket pulled up tight against her chin.

The crazy woman never slowed to see who was in my bed. She leaped onto Kaga and began pummeling the future mother of my child with both fists.

I grabbed Tess around the waist and lifted her into the air. Feet and legs flailed wildly, and she screamed obscenities before making death threats against her perceived competition for my affection.

Kaga sat up and grabbed the knife from its sheath next to her bed. Still half asleep, she slashed at Tess, driving her sharp blade across the sole of an expensive shoe. I spun Tess away from Kaga to protect her from the Indian's anger and skill with a knife. Tess continued to scream, but Kaga quickly understood the situation and backed up on the bed as far as possible from the melee.

"What's going on?" Clyde parted the curtains.

"Grab her feet," I shouted.

Clyde dropped his crutch and secured one of Tess's legs under each arm.

She kicked and twisted trying to break free from our holds. Her hand reached over her head and clawed at my face. This went on far longer than any wrestling match I saw in college. It was amazing how much stamina she had.

When Tess stopped fighting, she went limp in our arms.

"If we set you down, will you behave?" I asked.

She still thought she had jumped on Isabel and spoke over her shoulder to her foe.

"You can have him, you little whore. I've been rejected by this pig for the last time. Just wait, as soon as he finds another little tramp, he'll leave you, too."

Clyde released Tess's legs. She got her balance and looked around me to say something else, but was caught short when she saw a very pregnant Indian woman.

"Who's that?" she asked.

"She's my friend. Staying here until she has her baby."

"But . . . but she's an Indian. Why would you let—?"

She caught herself.

"Oh my God. Is that the squaw who helped you kill those two men in the desert?"

"I didn't kill anyone in the desert."

"Zeke and his brother. The Indian guide with them made it back barely alive. Said you salted their water, or did she do that?"

"No. I did it. They wouldn't be dead if you didn't send them after me."

Tess sneered. "Where did you learn a trick like that, city boy? Injun training?"

Tess brushed off her dress and refastened loose braids of hair using long needles that had held them in place before the altercation.

"Well, I guess this is goodbye, Colton," she said with disconnected coolness.

As she stepped, the heel broke off on her shoe where Kaga had slashed it. She stumbled, and Clyde caught her. Removing both shoes, the irate woman batted the curtain to one side, but spun around instead of walking through. Her eyes darted wildly, and her cheeks flushed red.

"Colton! Is that your half-breed kid?" she asked and pointed at Kaga's belly.

"I think you'd better leave, Tess. Nobody wants you around."

"It IS!" she said. "Now, it makes sense. You did it with this heathen, and now you're stuck with her half-animal, half-human spawn. Oh really, Colton, you could have done so much better. Even that little cowgirl was at least civilized."

Tess laughed maniacally as she left the store.

"That's one nasty human being," Clyde said. "I'm going to settle my affairs with her one day, real soon."

Chapter 55

"Are you okay?" I asked Kaga.

She leaned back against the wall with her arms wrapped around her abdomen.

"Baby active. She good. White woman not hurt me. Just surprise."

I was still secretly hoping for a boy.

"He must be as tough as his momma," I said with a smile.

Kaga caught my use of the male pronoun and shook her head at my hopeful choice.

"I gotta lay down," Clyde said. "Leg's killing me."

Fresh blood seeped through his bandages. He must have opened his wound during the scuffle. Kaga followed him into the storage room and gently pushed him down on his bed where she removed his dressings.

"Cole," she called to me. "I need more cloth, my medicine bag, and water."

Within a short time, she cleaned his injury and applied more poultice. Clyde remarked that it did not hurt nearly as much this time. He did use the excuse to imbibe more whiskey.

That night, while they slept, I put the final touches on my article about native remedies for infection and how they accelerated the healing process. Eastern medical professionals would challenge the worth of my observations, so I did not offer explanations, only observed results.

Early the next morning, the doctor looked at Clyde's thigh and was astounded by all evidence of infection gone. His open wound had mended up to the surface layer of skin.

"Where did you get these bandages?" he asked.

Clyde told him everything.

The doctor entered my room to check on Kaga. After giving her a good report about the baby's progress, he asked her about the poultice. His tone was very respectful, and he took notes while they talked. Her terms for the ingredients were all Lakota Sioux words, and she was unable to provide descriptions of the plants that could positively identify them.

"After the baby comes, would you be willing to teach me your knowledge?" he asked.

She nodded, an agreement I did not expect. She must trust him.

Three more days passed without trouble from Tess. I began to hope she was done with me, until the sheriff stopped by.

"Cole, you seem to know the widow Grumman. What can you tell me about her?"

"Is there a problem, sheriff?"

"Not sure. She stopped at the bank a couple days ago and withdrew all her money. Had a tough-looking hombre with her. From the teller's description, the guy's clearly a gunman. He's packing a modified Navy thirty-six, wears it low and tied tight on the leg. I'm worried that she might be in some kind of trouble."

Clyde heard our conversation and limped into the storefront. I was not sure how much to tell the lawman when Clyde solved my dilemma.

"Sheriff, I know Tess Winslow from way back."

"Tess Winslow? I thought her name is Nelly Grumman."

Clyde proceeded to tell the sheriff the whole story, including my part.

"Why didn't you boys tell me about this earlier?"

Clyde said, "I was planning to settle my uncle's affairs myself, but you folks give me a fine welcome in this town. This is the first real home in my life. I been thinking about that all week. It ain't right for me to take advantage of your trust. She's your problem now, sheriff. What are you gonna do?"

The sheriff considered all the information before deciding his course of action.

"Let's hope she left town. I realize there's no telling what she'll do with her history, but until someone sights her, I'm going to assume she's gone. If she does show up here, will you boys sit tight, and let me deal with her? I don't need any more gunfights in town."

"Yes, sir," I said, "but what if she doesn't give us a choice?"

"In that case, you boys do what you gotta do. Since you told me about her, I'll stand up for you, even if she forces you to defend yourselves or your property. Let's hope it doesn't come to that."

It felt good having someone else to worry about that evil woman. Now, I can wait for the birth of my baby and slip quietly into my new identity.

Chapter 56

Tess had vanished. Banker told me the farm she contracted to buy along the Cosumnes River reverted to the bank when she failed to show up for the settlement meeting. A wanted poster showing sketches of her and the unidentified gunman circulated around town. They were only wanted for questioning, so no reward was offered.

We pretty much stayed in the store as the sheriff requested. When I had to pick up freight from the riverboat, I kept my trips short and never wore my sidearm. I will admit, I felt naked without my gun, but a promise is a promise to both the sheriff and Kaga.

I got back from a freight pick up and Kaga was behind the counter waiting on my stool. How she got up on it, I don't know, but she can be a determined little woman.

"White-man bed too soft," Kaga said.

"What do you want me to do about it?" I replied with playful sarcasm.

"Fix it. Now!"

For a fleeting second, I thought she was serious, but she could not keep a straight face.

"Let me unload the wagon first."

It was hot outside. I removed my shirt and tossed it on the counter while several customers negotiated with Clyde over flour prices. An older woman, looking at bulk cloth, stared at my bare chest.

"Ma'am, I apologize for working shirtless. I know it's uncouth, but it's so darned hot outside, I hope you can forgive me. If you want, I will put my shirt back on."

"I've seen worse, young man. Most men who remove their shirts are an assault on a lady's eyes. At least, you have a nice body that does not offend this old woman's sensibilities."

She nodded and turned away. I think she took a quiet pleasure in what she saw.

Kaga grinned.

The store made up for early season slow sales when miners began accumulating gold and swamped us looking for equipment and supplies. Clyde excelled in deal making. I could see why he made so much money in less than five years.

I stacked new bolts of cloth that just arrived from San Francisco near the front door. The old woman immediately sorted through the flowered prints, thrilled to be first to see the new colors and designs. Bundles of exotic hardwood slabs went into the back room. They came from South America as prepaid goods for a fine-furniture maker in Lodi. Round trip delivery to his shop would take most of a day, and there was some urgency to the delivery. The craftsman enquired about his product every week during trips to Sacramento.

"Kaga, I need to take that wood to Mokelumne City, down near Stockton. Will you be okay if I am gone for the day? Clyde will be here."

"No problem. Doctor come later. Baby not come for few more weeks."

I discussed the wood delivery with Clyde and he assured me the business would be fine in my absence. His leg felt great since Kaga's remedy healed him, and he promised to keep an eye on her.

After loading the dense hardwood, I headed south, out of town.

It was a typical hot, dry Sacramento summer day. I took it easy on the horses, letting them set a comfortable pace on the dusty trail. About half way, I stopped at a public horse trough to let them drink. Mokelumne City was one of two ports with deep-water access allowing ocean-going schooners to dock, but my mercantile was the only store with overseas connections to fill his order. Otherwise, the wood could have been shipped directly to his town.

Mid-afternoon became hotter than normal. Heat exhausted me by the time I unloaded his hardwood.

"Thank you very much, Colton. The project waiting for this wood is worth a small fortune to me. You've made me a happy man."

"You're welcome, Michael. We're happy to be part of your success."

"Tell you what, son, I have furniture that needs to get to Sacramento. I'll pay you to back-haul it to my showroom. It will save me a trip and put extra money in your pocket."

Get paid to ride back to Sacramento versus enduring the heat for free? Easy decision.

We loaded as much furniture as my wagon could handle without over-taxing my animals.

The trip back was slow. Sun had baked the trail all day making it unusually hot. I unhitched my wagon near the Elk Grove stagecoach stop to let the horses wade through a shallow stream. After cooling their hooves and lower legs, they kept a good pace the rest of the trip into the city.

It felt good to unload the furniture. I thought about things I might buy for Kaga with the unexpected money. She never asked for anything, making it difficult to shop for her. Knives always caught her attention, so did hard candy in the store, but she could have anything she wanted from the store. I had to find something special.

Daylight was giving way to evening shadows when I turned in the horses and wagon at the livery. Plutus greeted me with his usual happy nudges, and nickering. We headed for home.

As I came around the corner, a large crowd stood in front of my store. The sheriff's horse and doctor's buggy were tied to the rail, along with a couple more animals I did not recognize.

The crowd parted to let me pass. I tied Plutus to the rail and spanned three steps at a time to get to my front door. Dozens of people packed the aisles between stacks of goods. They stopped talking when they saw me.

Curtains to my personal quarters were bunched to one side on the curtain rod. The sheriff talked with two people I recognized—one, a doctor from the hospital, the other, an undertaker.

I shoved people aside. The sheriff saw me coming and moved to intercept.

"Cole, where have you been?" he asked, more in urgency than inquisition.

"Just delivered a load of supplies down south. What's going on?"

I started past the sheriff, and he grabbed me.

"Don't go in there, son. Come with me. We need to talk."

"Is Kaga okay?"

My fear grew.

"Cole, come with me," he spoke firmly and grabbed my elbow.

I shoved the sheriff aside, pulled from his grasp, and forced my way into the room.

The table rested on its side against the wood stove. Clyde leaned back on the base of the trophy wall, his eyes open and locked in a stare to nowhere. Blood ran from behind his ear onto his collar where it soaked into the fabric of his shirt. A circular patch of blood surrounded a single hole in the lower abdomen of his shirt. His gunfighter-Colt lay on the floor next to him.

I picked up his weapon and sniffed it. It had been fired. A divot in the floor planks matched the impact of a large caliber bullet. I turned the cylinder. One round was missing.

Covers hung off my bed and scattered splashes of blood suggested a fight. The blade on Kaga's knife was broken half way up with only the handle and shank remaining.

The sheriff put his hand on my shoulder.

"Colton, your Indian friend is not here. We're trying to find her."

Chapter 57

"Tess was here," I said.

"How do you know?" the sheriff asked.

"Clyde told me."

"He's dead. What are you talking about?"

I told the sheriff about Tess's trademark way of killing. Clyde was gut shot and then assassinated. Tess's work.

"You're right, Cole. We have an eyewitness to Tess leaving. She took Kaga with her. The strange man Tess had with her at the bank was also with them. Your Indian friend's hands were tied, and he pulled her along with a rope tied around her neck."

"Let me talk with the witness."

The sheriff called a neighbor to the counter. I recognized him as a regular customer. The man was highly agitated and spoke quickly.

"That pretty lady—the one that helped you run the store a couple weeks ago—she drove up in her buggy. Then, that other guy, he looked like one of the gunman you killed in the big gunfight. That guy rode up on a horse. He was trouble. I could see it."

The man choked up until the sheriff consoled him, and he could continue.

"The pretty lady wasn't afraid of the gunman. Seemed to know him. They went into the store together. Maybe five minutes later, I heard a gunshot. It might have been two shots, but they were so close together, so I couldn't tell for sure. Bout two minutes after that, there was another gunshot. Then, the pretty lady and the ugly man come out with an Injun squaw. Her hands were tied, and he pulled her along with a rope around

248

the neck. They tied the Injun in the back of the buggy and covered her in a blanket. That squaw was pregnant."

"Which way did they go out of town?" I asked.

"Headed east, toward the mountains. That gunfighter mighta been shot because his left shirt sleeve was all bloody."

"How long ago did they leave?"

"Two hours, maybe two and a half."

"Thanks," I said and went back into my room.

I took my gun and belt off the peg and began putting it on.

"Colton," the sheriff said. "You can't beat them by yourself. Let me deal with it."

I ignored the sheriff, and kneeling by Clyde, I used my thumb and middle finger to close his eyelids. "Thanks for everything, buddy. I'll take care of your uncle's blood debt."

The sheriff blocked my exit.

"Get out of my way," I said.

"Give me your gun, son. I'm not going to let you get yourself killed."

"I'm going to get Kaga. Step out of my way, Marcus." I slipped the hammer loop off my gun and used my thumb to cock the hammer. "Sheriff, I've done everything your way up until now. I'm going to finish it my way. Step aside."

My feet spread slightly wider than my shoulders. The palm of my hand hung in the air an inch above my gun handle. I would not allow the sheriff to waste any more of my time.

"Kid, if you don't let me handle this situation, you will not be able to come back to this city. Cole, I like you. Don't go after them yourself. I'm deputizing a posse. Join us."

"I said, step aside!"

He relented.

I galloped away from the store on Plutus, following Tess's wagon ruts to the edge of town. Kaga had taught me to track. I could see that the gunman followed the wagon. His horse's prints laid over those of the buggy's horse and wheel ruts.

Headed due east. Truckee Trail, I thought.

I pushed Plutus, slowing from time to time to verify her trail. Last light faded, and I knew they would lay up at least until moonrise after midnight. It was too dark for me to continue, so I hung a feedbag on Plutus with oats from my grain sack. He drank half my water. I'd been up this slope several times recently, and I knew my horse would need to stay fresh. I hoped Tess and the gunman would not take such care of their animals.

I had trouble sleeping but closed my eyes to rest as best I could. When the first light from a sliver moon hit the horizon, I saddled Plutus and headed into Auburn on my way to Nevada City. At daylight, I stopped in the same stage rest where I watered last month. The keeper recognized Plutus. Ground here was rocky, and I could no longer be sure that sporadic wagon wheel impressions I saw were those of Tess.

"Nice horse, mister. Saw him a few weeks ago. I believe a doctor was riding."

"Good memory, I loaned him to the doc. Hey fella, I'm looking for a pretty woman in a buckboard traveling with a tough looking gunman. Have you seen them?"

"You must be talking about the marshal. He's traveling with a beautiful redhead and a prisoner, Injun squaw wanted for murder back in Texas. Said the good looking woman is his wife, although that don't make no sense to me. What would a handsome woman like that find attractive about such an ugly man?"

"He's not a marshal, and the redhead's a killer. The Indian is a hostage."

"Really? I traded three horses for the buggy and his quarter horse. Buggy's out back."

"May I see it?"

The tarp used to conceal Kaga was still in the back of the wagon. I checked it for blood. There was none, but several drops of blood were smeared on the quarter horse saddle.

"Did you hear where they are going?" I asked.

"Said they're headed to Texas. Needed fresh horses to make good time."

"How far am I behind them?"

"Not more than forty-five minutes."

"Good. I have to run them down."

The stable keeper looked at Plutus as my horse drank from the water trough.

"If any horse can catch them, that one can. They're riding a roan, a paint and a big quarter horse. None of them critters can hold a candle to that stallion of yours."

I tossed a gold coin to the man, far more money than was due. It was thanks for his detailed information.

Fortunately, long grades with infrequent water stops on Truckee Trail would slow their travel. I had to be careful not to run up on them too fast. With Kaga's life in the balance, I had no room for mistakes. Surprise was essential.

Chapter 58

After four hours of pushing Plutus harder than I wanted, I caught sight of the three-horse caravan. Tess rode the largest animal, a big quarter horse. The gunman rode the roan and led Kaga's small paint by its reins. Her hands were tied together around the saddle horn, and her feet were bound to the stirrups. A red bandana wrapped tightly around her head and was wedged in her mouth. She swayed in exhaustion as the horse walked carefully along the rocky path.

I kept my distance and searched ahead for ambush points.

They bypassed the turn leading down into the town of Grass valley, but I was in luck at dusk, when they turned down into Nevada City. Tess stopped at a small hotel off the main road through town. All three went inside. The hired gunman came back out a short time later and walked their horses to the local stable.

Good. They're spending the night in town.

I resolved that this had to end right here. It would be too difficult to handle both Tess and the gunman on the open trail.

After waiting until nearly midnight to enter town, the stable keeper remembered me from a few weeks before. I took a chance and told him why I was in town.

"Mister, please don't have no shoot out in my barn. I can't afford to pay for any dead horses."

"What about the sheriff? Think he will help me?"

"Might, if he's sober, but that ain't likely. Most folks in this town hate Injuns and don't want to get involved in gun fights, especially to save a squaw. You're on your own."

"Mind if a sleep in your hay bin?"

"Suit yourself. You got food?"

"No, left town too fast. I ate some jerk meat in Auburn this morning. Is there any place to get food at this time of night?"

"Come with me. Wife made too much stew. I'm sure we can spare some."

After a hot meal, I leaned back in the hay and wondered how Kaga was being treated. I wanted to break down the door to their room and set her free, but they could easily use her as a shield in that setting. It would be best to catch them in the open, on foot.

Morning came quickly after a night of fitful sleep. The eastern sky was already getting light when I rinsed my face in fresh pump water. I practiced deep breathing like Clyde taught me and checked all the chambers in my gun. I tightened my leg ties, and in case Tess got away, I saddled Plutus and tied him to a rail next to the hotel. He would be out of sight, but quickly available.

I leaned on the corner of a clothing store one building over from the hotel and chewed on a long stalk of hay.

Tess came out of the hotel first and walked across the wood walk into the street. She wore full-length, button-front riding pants and a simple off-white blouse under a light gray, tight-fitting vest. A Colt Baby Dragoon rested loosely in a cut-down holster on her hip. Clyde warned me about her weapon choice. That gun could clear the holster in less time than mine could be drawn. I hoped he was also correct about the poor accuracy of the Baby Dragoon's shortened barrel. She wore the gun at the perfect height in relation to her arm length to give her the fastest possible draw.

She'll get the first shot, I thought. *I have to get the killing shot.*

My heart jumped when Kaga stumbled out the doorway having been pushed by the gunman behind her. Her hands were tied in front of her. When he stepped in sight, he was holding a rope tethered to her neck. For the first time, I actually wanted to kill a man.

The gunman looked familiar. I suddenly recalled him as an Apache Indian tracker who lived in Tumbleweed. The last time I saw him, he was with Zeke and his brother when they tracked us across the desert.

253

He wore a Colt Navy, thirty-six caliber gun cradled in a deeply modified holster. Clyde taught me that the Navy model would be very accurate, but its long barrel would be a slower draw. It was hung too low on his hip, a flaw that would cost him a fraction of a second. On his left chest, a silver and gold marshal's badge made him look legitimate. I knew it was a fake.

To my great relief, Tess motioned for them to join her in the street, and they walked casually toward the livery. Overconfidence dripped from her posture. Smug in her belief that she got away with yet another murder, even the hammer loop for her sidearm was still in place.

They were a hundred feet away when I strode into the street directly blocking their line of travel. I squared to face them and lined up on Tess. Gunfights normally came at closer distances, but after Clyde explained that Tess's shortened barrel made it hard to hit a target beyond fifty feet, I chose this greater distance for our confrontation.

If my appearance surprised Tess, she did not show it. She was a true professional.

"Well, look what we have here," she said.

"Let the girl go, Tess. She has nothing to do with us."

"No? Why do you think I took her with me? I knew you'd follow."

"I'm here, so let her go. If you want to kill me, here's your chance, but let the Indian go."

"You should have seen your pathetic friend beg not to die. Stupid fool tried to draw on me. Poor dumb man was too slow. You can't beat me either."

Just like Clyde told me. Good fighters try to get into your mind to disrupt your reflexes with emotions.

"You murdered a good man with a shot to the side of his head. That's the only way you can kill a man. You're not good enough to do it with your first shot. You can't aim worth a shit."

"We'll see about that when you're rolling on the ground."

"You plan to murder me, too? You're sloppy, Tess. That's going to get you killed this time. I don't miss."

The gunman stepped behind Kaga to use her as a shield.

"Kill him, Tess. Kill him now," he shouted.

"You can't win, Cole. If you draw on me, he kills your whore and your half-breed kid. If you draw on him, I kill you, even if you get him. Then, I finish off your Injun and spawn. It's a no-win for you."

So cold. So calm. So confident, I thought. *I have to get into her head.*

"I never told you the real reason I left you, Tess," I paused as she visibly tightened. "You weren't good enough. Just a two-bit whore in a dust town. I used you and dumped you. You never meant a thing to me."

Redness spread across her face.

Tunnel vision narrowed my view to her elbow, watching for the slightest movement.

"Kill him, damn it, or I will!" the Indian guide called out.

The gunman was cracking. Tess knew it. I knew it. His panic would force our draws.

Tess's elbow moved.

DEAN SAULT

Chapter 59

Tess drew. Her muzzle flashed at the same instant as mine. Clyde's side-step technique saved my life as Tess's bullet grazed my left hip, hardly a lethal shot.

My aim was true, but I had not aimed at Tess.

The head of the gunman holding Kaga snapped back with the impact of a forty-four caliber slug entering his right eye socket. He dropped Kaga's tether and fell onto his back.

Kaga dropped to the ground.

Tess took a step toward me, trying to close distance to gain accuracy. Muzzle flash from her gun came at the same instant that I fired at her for the first time. Despite the distance, her bullet found its mark, impacting my lower abdomen. Oddly, I felt no pain, yet knew I had been hit. I kept firing as fast as I could stroke my gun's hammer.

Shells-on-the-tree practice with Clyde by the river taught me to empty my revolver quickly, making every shot count. Tess's body jerked with each of the next four rounds that slammed into her central torso in rapid succession. She fell forward, face bouncing hard on the dry dirt. Rolling onto her side, her dying act was to squeeze off one last shot—at Kaga, only a few steps away.

I tried to go to Kaga, but fast-growing gut pain dropped me to my knees. I saw Tess's body laying facedown in thick street ruts, blood seeping from under her chest to pool in wagon wheel tracks. The fastest female gunfighter in the country finally paid for her crimes, but, at what cost to me?

"Kaga!" I called out. My vision faded to black.

Chapter 60

My eyes took a minute to focus. Across the room, a woman slept in a chair next to a tall dresser topped in metal tools of some kind. Her head rested against the wall behind her. Bright lights forced me to cover my eyes. I tried to sit up, but excruciating pain forced me back down.

"Help," I said with an unexpectedly hoarse voice. "I can't get up."

The woman stirred.

"Ma'am, please help me."

She wore an odd-looking triangular white hat, a white uniform and carried medical equipment in her pocket. My call woke her, and she jumped to her feet.

"Mister Minar, it's good to have you back with us." She patted my arm. "I'll be right back. Don't try to get up. Let me get the doctor."

Moments later, strange faces surrounded me. One, obviously a doctor, took charge while others on his staff followed orders.

"Doc, where am I? Where's Kaga?"

"You're in a Sacramento hospital, Mr. Minar. Do you recall what happened?"

"Not sure," I said and told the doctor everything I remembered. "Kaga was on her knees holding her hands across her stomach. Is she okay?"

They told me I had been unconscious or delirious for almost two weeks. It seemed like I just closed my eyes and woke up.

"Where's Kaga? I want to see Kaga."

The nurse whispered to the doctor.

"Mr. Minar, I have been informed that your Indian friend left the hospital two days ago. She left against our recommendation."

I tried to rise.

"You can't do that, Mr. Minar. Your abdomen was damaged by widespread infection. If you rupture your stitches, the infection could spread. Please stay still."

"Need to find Kaga."

I persisted in trying to rise.

"Here drink this," the doctor said. "It will stop the pain."

I sipped a nasty tasting fluid. He was right. I felt no pain because that medicine knocked me out.

Each day, the medical people reduced my "pain medication" and gradually broke the news to me that Kaga had taken a small caliber bullet in the belly. The baby's body saved Kaga by stopping the bullet.

"I was told you are the father of the child. Is that correct?" the doctor asked.

"Yes. She was my baby."

"She?" he asked. "The infant was a boy. The sheriff gave him a proper burial in the city cemetery. I certified that your son was a Christian and white, otherwise they would not have allowed a heathen or Indian-blood to be buried there."

I do not think I ever thanked the doctor for his kindness. In hindsight, I wish I had.

For the next three weeks, they cared for my infection and helped me to get back on my feet. Kaga had been gone for a month, and if the fall rains started, it would make her trail impossible to follow. I was anxious to get going.

"Howdy, Colton." It was the sheriff. "Sorry about the loss of your son. What name would you like me to have them put on his grave marker?"

I thought for a moment.

"His name is Douglas Clyde Minar. Douglas was my dad's name, and you knew Clyde."

"I'll see to it his name gets engraved right away."

He fidgeted with his hat, rolling it along the brim in his hands.

"Colton, what are you going to do with the store. It's been closed since the . . . well, you know."

"Since Clyde died," I finished his thought. "Did someone give Clyde a proper burying?"

"Yeah. Mortician wanted his money, so I paid it for you. Wasn't sure you'd come back alive, but I could sell the store to pay off the city and casket maker. I'm sure you understand."

"I've got plenty of money. I'll pay his debts."

"About that money, my wife and I cleaned up the living quarters for you while you were unconscious. We took the mattress to be cleaned and found your gold stash under the bed. I never dreamed you were rich. I put your gold and some cash from the safe in the bank. It's waiting for you."

"Thanks, Marcus. You're a good friend."

"What are you going to do with the store?"

I sensed an agenda to his inquiry.

"Why do you ask?"

"Nice fella owns that new hardware store on K Street. Told me to tell you, he'd be happy to buy out your inventory at full wholesale if you decide to leave town."

"I've got some thinking to do. I'm sure you understand. Doc says I can get out of here in a couple days. Thanks for looking after me and the store."

I got out of the hospital on a Friday. The sheriff and his wife picked me up in their personal buggy, because the doctor asked me not to ride a horse for another month. Fall settled in and colored leaves began to blow along the sides of the streets. Chill from mountain air settled into the valley making me worry about Kaga. How was she handling the cold? I guessed that she went east or south to find wilderness where she could live. Thankfully, fall rain was late this year.

The store surprised me. Everything was neat, much more so than when Clyde and I used to keep it. Counter tops shined with recent polishing. They looked almost new. At the end of the counter, I saw my Colt forty-four and holster.

"Thought you might get rid of that while I was recovering," I said to the sheriff.

"Won't lie, Cole, I was tempted, but that's your decision. You know you're welcome to follow through with that false identity. Word spread real fast about you gunning down Tess Winslow and her sidekick. San Francisco paper used that "Maker of Angels" name in their article. Even sent a reporter all the way to Nevada City for eyewitness quotes. I suspect more gunmen will be coming to town, looking for you."

I spun the cylinder of my gun. All chambers were empty. I smelled the muzzle and it still smelled from the gunfight.

The sheriff's wife spoke hesitatingly.

"I hope . . . I mean . . . your Indian friend came by here while I was cleaning. She asked if she could leave something for you. I put it on the table in your room."

What would Kaga leave me? I wondered.

I pulled aside the curtains and saw two of her handmade animal skin pouches leaning against each other at the midpoint of the table. Opening the first, I saw it full of familiar dried purple flowers. The special meaning of those flowers brought a feeble smile. Most of the truly meaningful moments of my life happened with the scent from those tiny flowers.

The second pouch puzzled me. I shook its content onto the table. It was Kaga's bear tooth necklace. I touched my version of the same good luck charm. The large canine tooth made a noticeable lump under my shirt.

What does this mean?

Was it an ominous message about the future? Had our bond ended?

"What is that," the sheriff's wife asked.

"Bear tooth. Kaga gave it to me from a bear we killed. This one was hers. I have the other long tooth."

I pulled my own tooth from under my shirt and held the teeth side by side. She grimaced at the threat represented by such large teeth.

"In her tribe, a bear tooth brings good luck. Guess it didn't work."

Both necklaces went back over my head and produced two lumps under my shirt. I noticed the rawhide cords were different lengths making Kaga's tooth hang higher than mine.

"What's in the other bag," the sheriff asked.

I sprinkled a few of the flowers in my hands and breathed deeply on them before pulverizing them in my palms. I held out the result and suggested they smell the purple mash.

"That smells wonderful," the sheriff's wife said. "What do they call those flowers?"

"The term 'baby flower' is what Lakota call them."

The sheriff's wife smiled. She got it. Her husband took the meaning literally, like I did.

"Is that because they're so small?" he asked.

His wife elbowed him in the side. "I'll explain it at home, Marcus."

I spread a handful of bullets next to the flowers thinking, *Doc says I can't wear my gun, but there's no reason I can't clean and load it.*

"Thank you for the ride from the hospital. It won't be necessary to initiate that fake name. I'm leaving Sacramento. Please tell Mark Hopkins he can buy my entire inventory. I'll make him a great deal. I'll be leaving as soon as I can ride."

I ignored the doctor's advice and attempted to buckle my holster belt. It hurt too much.

Chapter 61

While my wound healed, I used the time to settle my affairs in Sacramento. The new hardware store in town bought my inventory, and I sold the building to my furniture-builder friend from Mokelumne City. He was thrilled to set up a real store in the big city and agreed to let me live in the back room until I was ready to leave permanently.

It felt odd having my days free from responsibilities. I still could not ride Plutus, but the stable owner hitched up my wagon every morning and dropped it by the store, so I could get around. I got to the point where my gun belt and holster felt good, but the doctor cautioned me not to push too fast with my recovery. Think he suspected I was secretly practicing my fast draw. He was right.

This morning, I got up before light, fixed coffee in Clyde's old pot. Yes, I learned to like coffee, and heated a pan of gravy to pour over last night's pan-biscuits. Nothing tasted right. I partially closed the damper on the stove and tossed a glass of water onto the remaining red embers. Steam billowed from both the draft vent and the cooking grill on top. Most of the coals vanished through the ash grate into the catch tray below.

Clyde's supplier of dried salmon delivered a bundle of meat wrapped in butcher paper for travel. I stacked two blanket rolls in the wagon, along with bags of water, grain for Plutus and everything I needed for travel. The door to my life in the mercantile closed for the last time.

It was still dark when I got to the bank.

"Mister Minar," the bank manager shivered in the cold by the front door. "How are you feeling this morning?"

"Feeling fine, Mr. Howard. Appreciate you asking. Mighty cold this morning. Thanks for opening up early for me."

"Yes, it is cold, and you're welcome," he replied as he unlocked the bank's front door.

Once inside, he lit several lamps and opened the main vault.

"Your gold is in this bin. We can convert it to US currency any time you wish and mail it to you when you establish a new home. Just send me a note. For security, here is a secret account number to include in any letters you send. This will authenticate your instructions."

He handed me a printed piece of paper.

"If you lose this, I will need a code word to positively identify you."

I thought for a moment. It had to be a name I would never forget and one that would identify me without question.

"Maker of Angels," I said.

He paused before writing it on the sheet.

"Yes," I said. "I'm sure. Maker of Angels."

He wrote it down.

"Do you need a little money to tide you over in your travels?"

"Yes. Five hundred in US currency."

He immediately started counting cash.

"And, that bag of gold."

I pointed at the largest of five bags filled with the precious metal.

"Mr. Minar, may I dissuade you from taking that much gold with you? Gold is heavy for travel and that is a small fortune. Very tempting for bandits."

"Why don't you let me worry about that. I can handle myself."

I patted my gun.

"Yes sir," he said, and his shaking hands accidentally dropped the pile of bills.

Was his nervousness over my weapon, or maybe my reputation? I really did not care.

He followed my directions and split the heavy gold into two smaller canvas bags, so I could lift either one without worrying about tearing my gut.

Light began to show on the horizon as I left the bank. My next stop took me to the livery. Plutus was saddled and ready to go as I requested. The owner tied my horse's lead rope to the back of my wagon.

"Here you go, my friend," I said and handed a twenty-dollar US note to the stable keeper.

"Sorry, Colton, I can't make change for such big currency."

"No change due, Mike. That money is my way of thanking you for all you've done for me. I don't need Thor, either."

I handed him a piece of paper.

"Here's a note of sale. You own Thor now, and all his tack. He's a good horse, so long as you let him know you're in charge. If you don't, he'll kick your ass."

I chuckled and slapped the reins on the backs of my wagon team. As I pulled away, he called out to me.

"When you coming back?"

I ignored his question, because I had no answer.

My last stop this morning gave me pause. I'd been here every day since I got out of the hospital, but this might be my last visit to the cemetery . . . and my son.

The sheriff's wife promised me she would care for Dougie's grave for as long as she lived. I loved what she did around his headstone, a white stone cross with his name carved in it. His date of birth and death were the same. She planted little flower bushes around the base of the marker and tied a small child's doll to one arm of the cross. Amazingly, the plants held delicate blooms despite the fall leaf-drop and morning chill.

I kneeled next to the outline of his burial hole and ran my fingers along the dirt strip where grass had not yet filled in. Mom's death was the last time I cried. Dad taught me to be a hard man, so I did not cry at his funeral, although I choked up and left the crowd of well-wishers, so I could make my own peace with him.

Tears filled my eyes. I fought them back. Despite never holding my child, I felt a heavy loss. He was more than my son, he was part of Kaga, the only person I'd come to love since my parents passed. My head nodded. I said the only prayer I could remember. It was a child's blessing mother forced me to recite every night before bed. It felt right.

I opened a small pouch tied to my belt and poured little purple flowers in my palm. Without crushing them, I sprinkled them along the length of his tiny grave. Most filtered into the short grass, but one petal caught in a light breeze and tumbled along the ground. A small brown bird with blue spots on its belly hopped along, pecking at the flower. Every time it tried to catch the fluttering petal, it missed and flapped it wings in frustration.

The antics of the little bird made me smile. I thought how my son would have enjoyed such simple entertainment by nature.

Leaving that cemetery was tough. I wanted to stay, but told myself there is nothing more I can do for him. My concern was for his mother.

Chapter 62

Early morning risers were starting to mill about as I left town. A few waved to me, not the normal greeting, though, it was like they knew.

The wagon ride to Old Dry Diggins was slow and easy. Some of the grades up the foothills were pretty steep, but I was in no hurry. I let my team set the pace and followed directions the miner gave me when he paid for the credit that I extended when his family stayed in the Fairgrounds. I felt sorry for him when his little girl died, but I think I had a better idea now of what he felt.

Around noon, I pulled up in front of a log-built home on a ridge overlooking a deep, heavily wooded ravine. Fog prevented me from seeing the bottom of the vast chasm, but the view was every bit as magnificent as he claimed.

"Hello!" I called out.

The front door of the house opened. Out came two of the man's younger boys and the mother I met in the refugee camp. She looked older now, worn by a hard life and undoubtedly beaten down by the loss of her child.

"Mister Minar," she said with a smile. "It's good to see you. Would you like to come in and sit a spell? Robby, run down the cut and get daddy. I'm sure he'd love to see our friend."

The boy disappeared over the rim of the canyon at a dead run.

"Malcolm's checking traps for small game for dinner. Been a little sparse lately, but we're making a living selling tanned fur skins and apple pies."

"Apple pies?" I asked. "I didn't know there were apples in these parts."

"Best in the country," she said with pride. "I sell apple pies and apple pastries to help out. Do you like pie?"

Within minutes, I consumed a quarter of the best deep-dish apple pie I ever tasted. Her husband barged through the front door, carrying a load of empty steel traps.

"Colton, it's so good to see you," he said and dropped the traps by the door. "I said you would always be welcome in my home, and I meant it. I see you've discovered my wife's wonderful cooking."

"That I have, sir. You're a lucky man."

"We have very little, but all we do have, we owe to you. My baby girl was so right when she called you our guardian angel, bless her soul."

It still hurt him as much as it did back then. He choked up for a moment.

"She's buried on the crest, over yonder, looking down on her favorite valley."

I tried to be thoughtful, "I'm sure it brought her peace."

"So, Colton, what brings you so far up the hill?"

I did not want to burden them with my recent life changes, so I told them a small lie.

"Had a customer die, and he did not have any kin. Before he died, he asked me to give his savings to the most deserving family I know. I brought you his leavings."

The wife lifted her apron to her mouth and began weeping.

"I'm sorry. Did I say something wrong?" I asked.

Malcolm sat hard onto a cut log seat.

"We ain't asking for no charity, Colton. I appreciate you thinking of us, but it feels like a give-away for poor folks."

I had to think fast.

"I didn't think of you as poor folks or for charity. I saw how hard you worked, and you paid back the store credit like an honorable man. That's why I came up here."

He looked confused.

"I'm leaving the area, maybe for a long while. I need someone I can trust to take care of his money for me, but I don't want you to sit on it. I want you to put it to work. Turn his life savings into more money and take care of as many people as possible. Would you be willing to do that for me?"

He looked at his wife and back at me.

"I wouldn't know where to start making that money grow. We are barely getting by on my trapping and her pie sales. How would I make that money grow?"

I ate the last bite of my pie and an idea hit me.

"How much do you get for a pie?"

She said, "Two-bits for a small pie and up to four bits for a big one."

"How much profit is in each pie?"

"Profit?" he asked.

I explained markups and production costs to the family.

"That won't work," he said. "We don't have enough apples. Besides, she can only make three pies a day."

"Can you buy more apples?"

"Yeah, but we don't have money to buy apples and flour. Besides, her small oven can't handle lots of pies, like you're suggesting. Sounds good, but it's just not possible."

I excused myself and brought in one of the bags of gold. I dumped it on the table.

"Oh, my Lord," she said.

"Take this money and buy all the apples you need. You've got a big level patch of land on the left that would be perfect for building a baking shed. I figure you can make fifty pies a day. Think you can sell that many?"

She was quick to see the possibilities.

"I can make that many pies, but we need a big market to sell them and that's down the hill in Sacramento. We've no way to carry them to market."

I took her hand, "Come with me. You too." I pointed at Malcolm and led them outside.

"That wagon . . . it's part of the deal."

I reached behind the wagon seat and lifted out the second bag of gold.

"Here's the rest of my friend's money. There's plenty to buy all the apples you need and to build a proper cooking room. You can have everything running by next year's apple harvest. How hard are you willing to work, Malcolm? It'll take you and your sons until next summer to build this commercial cooking room. Should be done in time for the first harvest."

Malcolm got excited.

"Do you think it might be okay if we bought some orchards? That would cut our costs a lot, if we owned the trees."

"It's up to you, Malcolm. All I ask is that you make this money grow and use the surplus to take care of your family and do good deeds for others. That's what my friend would want."

Malcolm dropped to his knees and sobbed. His wife buried his face in her apron and tears flowed down her cheeks.

"Mister Minar," she said, "we could never dream of such an opportunity. Our baby was right. You are a guardian angel."

I could not take any more emotions. This day drained me. Dad's stoic personality made sense to me now. It was so much easier in life to not feel.

Without further discussion, I loaded Plutus for travel, carefully mounted him, and left.

I found out many years later from the retired sheriff that the place Malcolm dubbed Apple Hill became the largest apple supplier and pastry bakery in the county. As the boys grew up, they built farms near their mom and dad and cultivated vast areas with apples and pears. The entire family donated heavily to charities like the Foundling Home in Placerville, and they set up the first medical treatment facility in that area for displaced miners.

Chapter 63

At nightfall, I entered the Chinese town on the river. They greeted me like family.

Yip Jing maintained the typical reserved temperament of his people, showing minimal emotion, yet I could tell he was glad to see me.

"Can you stay the night as my guest?" he asked.

"Thank you, Jing. I'm real tired and sore."

It was true. Riding in the wagon was not bad, but I had to keep reining in Plutus because it hurt my gut when he took up any gait other than a walk.

"Your friend came through here last month," he said.

"Kaga?"

"Yes. She did not seem well."

"You knew she was pregnant, didn't you?"

"Yes, but she demanded I not tell you. I wanted to, and I asked her permission, but she insisted. Please forgive me."

"I understand, Jing. She can be hard-headed woman."

He was noticeably relieved that I was not angry.

"Thank you for your hospitality. You should know, I will not be here in the morning. I have to keep moving. Was she on horseback?"

"No. She walked and carried a blanket roll on her back."

"Thank you, my friend. I think I know where she's headed, but I have to track her because I can't find it by myself."

271

The sister of my dead Chinese friend entered the room carrying a tray of hot tea and rice wrapped in seaweed. I was famished and ate everything on the plate.

Sleep came fast, but I woke well before first light. Plutus was restless, too. We rode out of town under a full moon. The trail south was easy until below Stockton. I stopped at each of the rancheros along the way, hoping for a report of a Kaga-sighting. There were none, but that did not surprise me. With her distrust of white men, she would stay to cover and circle around populated areas.

If I was going to track her, I would need to think like her.

Plutus kept increasing his pace, and I was feeling better each day, so I gave him looser reins.

The bear we killed held no more flesh, having been skinned by someone and the bones picked clean by scavengers. I stopped at the ranchero where we had spent the night. The owner remembered me and Kaga. He offered a room and food, both of which I accepted gratefully. At dinner, I caught my first break.

"One of my men spotted an Injun squaw down by the river. You met him. Bradley. Your squaw friend tried to save his brother."

"Where's Bradley? May I talk with him?"

The rancher sent a Mexican house servant out to the bunkhouse to fetch the man. We talked about the cattle business while we waited. Then, Bradley came in and sat across from me.

"Good to see you again, Texas Pete."

How the hell did he remember that fake name?

"Sorry for not trusting you when we first met, Bradley. My real name is Cole, Colton Miner."

The rancher stiffened up in his chair.

"You from Sacramento," he asked.

"Yes, sir. Why?"

"Does the name 'Maker of Angels' sound familiar to you?"

I grimaced.

"You don't act like a killer, boy. How'd you get that label?"

272

I really did not want to get into that right now.

"It's a long story, sir. Truth is, I never wanted to kill anybody, but they kept coming to pick fights, fights I didn't want. Every one was shot in self-defense."

"Thrity-four dead men? That's what they're saying down here."

"No sir. Not nearly that many. Rumors make it out to be a lot more than real."

Bradley had been listening intently.

"Shit, so you IS a real killer?" he said. "Damn, never would a guessed."

The rancher said, "Makes no difference to me. When a man tries to save the life of another man, he's okay in my book. Just one question."

"What's that?"

"I've never seen a fast draw. Would you mind showing me before you leave?"

"Would if I could, but I was gut-shot couple a months ago, so I can't move at full speed. How about if I show you some target shooting, and leave out the fast draw? First, I need some information from Bradley. I heard you saw an Indian squaw by the river recently."

"Yeah. Same squaw you was with when that bear attacked. She was digging clams on the river. Saw the shells on the ground after she seen me and run away. Just wanted to talk to her, but she disappeared into the brush. That Injun didn't even leave a track, and that was in mud! Thought I was seeing a ghost, but empty clam shells said different."

"When did you see her?"

"Two weeks ago. Had a blanket role on her back. Looked awful hungry."

I turned to the ranchero owner.

"I've got to get some sleep. Meet me by the back corral at first light, and I'll do some shooting for you. Then, I've got to hit the trail."

I woke up before light, but I made a promise, so I hung around. While I waited, I tested my abdomen. Practice quick draws lacked the explosive speed I had before the gut shot, but I figured it would still impress the rancher. I collected some targets from around the barn.

With extra bullets, caps, cap grease, and my gunpowder pouch lined along the top fence slat, I prepared my demonstration. The rancher showed up with a plate of flapjacks, sausage, and a cup of coffee for me.

"Thanks. I can use a good meal before heading out. You ready for a fast draw lesson?"

"Let's do it. Probably wake up the bunkhouse, but screw em. They'll just get more work done with the extra waking hours." He laughed.

I began the same way Clyde started with me.

"The first thing about fast draw is to learn to shoot from the hip. It's a lot faster than a full draw and aim. Watch that fence post."

I drew and fired three fast shots, all dead center and grouped within three inches of each other on the corral's corner fence post.

"Good Lord!" the rancher said. "That was less than two seconds."

A group of cowboys rushed out of the bunkhouse right after those shots, some pulling on gun belts over underwear. One of them wore his belt different than working cowboys do. He watched me closely.

"See those bucket handles and the curry brush on the fence?"

I wanted to get going, so I made quick work of the second demonstration.

I positioned as if I was facing a real opponent and drew. Items flew half way across the corral, being smashed by large forty-four caliber slugs.

The rancher whistled, impressed with my accuracy and speed.

I began to reload, so I could leave. To my surprise, my abdomen did not hurt at all.

"That's the fastest draw I ever saw," he said. "I can't believe you've got such accuracy without using a sight."

"I had a good teacher."

"He ain't that fast," one of the cowhands said. "I'm faster than that."

Oh crap, I thought. *Is this idiot going to be a problem?*

"You probably are, cowboy," I said to the one wearing his gun lower than the rest. "I'm really not that fast."

"You're that guy they call the Maker of Angels, ain't you?" he said.

Bradley scrunched his face, knowing he did wrong by telling the men in the bunkhouse.

"Nope," I said. "That must be somebody else."

The rancher stepped up to diffuse the situation.

"John, I'm not paying you to stand around jawing with my guest," he made a sweeping movement with his hand. "All of you . . . get some grub and head out."

They milled about for a moment and all left but the one hothead. He stood his ground, staring at me.

The rancher stepped between us, "John, you're new here. If you want to keep this job, you'll get your ass moving."

The man still did not move.

"Now!" the rancher ordered.

Again, the idiot stood his ground.

"Collect your pay, John. Get your things out of my bunkhouse. You're done here."

"Come on, Mister Black. I didn't mean nothing. He's staring me down. Guy's looking for a fight."

Amazing, I thought. *What's wrong with this jackass?*

The cowhand stomped away.

"Sorry, Colton. He just started here a week ago. He's already picked a couple fights, and I was getting ready to let him go, anyway. This was his last chance."

"I understand. That's what I was telling you. Idiots like that force the issue. I don't want to fight anyone."

"Why don't you give him a half hour to get down the road before you leave? I don't want you to run into him in the open. Let's get some more grub before you go."

I agreed and relaxed for almost an hour despite wanting to get back on Kaga's trail.

Chapter 64

My abdomen felt good, so I let Plutus achieve a full gallop for almost a mile as a test. I felt fine.

Two weeks behind a woman on foot. I thought. *She's got no more than two days before I intercept her. What will I do? What am I going to say?*

I had no idea.

Less than half an hour later, a bullet whistled over my head. Where did it come from? Who fired on me? I looked back in the direction of the gunfire sound.

Pretty obvious. The idiot's tracking me, but where is he?

I cut Plutus into a nearby thicket and dismounted. The river was in sight and low, having dropped during the recent drought. I ran along the sandy shoreline where I could cover ground quickly without being seen from the southbound trail. I used a heel-toe step that Kaga taught me for moving quietly.

The man's horse snorted. He was on the other side of a blackberry thicket that separated the river from the trail. I continued downstream looking for a game trail or opening where I could get back to the trail and come up behind the bushwhacker.

A deer drinking at streamside spooked. I watched where it penetrated the brush and followed its lead.

I came up behind the gunman. It was the hothead from the ranchero. His horse sensed me sneaking up and got agitated, but this genius smacked his horse with the reins demanding that the animal settle down. Reading animal warnings was obviously not his strength.

He stood in his stirrups holding his rifle and looking over some dense bramble that provided his cover.

Waiting until I got very close, I cocked my revolver. He stiffened in response to the recognizable metallic click.

"You wouldn't shoot me in the back, would you, mister?"

"Never know, do you, cowboy? Toss your rifle in the blackberries."

He did not react, so I fired a bullet past his ear. The horse reared up, and the rider tossed away his rifle at the same time.

"Get off your horse."

I must have gotten his attention. He instantly followed orders.

"Mister, please don't kill me. I was just trying to scare you."

"Why would you do that?"

"You got me fired at the ranch. I wanted to make you afraid. I could'a killed ya, but I didn't."

"You're more generous than me. I enjoy killing," I said trying to put the fear of God in this idiot.

"Please mister, give me a chance. I won't bother you again. I promise."

"Take off your clothes."

"What?"

"Take off your clothes and put them in your saddle bag."

He followed my instructions until he stood stark naked by the animal.

"Now run . . . run for you life. You've got ten seconds to get far enough so that I might miss you when I start shooting. You already know, I don't miss up close."

"But mister, I—"

"Run! You stupid son of a bitch! Run!"

He took off down the trail toward the ranchero.

I pulled out my knife and cut a foot-long length of blackberry bramble. I lifted up his horse's tail and shoved the thorns against his rear end, releasing the tail to hold it in place. That horse took off at a dead run and did not slow as he ran past his owner.

I whistled twice. Plutus came down the trail within seconds.

As we headed south on our mission, I was pleased that I did not have to kill that stupid man, but I also knew that if he gave me no choice, I would have prevailed.

Chapter 65

Rain I dreaded hit. It was cold and made travel difficult. I spotted one moccasin print that gave me hope. Other than that, I could only guess at her destination. She knew this country. If she thought I was following her, and she does not want to talk to me, she can end this forever.

Plutus splashed in ankle deep mud, while I hunkered under my poncho, thinking about what I might say to change her mind about leaving me. I may only get one chance.

I turned Plutus away from the river onto the long sloping prairie that led toward the mountain passes we had come through a year before. It was already cold here. I could only guess how much colder it would be at higher elevations. If she beats me to the passes, my pursuit is over. I do not have her knowledge of the countless cuts and canyons leading through the range.

Water ran off my hat in heavy streamlets. Even my horse folded back his ears under the relentless storm. Light was fading early under thick cloud cover. It was difficult for me to recognize landmarks. I slowly came to the realization I was lost. Mountains loomed not far away, but there was no more trail to follow.

Hope faded.

I released rein pressure on Plutus. In the dark, he needed to pick his own pace. He shook his head forcefully trying to shed water running into his ears. Then, he stopped.

I smelled it too. Smoke. Someone had a campfire, but in this rain, a fire would not burn.

Must be a house, I thought. *Maybe a settler.*

Plutus set a faster pace than I expected. His gait increased as we passed through deep grass and darkness set in. He knew something.

In the distance, the glow of a campfire stood out against the blackness. Plutus carried me, without hesitation, directly into the mountainside cutout where Kaga and I became intimate the first time.

Kaga sat cross-legged in front of a large fire with her blanket draped over her shoulders and wrapped around her body.

I dismounted and approached the fire.

"May I warm my hands by your fire?"

She nodded toward several bare sticks shoved into the ground as if waiting to be used.

"Are those for me?" I asked, not wanting to presume too much.

"I do not know," she said without looking away from the fire. "Are they?"

I took off my coat and hat placing them on drying sticks. Plutus needed care, so I removed his saddle, blanket and bridle, placing his tack across several sticks to dry.

Kaga did not say anything.

I sat down facing her.

"Can we talk?" I asked.

"Your clothes are wet."

She tossed me a dry blanket.

I peeled off my shirt and boots, placing them by the fire. My travel blankets were soaked, so I spread them next to the fire. After removing my pants and wrapping the blanket around my waist, I kneeled down facing her.

"Kaga, why did you leave me?"

She looked at me without speaking. Her eyes ran slowly from my hair to my face, along my bare chest and locked onto the two bear-tooth necklaces.

"Talk to me, Kaga. I need answers."

She reached out and ran her fingers across both bear teeth, lingering on them as she did. Tears welled up on her lower eyelids.

"Kaga, please don't cut me out. Why did you leave me?"

Her hand lifted from the bear teeth and fingertips traced my lips.

"Please, Kaga, I need—"

"Silent," she said and dropped her blanket off her shoulders.

She wore no clothes. Purple smudges of baby flowers stained her neck and chest, fading onto her breasts. Pushing onto her knees, she wrapped her arms around my body and pressed her full warmth against me. She pulled me backward onto her and took my earlobe in her lips. She whispered.

"What took you so long, white man?"

ABOUT THE AUTHOR

Dean Sault lives in Northern California with his mini-Dachshunds, Zack and Dink. He's been a writer all his life but did not publish his fiction works until releasing his science fiction tale in 2009, titled Space Chronicles: The Last Human War.

Since then, Dean has written a thriller (Faces of Hatred), a western-romance (Maker of Angels) and book one (Ghost of Lost Eagle) in his Sweetwater Canyon Series of western-romance-paranormal stories.

He enjoys contact with readers and can be reached through social media, his website, writing blog and by email.

Website – AuthorDeanSault.com

email – DeanSault@outlook.com

Faceboook – Author Dean Sault

Blog – deansaultpopcornwriting.blogspot.com/

Twitter - @AuthorDSault

LinkedIn member – Dean Sault

He also participates on GoodReads and Wattpad.

Made in the USA
San Bernardino, CA
07 November 2013